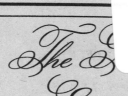

Experience

*I*t was almost . . . romantic, the husky way he was talking. The earnest look in his eyes.

Like they were two old lovers laughing on a special night, holding each other as they began to think of making love.

It felt real.

And the first rule of mistressing was remembering what was fake.

She was Eden's paid performer, not his lover.

She could flatter and flirt and beguile and seduce. She could writhe and moan and contort herself in ways he would remember on his deathbed. She could feign raptures of pleasure.

And the act of pretending made her safe. It reminded her this was her job.

It was time to remind Eden of that too.

SCARLETT PECKHAM

The Mistress Experience

SOCIETY OF SIRENS, VOLUME III

AVON

An Imprint of HarperCollinsPublishers

THE MISTRESS EXPERIENCE. Copyright © 2024 by Duchess of Peckham, LLC. All rights reserved. Printed in the United States of America. No part of this book may be used or reproduced in any manner whatsoever without written permission except in the case of brief quotations embodied in critical articles and reviews. For information, address HarperCollins Publishers, 195 Broadway, New York, NY 10007.

First Avon Books mass market printing: June 2024

Print Edition ISBN: 978-0-06-293565-6
Digital Edition ISBN: 978-0-06-293566-3

Cover design and illustration by Alan Dingman

Avon, Avon & logo, and Avon Books & logo are registered trademarks of HarperCollins Publishers in the United States of America and other countries.

HarperCollins is a registered trademark of HarperCollins Publishers in the United States of America and other countries.

FIRST EDITION

24 25 26 27 28 BVGM 10 9 8 7 6 5 4 3 2 1

For Grandma Pat, and all the other salty women who pass around their romance novels with a whisper and a wink

The Mistress Experience

Prologue

On a rainy night in Mayfair, a dim, wood-paneled gaming hell smelled like cigar smoke, whiskey, and the musk of the hundred damp men who mingled there, squeezing themselves around betting tables and barmaids bearing drinks, braced as if for a battle to the death.

The three ladies who stood at the center of this melee—the infamous radicals known in the papers as the Society of Sirens—had chosen the betting house for its name: the Queen of Hearts. It was an appropriate appellation given the prize of the auction underway: a month with Thaïs Magdalene, the most infamous, voluptuous, foulmouthed harlot in England.

"As you know," Seraphina Arden called out to the shifting, impatient crowd, "Miss Magdalene only accepts one lover a week, for one night, and never bequeaths her favors to the same patron twice. However, tonight she will do the unprecedented. She will offer herself as the mistress to the highest bidder for an entire delectable, ravishing—"

"Filthy!" Thaïs interjected from the hazard table on which she stood, nearly nude, modeling the buoyant-breasted, flame-haired, ample-arsed resplendence that made her so coveted by the gentlemen—and not a few ladies—of the nation.

"Yes, of course," Seraphina drawled. "For the right price, Miss Magdalene will provide unimaginable erotic raptures for one delectable, ravishing, *filthy* month."

The room rumbled with lusty men shouting their approval.

"The bidding will begin at a thousand guineas and go up in increments of five hundred," Cornelia Ludgate, Seraphina's fellow auctioneer, intoned over the din of the crowd. "And the proceeds of the auction will go directly to fund the Institute for the Equality of Women. So bid generously."

Whether the crowd of wealthy and dissipated men cared to support the ladies' cause was questionable. They were not here for philanthropy. They were here to win thirty nights with a woman commonly called *the best fuck in Britain*.

"Who will start the bidding?" Seraphina asked.

"A thousand," called a scrawny young man with thin whiskers, who looked like he was not yet out of school.

"You can do better than that, lad," Seraphina said. "Thaïs here will give you an education you'll cherish for the rest of your life."

"In bed," Thaïs added, fluttering her long lashes at the boy.

"I think that was clear, dear," Cornelia said to Thaïs.

"Don't vex me, wretch," Thaïs replied agreeably, plumping out her mass of curly ginger hair for the benefit of the crowd. "Not while I'm for sale."

"Fifteen hundred," an elderly man with a gold-tipped walking stick shouted.

"Oh please," Seraphina laughed. "Come up with a bid commensurate to the size of your staff, sir."

"Two thousand," called someone with a French accent from the back of the room.

"*Sois plus généreux*," Cornelia encouraged. "*Votre pénis vous dira merci.*"

"That means your cock will thank you, gents," Thaïs said helpfully, jutting out her hip to better display the outrageous curve of her famed rear.

"Three thousand," said a breathless man in front, his eyes fixed on her buttocks.

The bids reached five thousand in five minutes and doubled it in a quarter hour.

"Twelve thousand," shouted Laird Canaraugh, a burly Scotsman with hair as red as Thaïs's.

The three ladies exchanged a glance. This was better than they'd anticipated. They'd been expecting eight thousand guineas at the most.

"Thirteen," called out Faro Devon, the owner of the establishment, evidently so overtaken by the thrill of the hunt he'd decided to join in.

The bids kept coming.

Fifteen. Eighteen. Twenty.

And then, from a table in front, a man who'd bought Thaïs before and begged her to be his mistress to no avail, the notoriously dissipated libertine, poet, and heir to a vast shipping fortune: Colin Camberwell.

"Twenty-five," he yelled.

The room erupted in murmurs. Camberwell smiled serenely.

"Anyone care to venture twenty-six?" Seraphina asked.

No bids came above the racket of jealous men grumbling their disapproval.

"Going once for twenty-five guineas," Cornelia shouted.

"Going twice," Seraphina called.

"Sold!" Thaïs said. She hopped down from the table and sauntered over to Camberwell. "Well, look who finally got his wish."

"Worth the bloody fortune," he said.

He bent down, picked her up, and kissed her with the passion of a man who hadn't fucked in months—though this was unlikely in Camberwell's case, possessed as he was with a small harem of mistresses tucked around the country.

Thaïs wriggled away with a giggle. "Not for you yet, ya naughty devil. You'll be sending the fee to my solicitor before you have a taste of this."

"Oh, I'll have more than a taste of you," Camberwell said. "But that's where we can begin, if you like."

"Pay promptly, and your month will start on Monday next," Cornelia said.

"Gladly, Duchess," he said to Cornelia, who was, in fact, a duchess, though she rarely used the title, except in cases where nobility served her politics—thus not at a sex auction in a gaming hell in Mayfair.

He turned to Thaïs. "I think we'll while away the month in the Cotswolds. What say you to that?"

"More like the Cockswolds when I'm done with you."

Camberwell snorted. Cornelia shook her head.

"That was a weak quip even for you," she said.

"I liked it," Camberwell said. "Piquant."

Thaïs smiled. "He found it piquant. Quiet from Her Majesty, if you please."

"Time to retire, ladies," Seraphina said. "There is much to discuss."

Thaïs ran her hand down Camberwell's chest. "Until next week."

"I can hardly wait."

The women linked hands and wended through the crowd to the back exit, where Cornelia's carriage waited in the mews.

As soon as they were inside the coach, they all began to laugh with the universal glee that comes of securing a ridiculous sum of money.

"Unbelievable," Seraphina said. "I knew you were a prize, Thaïs, but twenty-five thousand guineas?"

Thaïs smiled. "Spoken like a woman who's never had me in her bed. Young Camberwell knows exactly what he's buying. I'm worth all the bullion in the sea, and he's an experienced seaman, if you catch my drift."

Cornelia groaned. "Please stop."

But Thaïs would never stop. Disgusting Cornelia with ribaldry was among her chief amusements.

"Don't squabble," said Seraphina, who found their amiable bickering tiresome. The three of them had been best friends for twenty years, and in all that time Cornelia and Thaïs had shown their love by competing to see who could provoke more irritation in the other.

"Do you like Camberwell?" Cornelia asked, a note of concern in her voice. "I don't wish for you to endure a month with a prig, even for untold riches."

"Oh, he's tolerable enough," Thaïs said. "Handsome. A bit dull beneath his antics, but he likes a jolly time and knows how to be creative. I'll be fine, if bored to death lolling in the country. Certainly worth the coin."

"Then it's done," Seraphina said with wonder in her voice. "We're finished. We've raised all the money we need to complete the Institute, and then some."

For two years, they had made it their sole purpose to create a place to support activists in the cause of women's rights and education, as well as a haven to train women in skills and give them apprenticeships to make them independent. They'd each employed their talents and salacious reputations—Seraphina penning a memoir detailing her scandalous life, Cornelia painting a series of portraits of whores dressed as Madonnas—to raise money for the land and the construction. With Thaïs's proceeds from the auction, they'd be able to open by the end of the year.

"It's wonderful," Cornelia said. "But I wish Elinor were here to enjoy it."

Cornelia's aunt, Lady Elinor Bell, was their benefactress, mentor, and the closest thing any of them had to a mother. It was she who'd educated them in the radical thinking that had led them to call themselves the Society of Sirens and devote themselves to fighting for female rights, employment, and education.

But she was not here. She was in Devon searching for her children, who had been kept from her since her husband, Viscount Bell, had accused her of insanity and adultery, and entered a bill in the House of Lords petitioning for divorce.

"She'll be thrilled when she learns the news,"

Seraphina said. "In the meantime, we have much work to do."

"Lord Jesus, can we celebrate a little?" Thaïs said. "Have a piece of cake? We're still in the bloody carriage."

Seraphina laughed. "You're right. I might be overeager to get started. I'll wait the ten minutes to get home before assigning our next duties."

They reached Cornelia's town house where her husband, Rafe, was waiting for them with Seraphina's lover, Adam. The men had arrayed a banquet's worth of food on a table in the drawing room, knowing the ladies would be famished by the time their late-night event was over.

"What's the news?" Rafe asked.

"Twenty-five thousand guineas," Thaïs clucked, twirling around the room—never mind that she was still partially undressed. She sat down at the table and began eating tiny honey cakes right off the platter.

Adam whistled. "Impressive sum."

"Enough to fund all the remaining construction, furnish the building, and hire teachers," Seraphina confirmed, making herself a plate of cheese and fruit.

"And to endow the place with enough funds to sustain it for at least ten years," Cornelia added. "Imagine what we can do. How many women we can educate and nurture. The speakers we can host and the politicians we can fund."

"If we move quickly we can get the first cohort recruited by autumn," Seraphina said. "Thousands of women have already written to express interest in learning trades. We'll have to write back offering formal applications."

Thaïs licked the honey from her sticky fingers. "We'll have to make the place comfortable for the girls who choose to live in the dormitory."

"And of course secure a final list of teachers and employers to guide their education, and come up with a plan for them to cooperatively share the labor of the house and gardens," Cornelia said.

"Let's make a plan to divide responsibilities," Seraphina said. "I'll handle the application process for the first class of one hundred, and see to it that the basic curriculum is established. Reading and writing for anyone who needs it, basic maths, civic education."

Cornelia nodded. "I'll hire the teachers and secure the employers willing to take on female apprentices."

"And what will I do?" Thaïs asked.

"Entertain a certain poet in the nude," Seraphina said with a smile.

Thaïs rolled her eyes. "I mean with my brains, not my bosoms."

"You can see to it that the place is beautiful," Cornelia said. "Adam will give you the architectural plans, and you can determine what we need to buy. Order furnishings and fixtures. You're so good at making people comfortable."

Thaïs frowned. "How will I do all that from the Cotswolds?"

"By correspondence," Cornelia said.

Thaïs scoffed. "I can barely write."

She had been raised in a brothel and received no formal education. Lady Elinor had taught her to read at the age of twenty-two, and Thaïs, while literate, lacked confidence in her spelling and penmanship.

"You are far more adept than you give yourself credit for," Seraphina said. "I love your letters. They're quite vivid."

"She means *vulgar*," Cornelia said. "Try not to curse in your missives to upholstery merchants."

Thaïs sighed. "I'll certainly not promise that, madam lady."

The three women laughed.

"It sounds like you have a plan," Adam said. "Shall we drink to it?"

They all raised their glasses—milky tea for Adam and Seraphina, wine for Thaïs, and whiskey for the others.

"To the Society of Sirens," Seraphina said. "May we expand our ranks."

Chapter One

Thaïs's body ached from her teeth to her arse after three days jostling about the countryside in Colin Camberwell's carriage. The vehicle was sumptuous, as Colin's driver had assured her, but weighed down by all her trunks—five of them, packed near to gaping—it could barely move.

Instead, it thunked along the unpaved roads and took her sit bones with it. Were her hind end not so generously padded, she might have snapped a hip.

She wished she'd packed lighter, for the sake of her sore body. But world-renowned courtesans did not slug about in daytime frocks; to provide the mistress experience Camberwell had paid for, she had to dress the part. And besides, she loved flouncing about in her high-class harlot costumes.

Over the years she'd bought a beautiful collection. Lacy underthings from Paris. Sheer peignoirs and silk chemises that clung here and floated there, begging to be torn off by desperate fingers. Daring gowns that just barely contained her tits, to provoke hungry stares at elegant suppers and sultry evening dos.

She'd also packed her favorite props. Cuffs, blindfolds, silk ropes, a dildo. Camberwell was known for seeking adventure in his bedchamber, and she liked to be creative.

Harlotry was an art she'd practiced her whole life, and she enjoyed a challenge.

But she did not enjoy this journey. Thank the screeching cats of hell it was almost over.

She looked out the window at the woods around the road. Greenery and bluebells and ancient trees. No sounds save for the clop of the horses' hooves and the rushing of the wind in the leaves.

Dull.

She preferred bustling streets crammed with hackney cabs and market stalls and raucous laughter and men shilling evening papers. Rolling downs, burbling brooks, and fields of wheat left her bored and sneezing. If she was going to step in shit, she'd rather it be in a gutter than a barn.

Of course, for twenty-five thousand guineas, Colin could drag her wherever he liked. And his estate was known for being like a palace. Hopefully she could wander about indoors barely dressed and avoid itching eyes and lowing cows entirely.

She was blessed glad Camberwell had won the bidding. The auction room had been full of characters she'd rather not spend a month with. Old gouty fellows that no doubt smelled of farts and meat breath, and a few clench-jawed men with violence in their eyes that froze your blood. God knew she'd dealt with both types in her day, but only for a night. A month with such a character was a different horse entirely.

Camberwell would be a breeze.

The carriage lumbered out of the forest—clomp, ouch, clomp, *bloody* ouch—until they reached a village with a smoother road. It was tiny as a pin and pretty as a fairy tale, if you liked that kind of thing, with houses built from golden stone boasting blooming gardens. The carriage turned off down a lane, taking them away from the village over hills of sheep-flecked farmland.

They slowed in front of a hedgerow, then turned off onto a pebbled drive to a small cottage under a grove of trees.

Odd, that.

The wee house didn't appear to be an inn for changing horses, and it certainly wasn't Colin's estate. It looked like a place a widow would live out her days, tending garden and reading books, God help her.

The coachman opened the door and offered Thaïs his hand to help her step down.

Step down?

She wrinkled her nose at the idea of it. She didn't know what they were doing here, but she did know it didn't concern her.

Besides, it was misting, which would cause her hair to frizzle. Colin had not paid a fortune for her to show up looking like she'd been romping in the rain.

"I'll just stay here while we're stopped, if you don't mind," she told the driver.

He frowned. "But we've reached our destination, ma'am."

Oh. Now she understood.

It was a prank.

Colin would be waiting at a window, laughing at

her dismay. Or perhaps he wanted to tumble her in this tiny house, pretending he was a farmer and she his willing wife. You never knew what fantasies a rich man would devise. She'd played everything from a mermaid to a milkmaid in her years on the divan.

She took the driver's hand and hopped down from the carriage. The garden smelled like the roses that bloomed in a blur of colors from bushes and off trellises. Quite lovely, though she preferred them arranged in vases where there weren't bugs or prickling thorns.

Behind her, the footman was beginning to unload her trunks.

"Oh, don't bother with that, my boy," she called to him. "We're having a confusion. I'll just go inside to have a word."

He looked at her like she was crack-brained but set down the trunk. "Aye, miss."

She bounded into the cottage, not bothering to knock.

"Colin," she called. "Where are you, you joker? Am I to be your naughty shepherdess?"

He wasn't in the parlor so she threw open the nearest door. "Camberwell," she said to the man bent over papers at a desk, looking deep in concentration.

He started and looked up.

He was not even slightly Colin Camberwell.

He was Lord Alastair Eden—as different a man as had ever walked the earth.

"My God," Eden said, clutching his heart. "You startled me."

"My God," she said at the same time. "What are *you* doing here?"

Lord Eden was about the furthest thing from a whoring rakehell she could imagine. She could not even imagine him *knowing* a whoring rakehell. He was the kind of man who would wince at the idea of knowing one. The kind of man who was pained by the ideas of whoring and rakehelldom entirely.

"Er, I rented the place, actually," he said, like he was a guilty boy confessing to a priest.

"Then what am *I* doing here?" she asked.

He stood up and accidentally knocked a few papers off the desk.

"Ah, damn," he muttered, bending down to gather them.

He was blushing.

Blushing?

They knew each other well enough, and she had never seen him anything but perfectly composed. They'd spent a week at the same house party the year before—courtesy of Rafe—and he'd been helpful in using his connections to smooth the way for building up the Institute. He was always stiff and reserved and perfectly dressed, with elegant manners and a dry wit.

Not the kind of man who blushed.

Now he seemed embarrassed to the point of stuttering.

"Miss Magdalene—" he bowed his head slightly "—I apologize for my rudeness. Welcome."

"Thaïs," she corrected. "And it's nice to see you, but where's Camberwell?"

He gestured to a chair. "Would you have a seat?"

She sat, hoping he wasn't here to tell her Camberwell had reneged. Or—what?—died?

But why would Eden know if he'd given up the ghost? How would a man like Eden—a leading progressive member of the House of Lords—even know a man like Camberwell—a fopling rascal who gadded about spending his father's money?

"You see—" Eden said, smoothing his coat. "That is—" He sighed and sank back down into his chair, like he'd lost the will to live. "Camberwell isn't here. He didn't pay for your time. I did."

He looked into her eyes, clenching his jaw sideways, like he was waiting for a blow.

She cawed out a laugh.

"So this *is* a rig. All right, you've gotten me." She looked around behind her. "Come out, Colin. You've had your chuckle."

Eden winced. "He's truly not here, Miss Magdalene. Thaïs. I'm afraid I'm serious."

She shook her head. Enough tricks. She could take a joke, but she'd not be the butt of one.

"I watched him win the auction," she said. "His own carriage brought me here."

"He stood as my proxy at the auction, for the sake of discretion. We belong to the same investment club, and he owed me a favor. He was kind enough to send his carriage for the sake of verisimilitude."

"For the sake of *wot*?"

"Uh, the appearance of truth. Lest others see you in my carriage and suspect the ruse."

He looked mortified.

Another laugh burbled up out of her, and she felt guilty for it, since he seemed so miserable. But faint Jesus, the hilarity. Lord *Eden*, wanting a secret shag.

"I'm sorry," she chortled, unable to stop laughing. Stopping laughing once she'd started was not one of her gifts.

"No, I'm sorry," he said. "For the dishonesty. You may, of course, decline to stay, given the false pretenses. I'll pay either way."

"No, no," she said, swallowing the dregs of her laughter. She liked Eden, formal and dry as he may be. He was quietly supportive of radical causes and kind and doting to his little sister, Anna, who Thaïs knew well. Swiving him would be more interesting than doing it with Colin, whose randy antics were predictable. She wouldn't mind seeing what Eden was like in the throes of ravishment.

"Shall we get started, then?" she asked. "Unbutton those breeches, and I'll see if I can fit under the desk."

"Oh no, please!" he said, gesturing for her to remain seated. "That won't be necessary. You see I'm—well, I have a rather specific request, and I'd hoped we could discuss it before we, er, consummate matters."

A specific request, eh? Intriguing. Perhaps she *would* have use for her bag of tricks.

She leaned back. "Very well, my dear. Tell me your wish, and I'll make it come true."

"I was hoping for . . . lessons."

Ah. She should have suspected.

"I see. You'll play the naughty schoolboy, and me your stern governess. That's easy enough." It would not be the first time a buttoned-up man wished to be bent over a desk for few raps on the rump.

"Not precisely," he said. "You see, I intend to marry soon, and I'd like to shape myself into the perfect husband. To do that, I wish to learn how to please my future wife."

She'd credit him this: it was not a request she'd ever heard before.

"Not to undercut my skills," she said, "but wifing isn't what I'm known for. A fine lady would be better suited for the role. A married one who can train a proper husband."

She'd fantasized, of late, about becoming such a person. Perverse of her, as her friends all said that marriage was a shackle. But how sweet, to be the wife of a doting man who'd cherish her for more than her looks and skills abed. Vow to keep her safe and comfortable. Put a baby in her.

But it was a rare man who clamored to sweep a whore off to the altar, especially one as infamous as her, and she'd not take just anyone. He'd have to love her like he loved life itself, and she'd have to love him back with the same vim.

Unlikely she'd ever be so blessed.

Eden laughed tightly. "I'd be called out for asking a married woman for demonstrations in what I wish to learn."

"Why?" she asked. Seemed to her that doling out manners lessons was all most aristocratic women ever did.

"Perhaps I should be more specific," he said. "I'd like to understand how to pleasure a woman intimately. My future wife will likely be a virgin, and I'd like to be able to welcome her into my bed with a minimum of awkwardness, and to make the matter enjoyable for us both. But I fear I have a deficit in this capacity. As of yet, that is."

It took her a moment to cipher out the meaning of this speech.

"You're a bad lover, you mean?"

She found this unlikely. He had the air of a man who was competent at everything he tried. Well, at least he had prior to today. At the moment, he seemed to wish to disappear to vapor.

"I, erm, lack the experience to say," he said.

"Do you mean you're a virgin?" she asked. Nothing shocked her when it came to sex, but she'd never have pinned him for an unspent lamb. He was well into his thirties.

"No," he said. "I did have a few encounters in my youth—none particularly, er, enjoyable, I'm afraid. My fault, I think. I fear I . . . lack an instinct for such proceedings."

He certainly lacked an instinct for talking about them. She felt rather soft for the poor hot-faced fellow. But she needed to know more to give him what he wanted.

"How long has it been since you fucked?" she asked, trying to make her voice more gentle and less bawdy, since he was so uncomfortable.

He shook his head grimly. "I've been celibate for years. Too much risk involved in casually undertaking something I don't particularly enjoy. Pregnancy, disease, you know."

Oh, she did, being a whore. But it was odd to hear he didn't *enjoy* sex. Plenty of people didn't, but they weren't the sorts to hire prostitutes.

Perhaps he'd been fucking the wrong people.

"Are you sure it's women you like?" she asked.

He nodded quickly. "It's not a question of attraction."

"How are the goods?" she asked. "They work?"

"Pardon?"

"Your cock. Does it get hard?"

"Uh . . . yes," he affirmed in a low voice.

"And you can spill?"

He winced.

"Yes."

"Well, then, this shan't be all too difficult, I'd reckon," she said brightly, wanting to cheer him up. "You're healthy, you're quick in the brains. Perhaps you just need a bit of practice."

He did not seem convinced.

He cleared his throat. "I hope so. In any case, I've done some studying in preparation."

"Studying what?"

He stood up and walked over to a carved wooden box sitting on a shelf of his bookcase. He took a key from his coat pocket and unlocked it, then took out a pile of books and brought them over to her.

"These," he said.

She opened one to a random page, hoping the text would not be too dense for her to make out.

Luckily, they were the kind of books with more pictures than words.

Pictures of people rutting.

Certain pages were marked with little scraps of paper. She turned to one and found it annotated in small, neat script, along with arrows indicating how a person might move to do the deed.

Poor, earnest fellow. He was trying to learn fucking from a book. Made her want to hug him.

She snapped it shut and put the pile on the desk. "You won't be needing these. You've got me."

She took his cravat and pulled him down toward her. "Here. Let's start with kissing."

He reared away like she'd grabbed him by the balls and not the neckcloth.

"I was hoping we might agree on a curriculum before we begin," he said.

"A curriculum," she repeated, trying not to laugh. "Believe me, you don't need a degree from university to have sex, milord."

"No, of course not. Nevertheless . . ."

His eyes pled with hers.

He was nervous. She'd been paid twenty-five thousand guineas to do little more than calm a man's *nerves*. Well, no problem, that. She could give him a damned list if he wanted one. Besides, she sensed he wanted to get used to her a bit. Some men needed to know a woman well before they wanted to bed her. Perhaps this was his problem.

"Very well," she said. "We have four weeks. We can take our time."

"Thank you."

"No need to thank me. I'm your whore."

That pained look returned to his face. "Don't call yourself that, Thaïs," he said. "You're a courtesan."

She rolled her eyes. "A courtesan's a whore like any other, milord, and there's no shame in paying for the pleasure of a cunny, whatever you call the owner of it."

It vexed her when people danced around the nature of her work, or thought that being an expensive prostitute made her better than an alley girl. She was proud of what she was and what she did, and didn't need to put a pretty name on it.

"Of course," Eden said, blushing.

That blush told her they would have to start things slowly. This was not a man who dealt frankly in matters of the body, even when it came to common speech.

"Now, as to your lessons," she said, putting on a prim tone of voice. "What say you we start with seduction? Flirting, that sort of thing."

"Ah, give me a moment. I like to write things down, to prepare myself for study."

He took a piece of paper from his desk and began a list in his neat hand. "One, *flirting*. And then?"

"Then a bit of kissing, once you have the hang of it."

He jotted this down, nodding.

"Next?" he asked, quill poised to take more notes. She had to school her face to keep from laughing at his earnestness.

"Touching *beneath the clothes*," she said with delicacy. She thought the phrasing would please him more than *groping*.

He nodded gravely.

"By week two the clothes come off, and we learn oral pleasures."

"And then?"

"Consummation of the marriage."

He blushed again but nodded, wrote it down, and put aside his pen.

"That's not the end of the course," she said. "Write this down."

He picked the quill back up.

"By week four: *ravishment*."

His eyes went wide. "Oh no, I would never wish to use force."

"Not *that* kind of ravishment," she chided. "The good kind. The kind that makes a woman's head explode."

"*Make woman's head explode*," he murmured as he wrote it down.

"And yours, of course," she added.

He did not look at her as he scrawled *and mine*.

Chapter Two

This was killing him. He was going to die here in the study of a cottage in Gloucestershire discussing the sexual explosion of heads.

He didn't know why he wasn't better braced for such a conversation.

Thaïs Magdalene was carnal-minded and foul-mouthed on her most demure day—he'd spent enough time in her periphery to know this. And he was not going to learn how to properly make love if he couldn't bring himself to talk about it.

But he loathed doing anything he wasn't perfect at, and the act they were discussing—one that seemed to come by other men most easily of all—was outside his natural gifts.

He could perform the basic mechanics to the desired conclusion well enough, if pressed, but the animal nature of it filled him with a paralyzing dread. He preferred to relieve his urges by his own hand, once a day, immediately upon waking. The matter dispensed with, he could go undistracted about the activities of his life that he was better at.

And he was better at most things. He strove to achieve perfection in everything he undertook. Looking after his investments and estates. Enacting legislation. Advocating for reform. Until recently, raising his little sister.

But now his sister was grown and married, and with her gone, his house was far too quiet. He wanted to fill it with a family of his own. He wanted a companion, and he knew he could be an excellent husband. He liked the company of women and enjoyed homely things like children and dogs. He was steady, responsible, rich, and capable of kindness—even love.

But he was inept in this one matter. And he couldn't in good conscience invite some poor young woman to his life knowing he was consigning her to a fate of being perfunctorily bedded by a man ashamed of his own inability to please her.

Such glaring imperfections were not to be tolerated. He had to fix this deficit in himself.

And he had to do it before the season opened in a month and he was plunged into the marriage mart. He planned to quickly familiarize himself with the young ladies coming out, court whoever was most suitable, and be married by year's end.

So he needed an education, and quickly.

A month with Thaïs was the ideal solution: enough time to take lessons from an expert he could study with in secret, without the entanglement of taking a mistress. That he knew and liked Thaïs was an added advantage. She was a good friend of Rafe and Cornelia. He'd spent a week with her at a country house party the previous year. He was certain he could trust her.

And thank goodness.

He was desperate.

"Well, we have a plan," he said. "I'll show you to your room and have the footman carry up your luggage."

"My room?" she asked. "We won't be sharing a bed?"

The idea had not occurred to him. He'd never—not once in his life—slept beside another person.

"Need we?" he asked.

She shrugged. "Would you not share one with your wife?"

He had not considered the question. He supposed it would depend on his wife's wishes. Though, left to his own preferences, he could not imagine such a custom would benefit either of their sleep.

"Perhaps let's table the matter until we . . . progress to later in the course of study," he suggested.

"As you wish," she said, though he gathered she frowned on his choice.

He gestured out the door. "Follow me."

He led her into the main room, pointing out the features of the cottage. It was pleasant but small. Downstairs, a kitchen, a parlor, and a windowed alcove for dining. Two bedrooms and a necessary above. He showed Thaïs to the larger of the two rooms, which had a sunny little nook overlooking the roses in the front garden.

She looked around. "Very nice. But no dressing room?"

"I'm afraid not. Do you need one? We won't be going anywhere of note."

"I packed for a month with Camberwell," she said. She gestured out the window, where five enormous trunks sat outside the carriage waiting to be hauled into the house.

Good God.

They'd barely fit up the stairs. And even if they did, they'd fill up Thaïs's entire room. Maybe the entire upper floor.

"I hate to inconvenience you," he said. "But perhaps you can take what you need from them, and we'll store the rest in the stables."

She did not look particularly enthused about this idea but nodded.

"As he wishes." She turned to go downstairs. "Send a maid to help me sort them out?" she called over her shoulder.

He gritted his teeth. He'd thought the bare-bones accommodations he had made for this month were adequate: he'd hired enough help to look after their needs in comfort without attracting undue attention from local strangers wondering why a supposed holidaying teacher would spend lavishly on servants. He'd not considered Thaïs would be expecting a lady's maid.

So much for being perfect. It seemed he was already failing as a host.

"I'm afraid I have no maid," he said. "Just a serving girl who comes in the morning to tidy and make breakfast."

Thaïs whirled around, agape. "You can spend twenty-five thousand guineas on a whore, but not spare a maid's wages? I'd have brought my girl from London if I'd known."

"I'm sorry. For the sake of discretion, I'd hoped to keep those who see us together to a minimum. I trust my servants, but the risk of gossip in this instance is too high. As for the serving girl, she thinks I'm a tutor taking a holiday in the countryside. A poor relation of Camberwell's. I'd appreciate it if you would not say otherwise."

"And who does she think *I* am? Assuming you don't mean to keep me locked up here in hiding."

"Of course not. I told her I was expecting my sister. A governess visiting from Lancaster."

She snorted and pointed at her reflection in the looking glass. "*Me*, a governess? You'd better hope your serving girl is blind and stupid."

Thaïs had a point. Even in her relatively modest traveling dress, her appearance was dizzying. Her prodigious breasts, either through some magic of corsetry or anatomy, swelled up and out over her neckline, promising to be unlike anything he'd ever seen except in the exaggerated drawings of his erotic books. Her waist nipped in dramatically, her hips and arse swelled bounteously, her plump arms promised of plump thighs to match. And her hair. That glorious, riotous red hair, set off by green eyes and skin so milky white it made him thirsty. And then, my God, those freckles along her nose and collarbone.

He was not one to covet women for their looks—his attraction tended to grow out of friendship—but there was a reason Thaïs was famous.

She simply glowed. One could not look at her without imagining what she might be like in the nude. Feel like in one's arms. Or, at least, *he* couldn't.

And then there was the flirtatious spirit she exuded. The way she held her body, the way she moved, the way she talked.

One took a single look at her and *knew* she was a fille de joie. A proud one, who reveled in the role of courtesan. Hattie Hart might, indeed, suspect Thaïs was not a governess. Especially if she went about dressed as she was now. But perhaps with limited contact and more modest gowns . . .

"You're a late riser, are you not?" he ventured, remembering how at Rafe Goodwood's house party, Thaïs had stumbled yawning from her room at noon, complaining it was not yet two. "Hattie arrives at seven. I doubt you'll even meet her."

Thaïs clapped her hand over her mouth, eyes huge. "Oh no," she said from behind her fingers.

"What is it?"

"You said she cooks breakfast. Who cooks the other meals? Not *me*, I hope. You'll never see your marriage bed as you'll die of pure starvation."

He laughed. "No, of course not. Hattie leaves a picnic for the midday meal, and I'll prepare our suppers."

She raised her auburn brows. *"You?"*

He nodded. "I enjoy cooking. It's quite soothing. I'll teach you, if you like."

She shook her head emphatically. "No thanks, unless it will help you in the bedroom."

Despite his stress, her pique amused him. "I tend not to prepare meals in the bedroom."

She threw up her hands, like this was all too much to endure speaking of a moment longer. He hoped it was not condescending that he found her irritation charming.

She was the most shocking person he had ever met, but he'd innately liked her since the moment they'd been introduced. She was warm but blunt and prone to irritation, crass but more funny than rude. As spirited a woman as he had ever met.

"I'll go down and rummage through my trunks," she grumbled in a rough accent that he suspected was her native one. Her speech was usually more refined, if always florid. It became less genteel when she was vexed.

"Let me help you," he said, following her downstairs.

She marched outside and over to her trunks, which she began unlatching, muttering to herself.

She ruffled through the first and pulled out a handful of transparent garments in bright colors that evoked a peacock's plumes. She tossed them to him. It had recently stopped raining, and the garments caught the golden-hour light as they flew across the garden.

"Wait," he said, horrified her things might fall onto the wet grass. He clutched them to his chest, realizing they were dressing gowns—or undressing gowns, as it were, since they were so sheer they'd not conceal the slightest bit of flesh.

The coachman and footman stared as Eden just barely caught the next round of projectile garments. Lace, this time, of the sort that went under a gown and was not meant to be seen by decent men in daylight.

"Thaïs, please stop for a moment," he said firmly.

She turned around, arms full of silk. "I'm fetching my meager wardrobe, if you please."

"Let's consolidate what you want into one trunk. Your things will get soiled."

"And no maid to wash them," she groused.

"I'll send out the laundry," he assured her. "I'm not a barbarian."

"Very well." She scooped the remaining unmentionables into the trunk with her night rails, and he deposited the items in his arms into the empty trunk. She moved on to the next one, which was filled with elaborate gowns fit for formal balls. Impractical, and sure to attract attention if she wore them.

"You won't have use for those," he said. "No need to unpack them."

She glared at him. "Then what would you like me to wear, milord? Shall I sally about stark naked?"

The footman looked down at his feet, and the coachman bit his lip to hide a smirk.

"Choose day dresses that will be comfortable in the countryside." By which Eden meant *inconspicuous*.

She rolled her eyes. "I brought gowns to suit Camberwell," she said. "Not to tromp around the downs."

"Surely you have *something*," he coaxed.

She flung open the lid of the fourth trunk to show him. "Shoes and jewels and the like," she said. She removed a pair of low-heeled boots and a set of satin slippers. Neither of them were ideal for country life, but at least she'd be able to walk around the garden should she desire air.

"And that one?" He gestured at the last unopened trunk. "What's in there?"

She grinned at him. "Have a look."

He opened the lid and peeked inside.

He nearly yelped.

It was filled with items that were clearly meant for sex. A jar of condoms, a carved marble phallus, vials of oil—

He slammed the trunk shut and whirled around to look at her.

She was utterly delighted at his horror. She sallied over to the trunk, opened it up, and grabbed the jar of condoms. "We'll be needing those," she said. "The rest can wait until we see how fast you take to schooling."

"My God, Thaïs," he whispered, glancing at the servants. "I asked you for discretion."

"Oh, Camberwell's men have seen worse," she whispered back. "From what I've heard he likes to spend his carriage rides riding women, if you know what I mean."

"It's hard not to know what you mean. Your description is quite literal."

She winked. "You bought yourself a plain-speech harlot, not a fair-tongued maiden."

He chose to ignore this, lest further conversation provoke more vulgarities for the amusement of Camberwell's men.

"Sirs," he said, addressing them, "would you carry these extra trunks into the stables? And then you may be off."

Thaïs gave them a bow that caused her breasts to come very close to spilling out of her dress. An unfamiliar feeling flashed through him.

Yearning. Sharp and undeniable.

It was the same feeling he'd gotten when he'd first seen her at Rafe's. A thump like he'd been tossed off a horse.

A mere *glimpse* of her figure aroused him. He almost wished he had not insisted on a curriculum that would bar him from touching her for days.

Almost. For who knew how he would fumble and embarrass himself when he got the chance?

"You've been a dream getting me here," Thaïs said to the servants, not noticing that her posture had very nearly undone her patron. "Thank you for a most pleasantful journey."

Eden picked up her remaining trunk and lumbered with it into the house. The effort eliminated the threat of his loins stiffening and her noticing. A profound relief.

"Need help?" Thaïs asked, following him.

"No, thank you," he grunted as he wrestled the enormous thing upstairs.

He set it down on the floor in front of her bed and stood there for a moment to catch his breath. She joined him. "Hmm. Quite strong, he is," she commented, running a hand over his arm. "I wouldn't have expected it."

He was surprised by how much this pleased him. Both her words and the soft pressure of her touch.

"You like that," she murmured, moving her hand up to his shoulders. "Are you sore? Shall I rub your back?"

The thought of it was tempting. But if he let her, he would stiffen for certain, and she would see. As much as he desired her, he was not ready to be so intimate with a woman he barely knew.

Not ready to reveal himself that way.

He forced himself to step aside. "No, thank you."

"As you wish," she said, and there was a gentleness in her voice that calmed him.

Made him want to be touched more.

Made it necessary to change the subject.

He cleared his throat. "I'm sorry I didn't convey to you the nature of our lodgings in advance, so you could be more comfortable. In the morning, I'll ask

Hattie to bring a seamstress to make you a few gowns. We'll say your bags were stolen on your journey."

"My, my, how devious you are, Lord Eden."

Not typically, but the lie was a harmless one.

"Perhaps you'd like to rest while I prepare our supper," he said. "It will take an hour. I hope you aren't famished."

"Not for food," she said with an exaggerated leer.

"I—well, excuse me, then," he said quickly.

Her laughter followed him out of the room.

Chapter Three

$\mathcal{B}$eing a whore was a bit like being a physician. You took the measure of a man, diagnosed him, and administered a treatment. And Thaïs suspected all Lord Eden needed from her was a bit of confidence. He was a handsome man, after all—tall and slender with black hair and olive skin and deep brown eyes— and he was rich. He could marry most anyone without learning a thing from her. These lessons were for him—to make him as assured in bed as he was outside of it.

She didn't need a month for this. A few nights of tips and tricks would do it.

She was not worried about making Eden a perfect lover. What was perfection, anyway, especially when every soul has their own tastes in bed?

What she *was* worried about was how in Satan's name she'd pass the time here.

In London her days were overflowing. There was her mess of friends, any one of whom might want to share a meal or a laugh. There were her girls, the young harlots she trained and dressed and fed so they could leave the streets for better-paying, safer bagnios. There was the Institute, which she and her fellow Sirens visited several times a week. There were her patrons. There was the theater, the pleasure gardens, the opera, the dissolute soirees.

Here there was—what? Sewing. Milking cows.

She put away her things, which took no more than a quarter hour seeing as how few of them she'd been allowed to keep. She would have loved to change into a pretty gown for dinner, were her finery not locked away in Eden's barn. She settled for dabbing her face and bosom with water from a pitcher on the bureau, spritzing herself with her spicy eau de parfum, and fluffing out her hair.

She was already bored.

She'd never been good at lacking for company. Aloneness made her itchy.

She'd make Eden talk to her.

She went down the noisy stairs—this whole house creaked like a listing ship every time she took a step across the ancient floorboards—and found him in the kitchen. He was at the long table in the center of the room, coatless in his white lawn shirt, sleeves rolled above his elbows, rolling out dough.

There was flour on his cheekbone and a few flecks in his hair, which had gone mussed as he bent over his task. It made a boy of him.

"What's all this?" she asked.

"Your supper," he said.

She eyed the ingredients arrayed in tidy little bowls around him. "What's my supper going to be?"

"Quiche. It's a pie of egg and cheese and—"

"I know what a quiche is, Your Lordship. I'm the fancy kind of whore."

"Of course," he said mildly, not ceasing the fluid

movements of his hands as he pressed a round of dough into a tin. She liked the way it made his forearms flex. "Forgive me. Not everyone is familiar with French cookery."

"Is that the kind of cooking you do?"

"Mostly. My mother was French. She taught me."

Ah. Half-French, he was. That would explain his olive skin.

"Why?" she asked.

He shrugged. "She enjoyed it. And I liked to help her."

Thaïs wrinkled her nose. "Lesson one for charming your future bride, hire a cook."

He laughed. "I do have cooks at the abbey and in London."

"The abbey?"

"Kendal Abbey. My family home. It's in Cumbria."

"Is it very fine?"

"It's large, if that's what you mean. It's surrounded by quite a pretty forest, on a small mountain overlooking a lake."

"How big?"

"Sixty rooms, or so."

She wished they were staying *there*.

"You'll want your ladies to know they'll be mistress of such a grand place. They like that sort of thing."

"Their mothers will already know," he said. "Believe me, they keep track."

Ah. Of course. Mothers. A class of woman Thaïs was not experienced with, being an orphan.

"I've thought more about your lessons," she told Eden. "I have a plan for your first week of schooling."

He looked at her with interest. "Oh?"

"We'll practice courting first. Conversation. Dancing. A stroll. A private call. And we'll practice your proposal."

He raised a brow. "Wouldn't that require knowing *who* I'm going to propose to?"

"Why?"

"I'd want to compliment her appealing attributes."

"You can compliment mine," she said, gesturing at her hips.

He blushed. "I would never comment on a woman's appearance."

"But you would notice it."

He focused intently on the onions he was chopping. "Well, I suppose one does."

"No harm in wanting a comely lassie. Tell us, what do you like?"

He shook his head, clearly embarrassed. "Looks aren't of particular importance to me."

Lies. No one was immune to a fair turn of the head.

"But if you could build a girl from scratch, you must have some druthers as to what she'd be like," she insisted. "You must know what you're looking for in a wife."

"Ah," he said. "Of course. She'd be young enough to bear several children, but not too young. I don't want a maiden fresh out of the nursery. She'd like the country, as that's where I prefer to spend my time when I don't need to be in London. She'd be sympathetic to progressive politics and educated enough to understand such things and take an interest. She'd be nurturing and kind, so as to be a natural mother to our children. And she'd be polite, with elegant manners."

In other words, imagine a woman completely unlike Thaïs, and one would have a perfect match. Ironic that *she* was the woman he wished to practice on. At least she understood politics, education be damned. And she could be polite when she chose to. Though, it wasn't a choice she often made. Being vulgar was quite a bit more fun, when you could get away with it.

"That's all lovely. But you still haven't mentioned what she looks like."

He slid a bowl of freshly washed mushrooms to her. "Would you mind slicing these?"

He was trying to distract her.

"I would mind, in fact," she said, sliding it back. "And stop dodging the question."

"I simply don't see why it matters."

"It matters because to make all those babies you're imagining, you'll need to want to fuck your wife."

She hoped to get a rise out of him, as his stubbornness was annoying, but he just looked at her calmly. "You're being crass deliberately."

"Sex is crass, I'm sorry to tell you," she said. "It's noisy, wet, and messy, if you're doing it right."

This *did* disturb his calm. He scrunched up his face in distaste. "Please stop."

"If you can't talk about swiving, I don't know how you plan to do it. But that's a lesson for another day. We're still onto the basics of courtship, where we'll be stuck for the whole month as you can't even admit what you fancy in a lady."

"Very well," he said, sounding cross. "She'd be pretty."

She snorted. "Let's be a bit more precise."

"She'd have ginger hair," he said quietly, to the table. "Freckles across her nose. A figure on the . . . ample side."

Well, no wonder he hadn't wanted to admit it. He was describing *her*.

She moved closer to him. "A bounteous bosom?" she asked.

"Uh, I suppose, er, yes."

She grabbed his hand and plopped it on her arse.

"A nice, fat rump?"

He snatched his hand away like she'd put it in the fire.

"Thaïs!"

She sighed. "I reckon we'll have to add rump-squeezing to the list."

"She could not possibly enjoy rump-squeezing."

"Says you, the female expert."

He did not reply. Instead he turned his back and carefully transferred the quiche to the bake-oven.

Convenient like.

"How long until supper?" she asked. "It's been a long day of travel, and I'd not want to starve."

"Ah, I'm sorry," he said. He grabbed a loaf of bread and cut her a slice, which he slathered with butter and sprinkled with salt. "Here you are."

Upon closer inspection, the bread was flecked with green. She dropped it on the table, disgusted. "It's moldy!"

He laughed and handed it back to her. "That's not mold, it's rosemary. My own recipe. Try it."

She took a tiny bite. It was delicious.

"You invented this?"

"I fiddled with a version my mother used to make."

She shoved more in her mouth. "It's heaven."

"Thank you."

She munched her bread and watched him mix oil into a bowl of mustard, vinegar, and something white he smashed and then cut into tiny pieces.

"What's that?"

"Garlic."

It smelled sharp and grassy. She liked it.

"You're not going to cook it?"

"I'm going to emulsify it and dress lettuce and herbs in it for our salad."

"Lettuce? Am I a rabbit, then?"

He stuck a spoon in the dressing and held it out to her. "Taste."

She delicately licked it with the very tip of her tongue. It was bright and tart.

"That's good," she allowed.

"It will be even better on your rabbit food."

She watched him tear bits of lettuce and other green things into a bowl with his bare hands, then concoct a mix of apples and cinnamon he put in a pot over the fire.

"What's that?" she asked.

"A simple applesauce, for pudding."

"I like chocolate for my pudding."

"Noted for next time."

He moved through the kitchen with as much authority as any cook she'd ever seen. She liked watching him. It was too bad that male cookery was not a quality sought after among ladies on the marriage mart, for he would find a wife in no time, his supposed lack of skill in the bedroom be damned.

Though, she was even less inclined to believe he was as ignorant in the bedroom as he claimed after watching him in the kitchen. He moved with confidence in his own body and had deft hands. And there was something sultry about the way he tasted this and stirred that and held out foods for her to inhale their aromas.

He made cookery look erotical.

The kitchen began to smell savory, and he removed the quiche from the bake-oven. The top had puffed up into a beautiful golden crown that made her mouth water just to look at.

"Can we eat it now?" she asked. Her stomach rumbled loud enough for him to hear.

"Not yet. It has to cool. Can I offer you a glass of wine?" He gestured at a bottle with an unreadable label she assumed was in French.

"Yes," she said.

He poured the pale liquid into a glass for her and then poured one for himself. He raised it, meeting her eye. "To you, for joining me here."

"To me," she agreed.

The wine was tasty, with hints of meadow and earth that should not have been delicious but were.

"Not bad," she said.

He smiled at her tolerantly. "I import it. I brought it from my cellar at the abbey."

She nursed her wine while he stirred his pot of apples, which made the kitchen smell spicy and sweet. She loved that smell; it was like the hug of a mother she'd never had.

At long last, he took a sharp knife and cut two large

slices of the quiche. It oozed with cheese. He added generous portions of the salad to both their plates, then offered them to her. "Could you put these on the table?"

"Am I the footman now?" she asked, but she took the plates anyway.

He followed behind her with bread, butter, and the bowl of steaming apples.

The dining table was small and round, and they sat beside each other.

"Please, begin," he said, gesturing for her to take the first bite.

She did not need to be begged. She chomped into the steaming quiche, and it was heaven: fluffy and gooey, with bits of mushroom and bacon and something herbaceous.

"Toothsome," she said.

He smiled. "I'm glad you like it."

He began to eat his own meal. He'd gone rather stiff, however. The ease he'd had in the kitchen was gone. Almost like he was at a loss to be alone with her without some task to keep him busy.

"Let's practice your gab," she said.

"My what?"

She assumed her finest accent. "Your conversation with the fairer sex, milord."

"Indeed, yes," he said quickly. He paused. "How would you recommend I begin?"

"You know how to talk to a lady, Eden. I've seen you do it a hundred times with right elegance." He had perfect manners, after all.

"Yes," he parried, "but never with a woman I've wished to marry."

"Well, it's no different. A girl's a girl."

"Very well." He brightened his voice. "Terrible weather today."

She rolled her eyes. "Rain. How seductive. Don't talk of the weather."

"Why? It's universally relevant and makes a strong impact on one's happiness."

"Not one's lust. Unless you happen to like swiving in a storm, no offense intended. We all have our little preferences. I suppose lightning gives the act a rather—"

He blushed. "Please stop. My future wife would definitely not talk to me of swiving."

"Not on your first meeting," she allowed. But he had gone red enough for her to take pity on him.

"Let's see," she mused. "Why don't you talk about your abbey? Great houses are magnets for fine ladies."

He nodded, looking less ill.

"We recently landscaped the rear gardens in the French style in Cumbria," he said. "And there's a fountain imported from Saint Petersburg."

"How beautiful it must be," she said, adding a high-pitched girlish croon to her most cultivated voice. "I'd *so* love to see it. Perhaps someday you will arrange a visit for me and Mama."

He burst out laughing. "Where did that accent come from?"

She glared at him. "You think I can only talk like a gutter-bred slattern."

"No, I simply wasn't aware you could also talk like a drawing room miss."

"Some gents like to whore with a gentle-bred lady. I have my tricks."

"Can you do others?"

"*Oui*," she said in a French accent. "I *adore* zees wine. *Magnifique!*"

"Needs a bit of work on the *R*s to pass as Parisian, but not bad."

"How do you know so much about what Parisian whores sound like, Monsieur Eden?"

"I told you, my mother was French. Although, er, not a whore. Obviously."

"More's the pity."

"We seem to have gotten off the topic at hand."

"Yes. Tell me more about your beautiful estate."

"Well, we have sixty acres. Much of it's grazing land, but we also raise livestock. Actually, we had quite an exciting year. A new blend of sheep feed has caused the herd to increase their weight by thirty percent in nearly half the amount of time we formerly—"

Thaïs reached out and put her hand over his lips. "No."

He looked flustered. "No?"

"We do not talk about sheep slop to women we want to marry."

He looked skeptical. "I agree it's not the most, er, delicate line of conversation, but animal husbandry is a large part of my life. Should I not be honest about that?"

"It's a part of your life your wife won't care about unless she's humoring you or happens to love lamb more than is good and natural."

"Plenty of women are interested in economics."

"Well then, wait for her to say, 'Why, Lord Eden, I'm so very curious about your sheep. Tell me, how long does it take you to fatten them up for the slaughter?'"

"That accent truly is very amusing. If I didn't know you, I'd think you grew up on St. James's Square."

"I grew up servicing the men of St. James's Square," she said.

The sparkle went out of his eyes. "Were you very young when you started?"

"Auctioned off at fourteen," she said jauntily, though the memory was not very pleasant.

"That's too young. How awful."

She shrugged. "Plenty of girls in the brothel weren't so lucky. The madam would have started me younger except she thought she could get more if she waited for my tits to come in. And come in they did."

He pointedly did not look at her tits.

"How was it that you were in a brothel at such a young age?"

"Usual reasons. Orphan. Fine-dressed lady found me on the streets and offered me a position as her serving girl. Didn't mention I'd be serving in a whore-house, and I was too young to know better anyway."

"How old were you?"

"Nine."

"Thaïs, I'm so sorry."

She disliked his pity. She'd done well for herself, her youth be damned. And everyone had a bit of trial in their past.

She waved his sympathy away. "Wasn't you who tricked me."

"I mean I'm sorry it happened to you. That you lost your parents so young and didn't have an adult to protect you from the procuress."

She shrugged. She'd long ago stopped crying on that account.

"What happened after you were sold?" Eden asked.

"The baron who took my cherry was nice enough. Kept me for a year. Then passed me on to a Swedish prince. Then a French merchant—lived in Paris for two years. After a few more stints as a mistress I got a reputation for being the delectable courtesan that I am, and I went on my own. One client a week, hand-picked, just like I like it."

"You like it?" He seemed so genuinely curious, she was not even offended by the question.

"Of course I like it. Wouldn't have done it this long if I didn't. I make enough to support myself in style working nought but a day a week. And I'm the best at what I do. As you'll know if you ever hop into bed with me."

Chapter Four

Eden had blushed so many times during the course of this meal that his face felt permanently scorched. He knew Thaïs was enjoying mortifying him.

A small part of him was drawn to her ribald speech. As much as it horrified his sensibilities, he'd never been spoken to with such carnal frankness.

He supposed the gentlemanly thing to do was admit it.

"I look forward to enjoying your talents," he said quietly, forcing himself to look into her eyes.

She slapped her hand across the table. "Finally, he confesses he has desires."

"I never said I didn't."

"Could have fooled me. You'll want to be a bit more direct with your lady on that subject, once you snare her. But you're learning."

"I hope I won't have to do something as ghoulish as snaring her. I'd fancied I could coax at least one person into marriage without having to break her ankle."

Thaïs laughed, which gratified him. "Well, your conversation is improving. All you have to do is talk to her the way you've been talking to me. Ask her questions. Listen to her, and then ask more. Of course, it goes both ways. You'll also have to talk about yourself, without droning on about hogs."

"Sheep," he corrected her. "I don't keep hogs, except for the—"

"Don't care! Tell me something *interesting* about yourself."

"About myself in what sense?"

"Well, how you grew up? Your parents, for instance."

He winced. "I'm afraid speaking of my parents may not win me any affections. Quite the opposite, in fact."

She looked at him with interest. "Why's that?"

"They were a bit notorious in their day."

She leaned in, green eyes alight. "For what?"

He hated to talk about this, but he supposed he owed it to her, after she had been so forthcoming about her childhood.

"Well, my father was a poet of modest repute," he said. "He never quite took to the responsibilities of a landowner."

"Didn't care for the sheep?"

"Er, not especially, no. Had a taste for opium. Spent all his money. Would have lost the abbey, were it not entailed. As it was, he let it go to seed."

"And your mama?"

"He met her in Paris on his grand tour. She was not of high birth—a baker's daughter. She was quite a lovely woman—very kind, very beautiful—but an erratic character. Sometimes she would wake me to dance in the garden in the middle of the night, sometimes she would stay in bed for weeks." He paused. "She took her own life when I was ten years old."

Thaïs's face went soft with sympathy. "Ghastly. Poor boy."

He nodded. "It was . . . difficult. My father, of

course, was beside himself. Sent me away to school, left the house and estate a shambles. He did recover a bit after a decade. Remarried. His wife gave birth to my sister, Anna, who of course you know. But they both succumbed to a fever soon after she was born. As Anna's guardian, I took on her care myself. With the help of a nursemaid and governess, of course."

Thaïs looked at him grimly. "You're right. You might save the family history for after the wedding."

He smiled. "Sheep it is, then."

She nodded gravely. "Sheep it is."

He stood, perhaps a bit too abruptly. He did not wish to answer more questions. It was melancholy, speaking of his parents. And it reminded him why he was here: to avoid repeating the mistakes of his father. He would not be an unsteady husband nor marry a volatile woman. He would find a girl trained for a stable kind of life, raised to be a wife and mother and run a grand home. And he would devote himself to being exactly the kind of man his father wasn't.

He picked up their plates and started walking to the kitchen.

"Need any help?" Thaïs asked, in the tone of a woman who did not in any way wish to help.

He shook his head. "Cleaning is a meditative activity. I wouldn't dream of letting you deprive me of it."

She puckered her lips. "I don't enjoy meditative activities, so I'll leave you to it."

He washed up quickly. He was scrupulous about cleaning as he cooked, so there was not much to do. When he went back into the sitting room it was growing dark inside. Thaïs had lit every lamp in the room and was sitting by a window, staring off at the dim rose garden. Her porcelain skin looked lunar in the lamplight. God, she was beautiful.

She noticed him staring at her and whipped her head around. "Ah, there he is. Best you come entertain me before I die of boredom."

"You needn't sit idle on my account. You're welcome to read, sleep . . ."

She shook her head. "I hate reading, and it's far too early to go to bed."

"Perhaps you have correspondence?"

"Perhaps not."

She looked at him expectantly. "She's bored."

"She?"

"The beautiful woman you kidnapped to live alone in your tiny house."

"Kidnapped! Is that what you think?" He had not considered the ethics of summoning her to this cottage without the full information about where and with whom she'd spend the month until she'd arrived thinking she'd been tricked. He felt guilty, even if there'd been no malice in it.

"Oh, don't yawp about it," she said. "You paid for the privilege of my company, so get your money's worth."

"I'm afraid I have letters I must reply to in order to give them to Hattie to post in the morning."

"What kind of letters?"

This he did not wish to tell her.

"Private ones."

She let out a hoot. "Sounds spicy. Come on, tell the girl. Perhaps I can use my magnificent brain to help you."

Upon reflection, this was not such a terrible idea.

"My secretary is preparing reports on young ladies for me to review. Once I identify which women I wish to meet, he'll determine which invitations to accept. Usually one's mother would perform this activity, but as mine is no longer living . . ."

Thaïs nodded sympathetically. "You need a female opinion. I'll help you as part of my services."

"Thank you."

He retrieved the missive on his desk and settled in the parlor to unseal it.

"Lady Sophia Greenwood," he read. "Eldest daughter of Lord Peter Greenwood, Earl of Lancaster."

"Elegant name," Thaïs said. "And nobility."

"Belonging to the aristocracy is not a detriment, but not strictly necessary," he said.

"Why not, milord?"

"Well, whoever I marry will receive my title. No reason for her to be born with one of her own. And plenty of girls have lovely manners and proper education, and that's all I require."

"What you mean is, you want yourself an heiress."

He shook his head. "No. My estate does well. I have no need of a wife with a large fortune."

Thaïs raised a brow. "So you're richer than I thought. I guess you must be, to pay such a sum for a month with me."

He hated to speak of money. "I made profitable investments."

"Fancy-speak for *being rich*."

"Would you like to hear the rest of the letter?"

She waved her finger at him to proceed. "I certainly would."

"Lady Sophia," he read, "is regarded as an elegant young lady with a pristine reputation and sterling breeding, as the daughter of an earl and granddaughter of a duke."

"A duke. Impressive. Too bad you don't care."

"She is eighteen years old, in good health, and considered a beauty."

"Nix. Too young."

He was inclined to agree. He was more than double Lady Sophia's age. He'd prefer a girl at least several years older than his sister.

"Perhaps she has maturity for her age, but I do think I'd prefer a woman who is older."

"Read me the next one," Thaïs said.

"Miss Emily Harper is the fourth child of Mr. Robert Harper, owner of the Standish Shipping Company."

"Fourth child. Means her mama was fertile. Good sign for you."

"Unfortunately, Standish Shipping is involved in trade with the slaving colonies. I'd want no association with such a family."

"Scratch her, then. Who's next?"

He read her three different descriptions, and she rejected all three on grounds of the women being, respectively, too old (thirty-two), too urbane (raised in Paris), too recently widowed (a year since her husband's death). He did not necessarily agree with these assessments, but it was amusing to hear Thaïs's opinions.

He enjoyed listening to the colorful way she expressed herself. She could have been a poet. A very vulgar poet.

"Thank you for your candor," he said. "This was helpful."

"Well, one of us has to be blunt about the options. It's your whole life we're deciding. 'Til death do you part is the bargain, so I hear."

Yes. His entire future was at stake. His legacy.

He stood up.

"Where are you going?" Thaïs asked.

"Forgive me for leaving you unattended, but I must write a reply now."

She groaned. "Dull, dull, dull he is. Letting me rot away lonesome as a stray mutt."

"You are far from a stray mutt. And perhaps you have some . . . handiwork? Sewing?"

She snorted. "The only handiwork these fingers do is under the breeches."

His mouth fell open.

She laughed. "Oh, don't act so shocked. I'm a *moll*."

He could tell she enjoyed riling him with ribaldry.

It was beginning to have an effect, in that he kept thinking of sex. So much that he needed to remove himself from her company.

"So you are," he said. "In any case, it's time for me to retire. I'm going to pen the letter in my room. Good night."

"Are you joking?"

"Not at all."

"It's eight o'clock, Eden."

"I keep country hours."

"Well, don't expect me to be up with you in the morning."

"I would never ask you for something so harrowing."

He dashed off his letter in a scrawl quite a bit more slapdash than his usual precise hand, then undressed himself and climbed into bed.

He closed his eyes. But sleep did not claim him.

He was too damned aroused.

Odd. Usually he slaked such urges in the morning and needed no further outlet the rest of the day. But the thought of Thaïs sitting just downstairs—Thaïs available to him whenever he dared to be intimate with her—made his skin tingle. He almost regretted attenuating this process. How pleasant it would be to go downstairs, take her by the hand, and . . .

He gripped himself, imagining it, and came quickly.

He hoped she didn't hear the gasp he made.

God knew that she would cackle at it.

Chapter Five

Thaïs awoke to the sound of birdsong. She removed her silk eye mask and squinted against the harsh, mid-day light that assaulted her eyes even through the filmy curtains. The small clock on the wall read half past noon. She groaned.

"Damn country sunshine," she grumbled to herself.

She pulled the curtains aside and slid the window open. Fresh, meadowy air hit her like she'd inhaled smelling salts. She was so used to the close, humid, smoky smell of London that the absence of stench made her homesick.

Eden was in the garden fussing with a rosebush. It looked like he was—yes, he *was*—cutting off flowers. Was the man making a bouquet?

"Are you a florist now in addition to a maid?" she called.

He turned around and his eyes bulged at the sight of her.

"Thaïs!" he cried, squeezing his eyes so tightly closed his nose wrinkled. "You must dress."

She looked down at her uncovered breasts and shrugged. "I sleep as God made me."

"Yes, well, you're awake now, and anyone could see you."

"No one's here but you, and you paid good money for the sight."

"Close the curtains and get dressed," he gritted out.

She sighed and stepped away from the window.

"Get dressed in bloody what?" she muttered, eyeing yesterday's gown lying crumpled on the floor. She'd worn it for two days traveling, and the idea of putting it back on made her skin crawl.

Which was ridiculous. Plenty of people wore the same clothes for a week without complaint. She'd spent many years as one of them.

"Ain't you the fine-kept lamb," she said to her reflection. Her *beautiful* reflection. She made a kiss at herself in the mirror. A woman as fine as this deserved a clean gown, and that was that.

She pulled one of the gauzy dressing gowns she'd been allowed to keep out of the wardrobe and shrugged it on, sashing it tightly at the waist so that she resembled a figure eight. She fluffed her curls and pinched her cheeks. "There she is," she said to herself, amused. "Eden's nightmare come to life." If the man wasn't going to put her properly to work at anything more fun than peeling carrots, she'd entertain herself by attempting to shock the prude right out of him.

She sallied down the stairs. "Milord?" she called. He didn't answer. A quick look around the house confirmed it was empty. She threw open the front door. He had migrated to a different corner of the garden, where he appeared to be pulling weeds out from around a bush with fluffy white flowers she didn't know the name of. A basket of roses sat beside the door.

"Now he's the gardener, is he?"

He looked behind his shoulder at her and let out a sigh.

"You're trying to shock me, aren't you?" he said.

She shook her head innocently. "Just came to say good morning."

"Good afternoon," he said, turning back to his weeds. "I'm amazed you slept through the roosters. They're quite loud."

"I'm frightful good at sleeping."

"So it would seem. Now, please go inside and put something on. You've made your point. The seamstress is coming at four o'clock to measure you for a few new gowns."

"Not going in until you've given me a nice, long look," she said. He sighed and turned back around. His eyes dutifully scanned up and down her figure.

"Lovely," he said. "Truly. Now, please cover up. Or at least go inside. Anyone could walk by."

"No shame in a woman's form," she said. "And no one can see through those hedges."

"Someone could amble up the drive. If I'm seen with a barely dressed woman and anyone discovers who I am, it will hurt my potential as an advantageous match. So please, honor our agreement and get dressed."

"Very well, you old prune."

She went back upstairs, put on a fresh shift, and donned her tired gown. Her stomach growled. She poked her head out of the window and called down to Eden, "I'm hungry."

He looked up, and his face relaxed when he saw she was dressed. It was the wrong reaction. She would not leave this place until his face relaxed when he saw her in the nude.

"Hattie left fresh bread and cold ham in the kitchen."

"Am I a plowman?"

"There's also cheese and apples."

She sighed loudly. In truth she didn't mind munching on picnic fare, but nagging at him was fruitful: his frustration made him loosen up.

"I'll make you something nice for supper," he promised.

"You better, Your Lordship. When are you coming in? We need to get on with your lessons."

"Eat. I'll be in soon."

She went down to the kitchen and found the promised luncheon on the table, arranged prettily on a tray. She cut herself a slice of bread and slathered it with butter. It went nicely with the salty ham.

Eden walked inside carrying the roses.

"Enjoying your luncheon?" he asked. He put the flowers down beside a basin of water and began to trim them with a knife.

"Are those for me?" she asked.

He smiled at her. "If you'll accept them."

"Right courtly of you."

"I'm glad I can do something correctly when it comes to courtship."

"You're going to do much more than bring ladies bouquets of roses when I'm through with you," she said. "Today, we'll dance."

He shook his head. "No need. I already know how to dance."

"You may know the steps. But do you know how to make a promise with your body?"

He squinted. "What does that mean?"

"Dancing done right is like pledging to a lady that there's more pleasure to come."

He looked distinctly ill at ease about making such a pledge.

"We don't have any music," he pointed out.

"I'll sing you a nice tune. Come. We'll practice in the parlor, where there's more room."

Chapter Six

*I*f there was one aspect of his boyhood education Eden's parents had not neglected, it was dancing.

His mother had been mad about dancing. She'd danced with his father every evening, with her lady's maid playing the accompaniment. But she hadn't needed music. She'd danced with Eden himself from the time he was a small boy, whirling him about the nursery in her arms as she hummed a tune. Later, she'd interrupt his studies or awaken him in the night to be her partner. During the years they could afford a governess, she enlisted the woman to play the pianoforte so she could teach him the minuet, the sarabande, the gavotte, and country jigs. She taught him silly dances of her own devising: galloping, twirling, jetéing in the air. Sometimes, she invited other children to come dance with him—those of farmers, villagers, or neighboring genteel families, it didn't matter.

But she had been his primary partner. She'd encouraged him, laughed with him, told him how graceful he was, how proficient on his little feet. She'd been beautiful and joyous when she danced. He loved it, but it also scared him. Because after these happy times, she sometimes became so melancholy that she'd disappear inside her room for days or wander about the house in a nightdress, her eyes blank, like she couldn't see him.

It could be months until, like magic, she wanted to dance again.

Thaïs, her hand in his and her eyes bright, offering to sing a song for them to dance to, was like a memory come to life. He let her lead him to the parlor, but he felt heavy on his feet, almost in a daze. When she looked at him, she cocked her head.

"Something wrong?"

"Just a memory."

"Not a nice one," she said. An observation, not a question.

He didn't deny it.

"What happened? Awkward on your feet? Stepped on some poor girl? Fell into the punch bowl?"

"Nothing like that. I'm quite a good dancer, in fact."

"Oh? Prove it."

She began to hum a minuet. He could tell she was a terrible singer. Utterly tuneless. Evidently, she could see this on his face, because she cackled. "Well, we're not at the opera, are we? I'm all the music you can get, unless you'd like to sing the tune."

"Never," he said. "I'm enjoying your performance."

"All it's for is to keep the time, and I know how to count. Not to brag."

He chuckled. "Very well. Please proceed with the accompaniment."

They took their places, and she once again began to hum. They bowed to each other and stepped forward, pausing to face each other and join hands.

As they began the first turn, Thaïs stopped humming.

"You're stiff," she said.

He disagreed. The minuet required impeccable posture. "I'm in form," he countered.

"Yes," she agreed, "but no one wants to dance with a wooden board, even if he's in form. Let's start again. This time, act like you *want* to dance with me."

He didn't, in point of fact. Or, he did, because it meant touching her. But that was a problem. It reminded him of last night. How he couldn't trust his reactions to her.

Nevertheless, he assumed the original position, facing her.

"You're looking past me," Thaïs said. "Look into my eyes."

He did so.

"Smile."

He did that too.

"Like you mean it. Like you're fond of me."

"I do mean it." He *was* fond of her, in his own way. Though, not like he hoped to be fond of a bride. There would be sweetness there. Not this charged combination of banter and veiled threat.

"Smile like you want to take me on the terrace and have your way with me," Thaïs said.

He frowned at her and shook his head. "Utterly inappropriate."

"Not if you're trying to win a girl. Do you want her to think she could be anyone, or do you want her to think you want to be dancing with *her*?"

"Her, specifically. Of course."

"Then tell her that with your eyes."

He looked directly into Thaïs's eyes and thought

about how she'd appeared in the window completely nude. It was not hard to want her. Her specifically.

"That's better," she said. "On we go, then."

She resumed humming, and they both walked forward. When they turned to face each other again he offered her his hand. This time, he shot her that same heated glance.

She smiled at him.

It made him realize she didn't often smile. She was plenty merry when she wanted to be, but usually she was so busy harassing him or talking that her face didn't reflect happiness. When she smiled, she reminded him of his mother. His mother in the happy times.

He smiled back.

"Clasp my hand like you want to take more of me," she instructed. "Like you suffer, holding just my hand."

He thought about his future with Thaïs, how eventually they would kiss, touch intimately, share a bed. He thought about his choice to delay this process, and his hesitation made him ache. He wanted her. It scared him to his bones, but he did. Every time he moved close enough to feel her skin, his body thrummed with a reminder of it. Every time he caught a whiff of her spicy scent, he wanted another.

They continued through the steps, with her occasionally breaking up her humming to give him instruction. As they danced on, she spoke less and smiled more.

He began to understand what she desired of him. To dance with a woman could be polite, but it could also be more like an intimate conversation. It could convey affection or longing.

Desire.

When they reached the final bow, Thaïs's face was soft, the smile on her lips subtle. It seemed she was genuinely pleased.

"You dance like a dream, when you put your heart into it."

Dance like a dream. It was the way his mother had danced. Perhaps this was why he could open up this part of himself. He'd inherited it from the woman who had loved him most. He'd lost it when she'd left him, but it was still there. He could have it back, if he let himself.

"Now's the part," Thaïs said softly, "where you whisper something in my ear."

He moved closer. Far apart enough for decency in society, but close enough to be within the range of hearing. "Thank you for the dance," he said. "I enjoyed it. May I have another one, later?"

She rolled her eyes. "How polite."

"Speaking to a young lady just out in society, one has to be polite," he pointed out.

"It's not what you say," she said, "it's the tone you use to say it. Ask me for another dance like you're asking me to join you on the terrace for a stolen kiss."

"But I would never ask for such a thing. It would be a scandal."

"Then make a scandal. But make it with your eyes, your voice, the lingering of your hand. Make a scandal only she's aware of."

A scandal only she's aware of. He liked this turn of phrase. Thaïs could be quite eloquent when she chose to be. It was charming, actually, how her register could change between the polite tones of the ballroom to the squawking of a street vendor in a second's time. She should be a ventriloquist.

"Let's take it from the final bow," he said. "I'll try again."

She picked up her humming, and they drew closer. This time, he didn't smile. He looked into her eyes intently. "Thank you for the dance," he said like he might say *Come to bed with me*.

"You're welcome," she whispered back shyly, in her cultivated accent.

"Would you permit me to ask you for another?"

Thaïs blushed. Either she could will herself to do so, or the intimacy in his tone had genuinely worked on her.

"You've done well," she said softly. "Perhaps now we should move on to stolen moments."

Before he could ask her what she meant by this, there was a knock at the door.

Chapter Seven

Eden darted away from her so quickly he knocked his ankle against a wooden table leg and cursed under his breath. It amused her, but not as much as it might have had she not been so thoroughly enjoying their dancing lesson. It was sweet watching him become more self-assured. It made her feel a little girlish. She knew about seduction—she was, after all, a genius at it—but it was rare indeed to be on the receiving end, given a whore was a sure thing. It was all playacting, but she liked the game.

"Steady there, milord," she said to Eden. "You need that foot for dancing."

He looked nervously at the door and put a finger to his lips to shush her. "That will be the dressmaker," he whispered. "She thinks you're my sister. She can't know we were dancing."

Thaïs nodded solemnly. "I'll tell her we were kissing instead."

His face contorted into horror, and she laughed. He was so easy to tease. It made her fonder of him.

"Remember," he whispered, "you're a governess visiting, and your luggage was stolen from the coach on your journey here from London."

"Aye, aye," she said, waving her hand. "I won't expose your perverted ways."

He walked over to the door and opened it. A plump blond-haired, blue-eyed woman stood there, holding a basket in one hand.

"Good afternoon," Eden said. "I'm Mr. Smith. You must be the seamstress Hattie recommended. Mrs.—"

"Sophie Gerity," she supplied.

"And who might this be?" Eden asked in a warm voice, peering down into the basket. Thaïs stood on her toes to see over his shoulder.

"A baby!" she exclaimed. The little creature was an angel, all wisps of blond hair and fat, rosy cheeks and eyes as blue as his mother's.

"What a precious darling," she said, edging Eden out of her way so she could get a better view. She reached down and put her finger to the baby's tiny pink hand. He squeezed it and her heart along with it. She adored babies, even strangers' babies, even—especially—ugly scrunch-faced babies. In the list of things she loved, they numbered only below her friends and money. And she needed money in part so she could, eventually, have a baby of her own. Perhaps even a whole family of her own, complete with a handsome, fawning husband.

It was her most secret fantasy: a family life.

"What's his name?" Thaïs asked the dressmaker.

"Charlie," Sophie said, smiling down at him.

"This is my sister, Miss Jane Smith," Eden said.

She nearly laughed. He'd given her the blandest name he could think of, obviously.

"Nice to meet you, Miss Smith," Sophie said. "I'm sorry to hear about your stolen trunks. Terrible, what people will do for a few pounds. But we'll have you some new gowns before the week is out."

Sophie didn't sound suspicious of their story. Eden must have noticed too, for she could sense him relax.

"A week? You must work quickly," Thaïs said.

"My sisters help me. There's six of us, and I'm the oldest and the only yet married. Youngest one is nine. No brothers. Usually they mind the little one when I make calls, but it's washing day at home, and they can't be spared. But he's a good baby. Hardly cries at all, except when he's hungry. But don't you worry. I fed him just before I left."

This woman clearly loved to talk. Just as well, as Thaïs didn't mind listening, and the fewer questions Sophie asked the better.

"I'll leave you ladies to it," Eden said. "Sophie, it was a pleasure to meet you." He withdrew to his study, closing the door firmly behind him.

"My bedchamber is upstairs," Thaïs said, using her fine lady voice. "We can do the fitting there."

"Such a lovely home," Sophie said as she followed Thaïs up the stairs. "A warm, sunny place to spend your holiday. Except for yesterday, when it was raining, of course. But the sun can't shine every day, can it?"

"How would we appreciate good weather if it did?" Thaïs asked.

"Exactly," Sophie said. "Undress then, if you would, and I'll take your measurements."

"Of course."

As Thaïs unlaced her bodice and shimmied out

of her skirts, Sophie continued to talk about the weather.

"Nasty out, it was, yesterday, and the day before. I was meant to deliver two ball gowns up to the old viscountess's house, but my nag wouldn't have made it up the hill. Have you seen the house, yet, Dunsmoor? Finest establishment in all of Gloucestershire if you ask me."

"A viscountess lives nearby?" Thaïs asked.

She was surprised Eden wasn't worried about being spotted by someone of his class.

"Well, a dowager. Getting on in age. Seventy if she's a day, and mostly blind, poor thing. Lift up your arms for me, love, will you?"

"And yet she still goes to balls?" Thaïs asked, shifting so that Sophie could measure her bust. "She must be impressive."

"Oh, the gowns aren't for her. They're for Lady Maria. That's her granddaughter. She's staying with her for the summer. Sixteen, I think, but the viscountess allows her to attend the local dances as long as she's chaperoned by her maid. Pretty girl. She'll marry well, that one, when she's old enough. Of course, I was married at fifteen, but they do it differently in the upper crust. She has to be presented to the queen. The queen! Can you imagine?"

"I certainly cannot," Thaïs said with a chuckle. That would be the day.

The baby gurgled, and Thaïs and Sophie both bent over to coo at him.

"You like children," Sophie observed.

"I do. I sometimes feel as though I'm a mother to my students." She did not add that her students were primarily young prostitutes who wished for training to be courtesans. She ran her own small charity to elevate such girls, taking on a few students a year.

"You have the hips for it," Sophie said, measuring around Thaïs's rump. "I have them too, good birthing hips. This one came right out, only three hours' labor. Of course, he's not my first. That's my little Molly, four years next month. Took six hours to get her out, but then, the first one's always hardest."

Thaïs imagined Eden overhearing this conversation and suppressed a laugh. "God blessed you," she said.

"Oh, indeed he did."

Sophie continued to chatter as she finished her measurements, telling Thaïs all the village gossip. She was so detailed that it made for a rollicking yarn, even though Thaïs did not know any of the people Sophie spoke of.

"Three gowns, then. Will that be enough?" Sophie asked. "Or maybe four, since you're here a month? Nice not to have to wear the same thing every day. I can do the first one for you in the next two days, the others inside a week, if I get the girls to do the stitching. They have nimble fingers. Our mother was a seamstress too, and she'd slap our knuckles if she caught us missing a stitch. Painful, but it worked, didn't it? It's her dress shop that I run. Well, mine now, I suppose. She passed a few years back, poor thing. A tumor, they said, though we couldn't see it."

"How awful. I'm sorry."

"It's nature's way. But we miss her every day. I'll send your first gown over with Hattie when it's done, save you a trip to town."

Thaïs thought of twenty-nine more endless days

stuck in this tiny cottage and nearly groaned. "Oh, you needn't," she said. "I can come collect it from your shop."

"No use," Sophie assured her. "Hattie lives next door, she does, and she'll be coming here."

"Thank you," Thaïs said reluctantly. "How kind."

"I'll see myself out, if you don't mind, since you're in your unmentionables. The baby will need to eat soon, and I'd best get home before he fusses."

"Very well," Thaïs said. "Thank you for coming."

Thaïs dressed and went downstairs, for lack of any other entertainment. Perhaps she could pick up where she left off with Eden. She'd liked their little lesson.

He was still in the study with the door closed. She considered knocking, but it would be more fun to barge in, and fun was scarce to be had in a cottage in the middle of nowhere.

He looked up from his papers when she walked in, spectacles on his eyes and a quill in his hand. A lock of black hair had fallen over his brow. She liked how his hair was tousled. She would ruffle him up when he finally allowed her in his bed.

"Mrs. Gerity is gone?" Eden asked.

"She is. Took her time. Quite a talker, that one. Chattered off my ear. Not that I minded. Full of gossip. Did you know the last schoolmaster here was sacked for fornicating with a barmaid at the carnival?"

His eyes widened. "No. How outrageous."

"*And*," she said, "the baker's wife is sleeping with the surgeon the next town over, and everyone knows except the baker."

He craned his neck at her, like he was not at all sure why she was telling him this. "Oh? I'll remember that the next time I eat bread."

"You don't want to hear about the village scandals?"

"Not particularly. We don't know any of the people and aren't likely to meet them."

"Here's one you might care to know. There's a dowager viscountess living a few miles away."

"Yes, I'm aware."

"You are? I'd think you'd be worried about being recognized."

"Camberwell mentioned it when he set me up here. Assured me she's half-blind and never leaves the house. I'm not acquainted with her anyway. Her son and I don't see eye to eye, as you know."

"Her son?"

"Lord Bell," he said, naming Elinor's estranged husband. A man so vile his very name sent the devil's fingers down her spine.

"Lord *Bell*?" she sputtered. "Elinor's *husband*?"

"The very same," he said.

"But he knows who you are. And he certainly knows who *I* am. Hates me and anyone else who loves his wife."

"He's a bastard," Eden said grimly. "But we needn't worry. Camberwell told me he hasn't been here in years. Not exactly the type to dote on his mother, unsurprisingly. And since we won't be going out, we won't be spotted."

She was hardly listening because suddenly she remembered Sophie had mentioned a girl named Maria.

Elinor's daughter was named Maria.

Which meant Elinor's missing daughter was living a few miles away.

"Gracious bleeding Jesus," she muttered.

"Excuse me?"

"Maria's there."

He looked at her blankly. "Elinor's girl," she explained. "Bell's been keeping El from her children. She thought they were in Devon. She's there looking for them. I have to write her."

His face softened in immediate sympathy. She liked him for it.

"Of course," he said. "Do it today, before Hattie picks the post up in the morning."

"Do you have another quill? I'll do it now."

He rummaged in the desk and produced a bottle of ink and a quill, which he sharpened deftly. He handed it to her along with paper.

"Thank you," she said.

She hurried to the parlor table to sit down and write her news.

Chapter Eight

There was an untuned orchestra's worth of racket coming from the parlor. Cursing. Incoherent grumbling. Scratching. The crumpling of paper. More cursing. Eden had never heard a person make so much noise writing a letter in his life.

He could not concentrate on his work. He rose to close the study door and found Thaïs sitting at the parlor table with ink smeared on her hands and splattered on her face, a pile of torn pages littered all around her. She was bent over a fresh page, writing with such concentration that the tip of her tongue was clenched between her teeth.

He heard the distinct sound of the nub breaking, and she slammed the quill down on the table in frustration, nearly knocking over the vial of ink.

"Fucking hell," she hissed.

"Thaïs," he said, "is something the matter?"

She looked up quickly, and some emotion flashed across her face. Fear?

No.

Shame.

A feeling he'd never imagined her capable of. He didn't like to see it.

"Can I borrow your knife?" she asked, wiping the

expression off her face and replacing it with a wry look that did not seem genuine. "I smashed the nib. Clumsy me."

"Of course."

He went back to his desk to fetch it. She reached for it with ink-stained fingers, and he thought better of handing her the pristine ivory handle. "May I do it for you?"

"If you like." She held out the quill. He reached in his pocket for his handkerchief and took the quill gingerly between two fingers, cleaning it off before he touched it.

"Sorry," she grumbled. "I made a mess."

"Quite all right." He whittled delicately at the nib until it was sharp and crisp, then handed it back to her.

"Thank you," she said darkly.

"You're welcome."

"Well, off with you," she said, making a shooing motion.

He walked back into his study, closed the door, and resumed working. But before two minutes had passed, the ruckus resumed, loud enough to bother him even through the walls.

He went back into the parlor and found Thaïs glaring at the page.

"You little bastards," she said, scratching out a word.

"Is the paper too rough?"

He bent over to look at what she was writing. She snatched the page away and held it to her chest. "No spying."

He backed away, but he'd seen enough to realize what the problem was: not the paper, but what was written on it. Her penmanship was childlike, many of her letters backward.

A surge of sympathy went through him. Of course. She'd told him she'd been raised in a brothel. She wouldn't have had an education. He was impressed she knew how to write at all.

"My apologies," he said. "I don't mean to intrude upon your privacy."

She waved him away. "Off with you. I'll be quiet as a mouse."

He hesitated. "Perhaps you'd like some assistance?"

She glared at him. "With what?"

"You could dictate, and I could write for you."

"Cook. Gardener. Secretary. Will His Earldom never settle on a job?"

She clearly did not want his help, and he wouldn't force it on her.

"I'll leave you," he said.

He retreated to the study, shut the door, and braced himself for the cacophony to continue. But this time, there was silence.

And then the door swung open.

"Fine," she said.

"Fine?"

"I'm not good at my letters, if you must know."

She looked at him pugnaciously, like she expected him to chastise her for this.

"I'm good enough at mine," he said. "Let's collaborate, shall we?"

"Enough of that," she snapped.

"Of what?" he asked, bemused.

"Don't talk to me like I'm a baby. You only make it worse."

"Make what worse?"

She slumped down into a chair and folded her arms over her chest. "How I barely know my letters. It's embarrassing."

This was why he supported female education. Why he had bid so generously to support the Institute Thaïs and her friends were building. Every child deserved the basic ability to read and write.

"Thaïs, there's nothing to be ashamed of," he said. "I'm happy to help. And I'm sure your missive will be more interesting than the one I'm writing to my land steward."

She did not quite grin, but at least the humiliation left her face.

"What's the going rate to hire an earl to write my letters?" she asked.

He smiled. "For you, I'll do it for free."

"Very well. Are you ready?"

He took out a fresh page, dipped the quill in ink, and nodded.

"Dear Elinor," she said, "you won't believe who I'm here with. Not Camberwell. It's Lord Eden. It turns out he's a right lecher."

He did not, of course, write this down.

"How droll," he said.

She cackled.

"I'd ask you to keep my involvement out of this," he said.

"Just a little comedy. But look at you, red as a cock in the morning sun."

He hoped she was referring to the poultry and not the genitalia.

He had his doubts.

"Do you actually wish to dictate a letter, or shall I go back to my correspondence?"

"What have you got? Any more news of your young ladies?"

Actually, he had. A fresh batch had arrived in the morning post.

"That kind of information is only available to those with no interest in mocking me."

"But mocking you makes you so cross and scrunches up your brows, and I like the looks of it. Much funnier than when you're calm and handsome."

Handsome? He had no problem with his looks, but the compliment (such as it was) surprised and pleased him. He hoped she didn't notice.

No luck.

"Oh, but he likes that, he does," she cackled. "Blushing clear up to his hair."

He leaned back in his chair and glared at her.

"I rescind the offer to help you."

"No," she said. "You don't. I'm learning you're softhearted. Should have gathered it from the way you dote on Anna. You'll take pity on the poor ignorant moll and do as I tell you."

He very much would. But he continued to glare at her, since she seemed to find it amusing.

"Well then, tell me what to write," he said sternly. "I don't have all afternoon."

"Aye. Soon you'll be needing to make my supper."

"Focus."

"Fine, fine! Just having a laugh. Someone around here has to." She cleared her throat. "Are you ready?"

He nodded.

"Dear Elinor," she began.

"Dear Elinor," he repeated, writing down the words.

"I've just arrived in the Cotswolds, and I have the most amazing news. Maria is here. She's staying with that old rat—"

"Slow down!" he said, trying to keep up. "A man can only write so quickly."

"I don't pay my secretary such a fortune to yell at me."

"I'm not yelling. *I have the most amazing news.* Pick up from there."

"Ma-ri-a. Is. Here," she intoned syllable by syllable.

He rolled his eyes. "Why are you making this so difficult?"

She shrugged. "Can't help it."

"You can."

"Very well, my liege. Write this. She's staying with that old rat—"

"Need you curse?"

"*Rat*'s not a curse. If you want to hear a curse—"

He held up his hand. "*That old rat.* Carry on."

"That old rat, the widow Bell. Your mother-in-law."

He finished the sentence and looked up at her expectantly. "What next?"

"What's the name of the house? Sophie said it, but I forgot."

"Dunsmoor, I believe."

"Ah! That's it. Tell her the bloody old crone is holed away at Dunsmoor House."

"Lady Bell resides at Dunsmoor House," he said, writing down his version of the words.

"And you must come here right now," she went on. "We'll find a way for you to see her."

He did not write this down.

"Thaïs, Lady Elinor cannot come here. Obviously."

"Wot? 'Course she can."

"No. She must not. No one is to know we are together."

Her mouth fell open. "Don't joke on me."

"I'm not. It's absolutely impossible. We must be completely discreet."

She narrowed her eyes at him. "Don't be a prig, Eden."

"I'm not being a prig. I'm being careful. Which is the entire reason I paid you such a handsome sum of money for your time."

She shot up from her chair. "Don't talk to me of money. You have plenty of coin, I'm sure, throwing it around for me the way you did. Elinor's in agony missing her children, no idea where they are. Hasn't seen them in two years."

"Which is appalling, of course, but—"

"Imagine if your Anna disappeared for two years," she said. "How would you feel?"

He inhaled sharply at the idea of his sister—as dear to him as his own child—being taken and kept away from him.

"It would be very painful," he admitted quietly.

She nodded. "I'd think it would."

She was right. To withhold this information would be cruel.

"If Elinor comes here, can she be trusted not to divulge that you and I are here together?" he asked.

"She'd be so grateful you could swive me right in front of her and she wouldn't say a word."

"Christ," he groaned. She was being deliberately insufferable for her own amusement. "Please, Thaïs."

"Oh, don't worry," she said gaily. "I'll be sure to tell her you're the type of man who pays a whore *not* to fuck him."

That cut. He knew she was being playful, but his situation pained him. He said nothing.

"Oh, don't be sour," she said, but her tone was uncharacteristically uncertain.

"I don't appreciate mockery any more than you enjoy it," he said.

She looked chastened. "I'm sorry. Truly. You're right. That wasn't kind."

Her eyes were heavy with regret, which made *him* sorry.

"Let's forget it. If you wish for Elinor to come, I'll see to it that she is welcome here."

"Thank you, Eden. And trust she will go to the grave with anything I ask her to."

"I suppose not much can shock her if she spends so much time with you. Certainly not a man wanting a little bedsport in the country before he weds."

He winked at her, and she winked back at him, and he liked being on the inside of a joke with her.

"Now," he said, "tell me what to write."

Chapter Nine

Thaïs went to sleep feeling almost tenderly toward Eden, who had entertained her with a game of checkers after their spat and made a delicious ragout for supper, after which he read her more of his courtship letters.

She had pleasant dreams.

That is, until they were interrupted by god-awful pounding on the door.

"Go away, whoever you are," she groaned, placing a pillow over her head to ward off the bright light shining through the windows.

"Thaïs," Eden called. "It's nearly noon. Wake up."

"Crack of dawn. Come back in the morning."

"Two o'clock is not the morning. It's time you get on country hours. It's a beautiful day. Let's take a walk."

She tore herself out of the nice, soft sheets, stomped to the door, and swung it open.

"Go away."

"Christ," he yelled. "You're naked!"

"I know!" she yelled back. "I sleep that way. I told you."

He slammed the door shut.

She threw it back open.

He was leaning against the wall with his eyes closed, rubbing his temples.

"Oh please. You look like you set eyes on the devil, not a woman in her natural state."

"Put something on."

"If you're going to drag me out of sleep, you can't be scandalized I'm not all dolled up in a gown and bonnet."

"One assumes that a person will wear a nightdress."

"What frowsy nightdresses did you find when we went through my apparel? I sleep the way God made me. Naked as the day I popped out of my mother's—"

"Enough!" he cried.

"You can open your eyes," she said. "I put on a shift, you prude."

He did, and they bulged when he discovered she was a liar, and she laughed as he squinched them back together. He turned around and walked toward the stairs, away from her, muttering, "You are truly unbelievable."

Was she mistaken, or did she hear the slightest speck of a smile in his tone?

"That's what a man gets for waking up his wife before her rising time," she called to his back. "And a doting husband would bring his little wife her breakfast on a tray if he had to interrupt her sleep. Remember that for next time."

She laughed to herself as she walked back to her room. Eden really was so shockable. A true delight to trifle with, being so stiff by nature. Perhaps she shouldn't torture him so much. But was this not why she was here? No lady wants her husband to shrink away in horror at her body. Not exactly flattering. She was going to train him to be what he claimed he wanted to be, even if she had to scare him a little to do it.

She crawled back into bed and closed her eyes

against the light, but the damage was done: she was awake. She put on her gown—the same damned respectable traveling dress she'd been wearing for days—and fluffed out her hair.

In truth, she was quite rested. Eden had gone to bed early after reading her more of his dossiers on potential wives. She'd rejected them all—the first girl being a Philadelphian too colonial to fit his English ways, the second being Scottish, and therefore likely too lively for his delicate sensibilities, the third being a thin brunette who would not satisfy his lusts. He had, of course, denied his lusts were so specific, to which she'd replied that if they were not, why did he have a long list of requirements and a man sending him descriptions of women on paper, as paper would not tell him if a woman caught his eye or pleased his mind? He'd had no answer to that and instead had bade her goodnight at the raw hour of nine o'clock, leaving her so bored and unoccupied that she went to sleep at ten for lack of better occupation.

If she was not careful, he would bore her into keeping country hours indeed.

She needed to quicken the pace of his sexual education, just to keep herself from going mad. A woman could only play so much patience before her brain slopped into mush.

She found Eden downstairs in the kitchen, eating bread the maid had brought from town.

"Well, you've gone and roused me. Now you have to feed me."

Wordlessly, still chewing, he cut her a slice of the bread, slathered it with honey, and handed it to her.

She took a bite. It was delicious.

"Have you recovered from the sight of my bosoms?" she asked through a mouthful.

He gave her a long-suffering look. "Thank you for donning clothing before coming downstairs. I know it goes against your principles."

She grinned at him. "I don't have principles."

"You do, actually. The political variety. It seems it's only when it comes to harassing unsuspecting gentlemen that you lack them."

"Well, start suspecting. Now, where's my tea?"

He gestured at the teapot. "What's mine is yours."

She picked it up to pour herself a cup, but there was nothing in it.

"You drank it all."

"Yes, hours ago."

"Well, make more!"

"You have free range of the kitchen. I assume you can boil water in a kettle."

She *could*, but she didn't want to. She liked watching him do it.

"My husband woke me up and yelled in horror at my body. He'll have to pamper me to make it up to me."

"I didn't yell in horror at your body. I yelled in surprise at the impropriety."

"Seeing your woman naked is plenty proper. You disturbed your wife's rest and hurt her feelings, so you'd better fill the kettle."

He shook his head, but he filled the kettle and put it on the grate.

"I'll give you tea on one condition," he said.

"And what's that?"

"You take a walk with me."

She shook her head. "We've talked about this, Eden," she said. "I don't take walks."

He rolled his eyes at her, which, the better they knew each other, was becoming a regular gesture. Though, she had to admit, the wry way he did it was not without charm.

"You walk in London every day," he said.

"That's London," she countered. "This is the bloody countryside."

"Some would argue that walking in the verdant, peaceful countryside is vastly superior to dodging muck and sewage and pickpockets."

"Not me. I like muck and sewage and pickpockets."

He leaned against a cabinet and examined her, smiling a little. "Somehow, I don't doubt that. Let's try a different tack. A wife must obey her husband."

She snorted. "Not a happy wife. There's a lesson for you to take to heart."

He sighed and shook his head at her. "Thaïs, in all seriousness, taking a lady on a stroll through a park is a ritual of courtship. I've paid you handsomely to practice just these things. And you've been cooped up in this house for days. I'd hazard it's making you irascible."

"I'm irascible by nature."

"I won't argue with that. Let me rephrase. Staying cooped up is making you *more* irascible."

She could see that he was not going to let her win, and she dearly wanted tea.

"Fine, milord. As you wish. But you're not going to like it."

Chapter Ten

Thaïs Magdalene was many things, but dishonest was not one of them. She really, truly hated walking in the country. And she took every opportunity to let him know it.

They'd been out twenty minutes and barely made it a half mile.

First, she insisted that his pace was too quick.

"No lady wants to gallop," she said, walking so slowly that it barely qualified as movement. He knew this was not owing to some disability. She moved faster just walking through the parlor to the kitchen. She was doing it to prove a point.

Nevertheless, he slowed down to her turtle's pace without complaint. If they were going to engage in a battle of wills, he had nothing better to do than to win it.

Next, she decided that the "rocky path" hurt her feet, despite the fact that the path was mostly smooth.

"You're wearing sturdy enough boots," he said. "And we're not going far."

"My feet are delicate. And besides, it's very bright. My skin is turning red."

"Why didn't you wear a hat?"

"Because all my fashions are too slutty for your ways."

"A hat can't possibly be too scandalous."

"For you, anything can be too scandalous. Find me some shade."

He took her elbow and led her off the footpath onto the grass, near a grouping of trees.

"We can sit in the shade, if you prefer, and enjoy the fresh air."

She sneezed violently. "The grass gives me hay fever."

He suspected she was faking it. But when he looked over at her, her eyes did indeed seem red and watery.

She sneezed again. "Damn you, Eden."

He offered her his handkerchief.

She took it and noisily blew her nose, then offered it back to him.

"No need. Consider it yours to keep."

"Can't handle a little snot?"

He sighed. "I can see you're not going to relent. Let's turn around and go home."

"Let's!" she said jauntily.

He noticed her pace was considerably fleeter now that she'd gotten her way. Not a peep to be heard about the rocks or the sunshine. Of course, she had other things to peep about.

"I'm bored," she said. "Should you not be making conversation to entertain me?"

"It's been difficult to get a word in edgewise."

"A gentleman needs to be able to direct the conversation with his lovely."

She had a point.

He gestured out at the downs in the distance. "Do you see those sheep?"

"Hard to miss."

"They're Lancashire Golds. I told Camberwell about them. I brought a heard to the abbey half a decade ago, and our supply of wool doubled. They have thicker coats, you see, and—"

She yawned dramatically. "Your wife does not want to hear about your wool supply, milord," she said. "We've covered this."

"The kind of woman I aim to marry *would* care about agriculture," he countered. "She will, after all, be mistress of the estate and share in the gains of it."

"Well, add *loves farming* to your endless list of requirements."

"My list is not endless."

"It's not short either."

"Do you truly think I'm being unreasonable by desiring to share my life with a woman who takes some degree of interest in my principal occupations?"

She considered this. "Maybe you're right. But the more rules you have, the less likely it'll be you find a girl this season, won't it?"

"Well, yes, I suppose."

"So you have to decide if she really wants to hear about your apple trees and goat breeding."

"I have not mentioned apples or goats."

"Yet."

They were nearing the cottage, and he was not yet ready to abandon the outdoors. Despite Thaïs's grumpiness, he did enjoy her company. And there were gems in her perspective, even when she primarily shared them just to needle him.

"There's a pretty lake just past those trees," he said,

pointing to a few nearby willows. "Would you mind very much going to look at it? It isn't far."

"I mind," she said firmly.

"If you were a lady I was courting, you would acquiesce to my invitation gladly. This is exactly how such things are done."

"Fine," she grumbled. "If we must."

They turned off the main road onto a narrower footpath. It was slightly rougher, and she stumbled over a gnarled tree root. He took her elbow to right her.

"Let's turn around before I break my neck," she said.

"We're almost there. Here, take my hand."

She did so, and her skin was soft—much softer than his own. Between his cooking and washing up and gardening, and all the riding he liked to do while Thaïs slept in the morning, his hands were calloused. She noticed.

"Your paws are awfully rough for a gentleman."

"Does it bother you?"

"No. But it might bother *her*. Delicate lady skin and such, not wanting to be scratched up."

He'd never thought of that, and it concerned him. He'd hate for his bride to find his hands were uncomfortable to the touch or unpleasant to look at.

"I suppose I could take to wearing thicker gloves while riding. And I won't be spending much time in the kitchen once we're back in London. Cold water is not gentle on the skin."

"Butter," she said decisively.

"Pardon?"

"Rub butter into your hands at night before you go

to sleep. An old whore's trick. Softens the skin right up."

"I'll have to try that. Though, it might make one smell rather odd."

"No harm in the smell of butter. Unless it's rancid."

"I don't imagine I'll take up the habit of smearing myself in rancid butter, so I suppose I'm safe." He pointed at a glimmer of light through the cluster of tree trunks and willow fronds. "That's the pond."

"Beautiful. Let's turn around."

He pulled her by the hand. "No, come. You'll like it."

The pond was in a shaft of sunlight, surrounded by wildflowers. A few geese lolled placidly on the shore.

"Pretty, is it not?" he asked.

She shrugged. "I suppose it's nicer than the dusty path. I hate those birds, though. Evil creatures."

"Geese?" he laughed. "They're perfectly harmless."

Something splashed in the water, and she walked a bit closer to take a look. "Turtles," she said, in a tone that—shockingly—implied she actually liked them. "A whole family of them."

She bent down to peer closer. "Aww, a baby! What a funny little creature, with his tiny fat legs."

Her foot edged so close to the pond that she disturbed the water. It was charming to watch her actually enjoy something in nature. She had an endearing attraction to babies, it seemed—regardless of the animal.

The goose nearest her looked up at the sound of the splash and stretched its wings.

And kept stretching them.

He stretched to his full wingspan, rising to his feet.

"Thaïs," Eden called, as she was not paying attention. "You might want to step back."

She paid no mind to him, peering even closer at the water and making cooing sounds at her new friends.

The goose let out a tremendous honk and stalked toward her, beak first.

"Thaïs, move," he said, lunging in her direction to pull her away from the bird. She looked up, following the sound of his voice, just in time to see the bird charging. She turned and ran.

The goose ran after her, flapping his wings.

"Get it away," she squawked. "It's chasing me!"

He was already behind her, yelling and flapping his own hands to scare the bird away.

It worked—the creature flew into the air, though not without a menacing caw—but Thaïs had tripped over another root and landed on her hands.

"Beast," she yelled at the bird. "I hope you starve this winter and fall into the sea!"

He rushed over to her and bent to his knees.

"Are you all right?" he asked.

She gestured at her sprawled body with her dirty hands. "Does it look like I'm all right? Help me up."

He put his hands around her waist. She was so soft beneath his palms, her flesh giving way to the firm pressure of his touch. It made him want to press her to him, so he could feel all her curves against his lean physique. But that, of course, would be inappropriate when she was moaning in pain.

He looked her over. She was rumpled, her hair awry, with a bit of dirt on her face.

"Poor girl," he said. "Where are you hurt?"

"Everywhere," she moaned. That she was capable of such drama reassured him that she was not seriously injured. Still, he felt for her. He reached out and rubbed the dust off her shoulders, then smoothed her hair.

She stuck out her lower lip sadly and let him tend to her without complaint. He licked his thumb and rubbed away the mud below her eye. "There you are. Good as new."

"Tore my dress," she complained. "The *only* dress His Lordship will let me wear."

"I'm sure Mrs. Gerity can mend it. More importantly, are you in much pain? Can you walk?"

She tested out her ankle and winced. "I can. Won't enjoy it, though."

"Here," he said, pressing her against his side. "Lean on me. It isn't far home. And if it hurts too much, just say so, and I'll carry you."

She laughed. "You can't carry me. I'll topple you right over. These bosoms weigh me down, not to mention my ample arse. And you, just a skinny thing."

"I might surprise you."

"Maybe I'll let you try in bed, where it won't hurt if you drop me."

He did not comment on the idea of them in bed, though it was an increasingly appealing one. Now that he knew her, the prospect of being intimate with her filled him with more curiosity than fear.

She shuffled along well enough on the way home, favoring one ankle but not quite limping. It was nice to walk with her in companionable silence, her warmth tucked against his side.

When they reached the cottage he helped her inside and onto the settee to rest.

"You're a good nurse, milord," she said, smiling up at him. "You should trip all your ladies, so you can tend to them."

"I didn't trip you, if you recall," he said. "Your fascination with turtles won you the enmity of a goose."

"Very well, get all your women goose-attacked."

He chuckled at the idea of subjecting a succession of pretty, aristocratic girls to angry, territorial birds. "I think that will result in my dying a bachelor," he said.

"That would be a shame."

She did not add a barbed comment. She just smiled at him.

Was she being . . . *nice*? How novel.

And, well . . . nice.

"You're not bad company, Eden, if I'm honest," she said. "And if you were courting me, and we were just back from a stroll together, and you'd gotten me all buttered up and snug, I'd want you to steal a kiss."

This was not what he'd expected her to say. "That would be rather rude of me, to use an injury to molest you."

She clucked her tongue. "Kissing is not molesting unless the lady is unwilling. Which, after that, she wouldn't be, unless she didn't like you. And if she didn't like you, she'd make it clear after you made her tramp through the forest and nearly broke her ankle."

"I'm not sure I agree that that's what happened. But for argument's sake, say I should attempt to kiss her. How would you suggest I go about it?"

"Well first, make sure there's no one around to catch

you. You don't want to get yourself trapped in a bad match, or her either."

"It goes without saying that I would not kiss her if we were in danger of being discovered. But even if we were so lucky as to have privacy, how would I know if she wanted to be kissed?"

"First, look into her eyes, and see if she looks back at you."

He looked into Thaïs's eyes. She looked back at him with a winsome expression.

"Now look at her lips, and see if she looks at yours," she instructed.

He lowered his gaze to her pillowy lips, which were always pink and shiny against her creamy skin. He had never allowed himself to stare at them, and now that he did, he didn't want to stop.

He peeked at her eyes and saw she was looking at his mouth, leaning closer than she had before.

"Now touch her, and see if she moves away," Thaïs said softly. "Mind, you have to feel your way through it. Use your senses. You're a bright fellow. I doubt you would ever think that a woman wanted to be kissed if she didn't. And you can always ask her."

"Ask her?" He was not aware such a thing was done.

"Yes. It's quite simple. Try it."

He was not sure how such a question should be phrased. He tried the most literal route.

"Uh . . . may I kiss you?"

His voice cracked on the word *kiss*, and he winced, but she didn't comment on it.

"Yes," she said simply.

He was not sure what to do.

"Kiss her, then," she coached.

He leaned down and pecked Thaïs's cheek.

"Not like that," she said, grabbing him by the back of the head. "On the lips."

She held him close, so his mouth was half an inch away from hers.

"I won't be doing it for you," she said, looking into his eyes and then down at his lips.

He closed the distance between them and brushed his lips against hers.

God, they were soft.

He felt something flutter in his chest and darted back away from her.

"Sorry," he said, a little breathless.

He was not in the habit of kissing. It had been years.

She leaned back her head and groaned. "Now he's apologizing? Eden, for Christ's sake. I gave you permission. Take it, and do it like you *want* to. Women *want* to feel wanted. You want to thrill the girl. And you also want a taste of the goods. There should be a spark between the both of you if it's a good match. If you don't want each other before the marriage, I'd reckon you'll not want each other after."

He was conscious she was lecturing him on taking liberties, a thing he lived in horror of, yet everything she said was reasonable. It did follow that if a woman agreed to be kissed, he should take her at her word that she wished for it. And it was logical that there should be attraction between him and any woman considering being his lifelong helpmeet. If he wanted to be a perfect spouse—and he truly did—he must find a woman he suited and who suited him. Otherwise, he was setting himself up to fail.

"May I try again?" he asked.

"I'm a sure thing, Your Lordship. I have all month."

He took a deep breath. "Thaïs, I'd like to kiss you. Would you grant me that honor?"

"I would, Lord Eden," she said in her faux-genteel accent.

She looked into his eyes.

He looked at her lips.

They were lovely lips, fat at the bottom and bowed at the top. He so wanted to feel them under his. Truly feel them.

And so he did.

And for a moment, just a moment, he lingered there and let himself enjoy the nearness of her. Her scent. The way her curls brushed against his cheeks.

He broke apart from her and then—as if pulled back by a thread—felt compelled to kiss her again, more slowly.

It was lovely.

So lovely that if he did not move away he might do it a third time, and that would be beyond the pale.

He pulled back.

Thaïs opened her eyes, her lips even pinker from his kiss.

"Not bad, Your Lordship. I'd have you to bed. Shall we go upstairs and do some more advanced lessons?"

The idea of this jolted him back into himself. He stood up abruptly.

"It's time for me to make supper."

"Supper can wait. Live in the moment. Let yourself want me."

He didn't need to let himself. He already did.

But being too eager was worse than not being eager at all.

He should know.

"The chicken won't pluck itself, and I doubt you want to help me," he said.

She wrinkled her nose.

"I'll pledge to that."

He smiled at her. "Thank you for the lesson, Thaïs."

And before she could respond, he left the room.

Chapter Eleven

Another day, another bloody noontime knock.

If Eden kept making such a racket every morning she was going to get used to this, and a lifetime of training herself to spend half the day asleep would be for nothing. And what a waste, for spending half the day asleep was a whore's special perk. Not to mention a necessity, when she spent half the night awake.

"I'm not getting dressed for you," she called. "Come back in two hours."

"The dressmaker sent word she's coming at one o'clock. I thought you might want to be awake for that."

"Fine, fine. I'll come down once I clear the crust from my eyes."

"Charming. But I brought you breakfast. Shall I leave it outside the door?"

Thaïs smiled to herself. Breakfast in bed? He was paying attention to this lesson, at least. If she taught him nothing else, he would know to bring his woman tea when he wanted to get on her good side.

"Come in. I'll stay under the covers to protect your eyes from the sight of female flesh."

The door opened slowly, and he edged inside, carefully balancing a tray. She spied a steaming mug of tea, a plate heaped with bread and eggs and rashers, and a dainty little vase with a single rose.

She grinned. "This looks so good I'd let you climb in bed with me and share it, if you wouldn't count it as a punishment."

A look crossed his face, and she could not quite tell if he was scandalized or tempted.

She hoped he was tempted.

He'd begun to show promise with that kiss yesterday. She could sense that he was nervous. That even leaving his notions of politeness aside, he hated doing anything he was unsure of. That he might even be a little scared of admitting that he wanted her.

It was her job to see these things. So she would keep coaxing him, step by step, to be the man she suspected he was deep down. A man who could be right randy if he gave himself permission.

She sat up, keeping the blanket over her breasts, and took a bite of her eggs. Heaven. "What have you put in these to make them taste so good?" she asked.

He shrugged. "Oh, nothing special. Butter. A touch of cheese. Chives from the garden. I'm glad you like them."

"You can make me these *nothing special*s every day. Good husbanding here, Lord Eden."

He held up a letter.

"You also received this. It's from Lady Bell."

"Oh, thank deuces. I was worried she'd left Devon before my note got to her. What's it say?"

He hesitated. "Are you sure you wish for me to read your private correspondence?"

She snorted. "You're better at reading it than I am. And who are you going to tell my secrets to? Hattie?"

"I appreciate your trust in me," he said drily. "Most flattered."

She took a bite of buttered bread—he'd toasted it over the fire to make it nice and craggy—and waved him to hurry up and open it.

He carefully broke the seal and smoothed it out, taking far longer than she'd have.

"Well?" she prodded.

He cleared his throat.

"My dearest Thaïs,

"I am beyond grateful, my darling, that you have solved the mystery of Maria's whereabouts. What luck, that she should be so near you! I had assumed that Bell would not entrust her with his mother, her being nearly senile, but of course, I somehow flatter his intelligence. His carelessness is my gain, I hope.

"I am leaving Devon this morning, and hope to arrive to you by Thursday afternoon. You are kind to offer me a bed. I hate to disturb your time with your paramour, but for the sake of discretion, I will most gratefully accept your hospitality. And as you ask, I will of course keep his identity private.

"In the meantime, let's both think about how we might arrange a meeting with Maria without raising the suspicion of her grandmother or any others that might be staying with them who could pass on word of my visit to Bell. I suspect it won't be easy, but I am desperate and willing to take a risk if I must.

"I love you, my darling—
"E."

Eden folded the letter and looked up at her, his face soft with sympathy.

"Poor woman," he said. "My heart goes out to her."

Thaïs nodded. She felt a little weepy.

"I'm afraid it will be quite complicated, finding an overture for a meeting with Maria," he said. "I share Elinor's concern that Bell might be alerted and act against her if he learns of it."

Thaïs slurped down a hot sip of tea. This was not among her worries. "That's because you and Elinor are not lying scamps like me."

He leaned back against the wall, examining her.

"Are you a lying scamp?"

"Sure am, when I need to be. And thank the Lord for that. I have a plan."

"Dare I ask?"

"Do you have a few shillings handy?"

"Of course," he said, digging in his pocket for a change purse and producing several shiny coins, because rich men thought nothing of keeping a small fortune on their persons even when doing nothing more expensive than lounging in the country.

"I'll be needing that," she said. "I'm going to bribe Sophie Gerity."

He put the money in her palm. "I don't approve of bribery, but to be honest, I can think of no better strategy. I'll leave the matter in your hands."

"Good. Now, off with you, and take this tray. I have to make myself pretty."

He took the tray.

"Thaïs?" he said, pausing in the door.

"Mmm?"

"You're always pretty."

She started at the compliment.

She knew she was pretty, of course. But to hear it from him—not just the sentiment, but his willingness to admit he felt this way—made her smile so deeply she flushed.

"Thank you, milord. Now, off with you."

As soon as he was gone, she rose and put on a shift and stays. She glared resentfully at the loathed day dress before shrugging it on. At least Sophie'd bring another one to add to her paltry wardrobe. With each hour in the increasingly tattered-looking thing, she longed to go to the stable and dig out an alluring gown to flounce about the house in. If Eden thought she was pretty in this drab, filthy thing, imagine how he might feel if he saw her in something that set off her beauty.

He might even dare to touch her without her ordering him to do it.

She saw Sophie approaching on a horse-drawn cart, no baby with her this time. Thaïs waved at her out the open window. "Good day, Mrs. Gerity. You're just the woman I hoped to see. Come right upstairs."

"I have two gowns ready for you," Sophie said when she entered the bedchamber. "Simple, they are, but I thought you'd want them as soon as could be."

"Oh, you're an angel," Thaïs said. "I would have kissed your feet for one."

"I knew you must be getting awfully tired of making do. I had the girls work extra time. There will be two more ready for you by the end of the week. Shall we try them on, then, and see how they fit?"

Thaïs unwrapped the gowns from the brown paper—simple muslin day dresses, like a farmer's daughter might wear to town. One was green, the other white and sprigged with yellow flowers. Exactly what Eden would want her in.

"They're perfect," Thaïs said.

"I thought the yellow would suit you. Redheads look so nice in yellow. And the green will bring out your eyes."

Thaïs put the green one on, and it fit perfectly. The second was a bit long for her, so Sophie set about bringing up the hem.

"Your work is beautiful," Thaïs said, smiling at herself in the mirror. "I wish I had occasion to order a finer gown. Sadly, the life of a governess doesn't call for much in the way of finery."

"Oh, I do love to fuss over gowns. You should see the ones I'm making for Lady Maria. Did I tell you about her? The granddaughter of—"

Thaïs held back a smile. She'd planned to bring up Maria herself, but all the better for Sophie to do it for her.

"Ah, yes, a dowager viscountess, was it?" she said.

Sophie nodded. "Silk gowns trimmed in my best lace."

"I'd love to see them." Thaïs sighed. "In fact, I'd love to see *her*. I've never met an aristocratic lady."

"Is that not who governesses work for?" Sophie asked.

"Not me. My family owns a furniture factory." She lowered her voice. "They're wealthy, to be sure, but not titled. I've always been curious to meet a true fine lady."

"Oh, you would love Lady Maria," Sophie said. "Most graceful girl you've ever seen, and such manners. Very kind."

Thaïs had known Maria since she was a baby and knew that this was true. Still, it was nice to hear that Elinor's daughter was as lovely to a local seamstress as she was to her mother's closest friends.

"I don't suppose she ever comes to your shop?" Thaïs asked. "I'd love to get a glimpse of her."

"No," Sophie said. "I call on her at home. It's a bit far out, but they pay me handsomely for my trouble, and I like to see the gardens in bloom."

Thaïs flashed a conspiratorial smile. "Do you think she might come to the shop if you asked? Like if you were, say, injured, and could not travel?"

Sophie shrugged. "Perhaps. But I'm fit as a fiddle."

"Oh, I have no doubt. But perhaps you could say you have a bad ankle. I have a bit of extra coin, you see, and not much to spend it on. I could share a bit with you for the chance to see a viscount's daughter."

Sophie pursed her lips. "I don't like to be dishonest."

"Oh, I'm sure you don't. Just a thought, as my mistress gave me more than I can spend."

Thaïs gestured at the coins sitting on her dressing table.

Sophie's eyes went wide.

"That's quite a sum."

"My mistress is a generous woman, and this is the first holiday I've had in two years' time. She bade me enjoy myself."

"Well," Sophie drew out, "I suppose there would be no harm in asking Lady Maria to come to town. Her grandmama has a carriage, and she might enjoy the diversion, being confined to her house these last months."

Thaïs clapped her hands in delight. "How soon could you invite her?"

"I have a gown to fit her in on Friday. I'll write today to see if she can make a call and pass on word to Hattie if she agrees."

"That would be perfect. I can collect my other gowns at the same time and spare you a trip here."

Sophie smiled. "Splendid. Now, turn around. Let's see if the seams are even."

Chapter Twelve

Eden heard the dressmaker leave, then Thaïs's footsteps coming down the stairs. She was humming a jaunty, if tuneless, melody. She truly could not sing, even without lyrics. It was endearing that she did it anyway.

She threw open his study door, as he knew she would. He looked up from his accounts. She was beaming like a child with a boiled sweet.

"Your wife's a bloody genius," she said, perching on the edge of his desk.

"What did you do?"

"Convinced Sophie to get Maria in her shop on Friday. As long as the girl agrees—and she's a cheerful, sociable thing, so why wouldn't she?—I'll bring Elinor to town, and they'll be able to have a secret meeting."

"Very clever."

"Are you proud?" She batted her long lashes at him.

"I am," he said, somewhat honestly. He would not usually approve of bribing people to tell lies to children, but in this case, it was for an honorable cause. And he could not help but be impressed at Thaïs's ingenuity.

"Give us a kiss," she said, scooting closer to him and puckering up her lips. "I've earned a bit of love."

He stiffened at that word. *Love*. It made him uncomfortable, the idea of them sharing such a connection, even if she was using the word glibly.

"You're crumpling my papers," he said.

She let out an annoyed breath.

"Is that what you'll tell your wife when she comes to you happy and proud, wanting a kiss?"

He hoped he wouldn't. He could see how that might sting.

"I, er—no?"

"No," she said decisively. She leaned forward and smacked her lips at him.

He bent down and put a light kiss on them.

God, she was so soft. And she leaned closer, like she wanted more from him.

But he had no idea what to do next.

He moved away, annoyed with himself for his own clumsiness.

She didn't move. Her eyes stayed closed.

"Is that all I get?" she asked, without opening them.

"I, uh . . . You want more than one?"

She opened a single eye and squinted at him. "Yes."

He leaned back in and gave her another peck.

She opened her eyes and rolled them at him. "Oh, for Christ's sake. Won't you even try? You did it earlier."

That was the problem. He'd gone as far as he knew how.

It was excruciating, this business of lacking skill. As much as his body wanted to be near hers, his instinct to flee the room was just as strong. Which led to this awkward paralysis, which was just as humiliating as the lack of skill itself.

"I'm sorry," he said. "It's difficult for me to . . . venture into learning new skills."

"Your problem is you won't relax," she said. "And if you won't relax, you can't be taught. Romance isn't in the mind. It's in the body. In the heart."

She put her hand on his chest, where his heart beat rapidly underneath it. It felt so *good*, so why was he so determined to get away from it?

"Perhaps we can try again later," he got out. "It's the middle of the day, and—"

"And you spend the evening cooking, then go to bed as soon as supper's over and won't let me join you there. So when do you think your lessons ought to happen?"

He sighed. She was correct. He was avoiding her attempts at initiating physical intimacy. He would not improve if he could not bring himself to try.

"You're right," he said. "The responsibility to try is mine entirely. You have acquitted yourself admirably, and I'm grateful for your persistence."

She gave him a wry look. "Gratitude is not going to get you a happy wife, milordy."

"No. I realize that."

How to explain in a way that would make sense to her?

"You see," he said, "I'm afflicted with reluctance. I want to learn the skills you offer, but I have no natural aptitude."

"And how would you know if you won't try?"

"I *have* tried. My past experiences do not reflect well on my innate skill, and I hate to impose my boorishness on others."

She burst out laughing. "You couldn't be boorish if you were an actual wild boar with tusks and all. You'd be as polite a boar as ever lived, going through the forest on the tips of your hooves asking the grubs permission to eat them."

This image would be amusing if he were not so acutely uncomfortable.

"Nevertheless, Thaïs, I'm terrible at intimacy."

"No. You're *scared* of being terrible. You can't be terrible at something you don't know how to do. And you'd never have learned how to do anything if you hadn't tried it first."

"I'm quite good at most things I try. And I devote myself to becoming perfect. This is different."

"Ha!" she squawked. "There's no such thing as perfect. Even from the likes of you. Especially not in matters of tomfuckery."

"*Tom*?" he inquired blandly, because he was at a loss to understand his own stubborn behavior. His resistance to attempting to learn might be counterproductive to his own goals, but it went bone-deep.

His dodge did not deter her.

"You're good at arguing with me," she said. "If you put in an inch of the effort into learning your lessons that you do avoiding them, you'd be fucking everyone in town."

"Ugh. That notion is revolting. Imagine the crabs."

She snorted. "Well, I don't have crabs, and it's impossible that you do, so maybe let's just plunge in and have a frig and see if you're as bad as you think. We have nothing else to do, and there's two perfectly good beds in this house with no one in them."

The idea of going to bed with her at three in the afternoon, light streaming in the windows, the country breeze dancing on their skin, was so wild he wanted to laugh at the idea of it. It sounded wonderful, for a different kind of person. One he could not fathom ever being.

"Oh, don't look so bloody *hopeless*," she clucked at him. "Let's make a deal. You can teach me something I don't know how to do, and then I'll teach you something you don't know how to do."

This caught his attention. He liked to teach. And he was good at helping others learn.

After this miserable conversation, it would be restorative to do something he excelled at.

"What would you like me to teach you?" he asked.

"What are you good at?"

He considered this. "Athletics. Greek and Latin. Politics. Philosophy. Accounting. Land management. Agriculture—"

"Everything except bedsports," she cut in.

He nodded. "Essentially."

"You forgot cooking."

"No, I didn't forget. You interrupted my list."

"Well, I'm not about to sit for a lecture on accounting, joyful as it sounds. So how about you teach me how to bake a cake."

Chapter Thirteen

Thaïs had as much desire to learn how to bake as she did to fall down a flight of stairs. Never let it be said she did not work hard for her money.

She followed Eden into the kitchen, where he was pulling down two aprons from hooks on the wall.

"Put this on," he said, handing one to her.

"My gown can't get dirtier than it already is," she said.

"I'd beg to differ."

He wrapped his own apron around his waist. It was yellow with a ruffle at the bottom, clearly designed for a woman.

"Well, don't you look pretty as a peach," she said.

He drily flounced up the skirt of the apron. "Thank you."

"What are we making?"

"We don't have many ingredients, so it'll have to be something simple. I think we can cobble together a honey sponge. And they're easy to make."

"Lord knows I'm easy."

He ignored her quip and went about lighting the fire beneath the cast-iron bake-oven. "This will heat while we prepare the batter," he said. "Next, I like to collect my ingredients and set them out neatly."

"I didn't expect you'd want to make a mess," she said.

"A certain amount of mess is inevitable, I'm afraid."

"In baking as in frigging."

He shook his head. "I knew you were going to make that joke."

"Well, then you know more about sex than you own up to."

He gave her a wry smile. "She says, before she sees him attempting it."

She liked how quick he was in returning her humor, even when it was dirty. It would serve him well in flirting with the ladies, could he ever bring himself to try.

He took a canister off the shelf and set it on the long wooden table in the middle of the kitchen. "Flour," he said.

"I suspected we'd need the stuff."

"Very keen of you."

"I'm not a total dullard."

"We'll also need a block of butter, a cup or two of honey, and ten eggs."

"*Ten* eggs?"

He nodded. "The lightness of the eggs helps to raise the sponge and make it fluffy. But it takes a bit of work. You'll see."

He took a rectangular pan off a shelf and handed it to her. "Coat this in butter so it doesn't stick."

"How?" she asked.

"With a clean rag."

He handed her a towel out of a drawer and passed her a plate with a large slab of butter. "Wipe the butter on the cloth, then smear it on the baking dish."

It seemed wrong to dip a clean cloth into butter, but she liked doing perverse things. "Like this?" she asked, scooping off a mound.

"Yes. Now rub it onto the dish in a circular motion."

She smeared a thick line onto the copper and reached for the butter to add another dollop.

"Not yet," Eden said. "First smooth that out. You only need a thin coating to keep the cake from sticking."

He watched her carefully spread the butter over every bit of the pan. "Well done," he said.

"A child could do that."

"Baking isn't difficult. It just requires patience."

"You know what else isn't difficult?"

"Too obvious," he said. "Your humor could be sharper."

"Yet there's a smile on your face."

He shook his head. "Now, time to measure out the flour."

He gave her a copper scoop to use to dig out a heap of it. It was the white, powdery kind that she knew was more expensive than the coarse brown stuff used for bread.

"Why white?"

"Because cake has a delicate crumb."

"How much should I put in the bowl?"

"Three scoops," he said.

"How do you know?"

"I've been making this cake since I was a child. There's a ratio of the flour to the butter, eggs, and honey. I'll show you."

He taught her how to sift the flour to add air to it, to cut the butter into a separate bowl, then to stir it with a wooden spoon until her arm ached so badly she refused to do it anymore. "Your turn," she said. "My wrist is dead. And I need that wrist for pleasuring your—"

"Use your left hand to give the right one a rest," he said. "Unfortunately, baking takes a great deal of effort. You'll have to build stamina."

Before she could make the obvious joke, he said, "Yes, yes, so will I, in bed. I know. Luckily I have a vigorous constitution. Keep stirring."

She liked him like this. Relaxed enough to joke—and about sex, at that. She should make him bake every hour of the day. Perhaps then she might eventually get the breeches off him.

Once the butter was fluffed to the ludicrous creaminess that he demanded, he had her measure out honey from a glass jar and mix it in. Thankfully, it combined into the butter without too much effort, as her arm was throbbing, and he was ignoring her complaints.

"Finally, Satan's work is done," she said, pushing the bowl aside.

He gave her a sympathetic look. "I regret to inform you that his work is only beginning. You have yet to whip the eggs."

"I only whip bottoms, and only for men who like that sort of thing."

"I don't know what you're talking about, and I cannot say I wish to. Now, watch closely, as this step requires a bit of skill. We're going to crack the eggs into two bowls, to separate the whites from the yolks."

"Impossible," she said, meaning it. "I don't do witchcraft. Don't want the demons after me."

"It's easy, with a bit of practice. Watch me."

He carefully lifted a big brown egg out of the basket of them on the counter and cracked it against the edge of a bowl. He put his hand directly below the egg and let the clear part drip through his fingers, leaving the bright orange yolk gingerly cupped in the palm of his hand.

"See?" he said as he slid the yolk into the other bowl.

Oh, see she did. And she didn't like the looks of it one bit.

"Disgusting," she said. "I shan't be touching slime."

"You eat this slime for breakfast every morning, and with an appetite, at that."

"It's *cooked* in the morning, and I don't have to touch it. And it's rude to comment on a lady's appetite."

"Rude to call an innocent egg disgusting. But very well. I'll show you again, and then you can try yourself."

The idea of it made her want to gag.

He repeated the process, and she continued to be revolted by it.

"I don't want to do that."

"Try it once," he coaxed. "And if you don't like it, I won't make you do it again."

She wanted to point out that *try it once* was the very request he kept denying her, but she was too disgusted by the idea of touching that awful broken egg that she didn't have it in her.

He wiped his hand on a towel and took her left hand in his. His touch was gentle. "Open your palm," he said.

He had a nice way of touching her. His grip was firm and knowing, but the pressure of it almost tender. It was like being guided by a lover.

She did what he asked. She was a bit sad when he stopped touching her.

"Now crack the egg against the bowl with a quick wrist, so the shell breaks but doesn't shatter. And just as fast, hold it over your hand to catch the drips."

She clenched her teeth and broke open the egg. She didn't like the crunch it made. She quickly moved it over her left hand and let the innards drip into her palm. Cold liquid like snot oozed onto her hand.

She screamed and flung the egg onto the floor.

Eden stared at her, his mouth open.

"Horrid, vile thing," she spat out. "I can't believe you made me touch it."

He doubled over laughing.

"Don't *laugh*. I don't laugh at you when you shrivel from a kiss, do I?"

"No, you're very kind," he said, still laughing. "But then, I don't throw you on the floor."

"Maybe you should," she muttered.

"I think we'll have to try that again," he said, bending over to scoop the egg mess into his once-clean cloth.

"I'll be having nothing to do with it," she said.

"Very well. I'll separate the eggs. But you're not getting out of the rest."

She folded her arms and glared at him, though she had to admit that his skill with this sick practice was impressive.

When he was done, he had two bowls, one with whites and one with yolks.

"Easy," he said.

"Smug, you are," she said. "What's the point of all this, anyway?"

"We have to beat the whites to fluff them up. It makes the batter nice and light."

He took a fork, stuck it in the bowl of slime, and began to whip it quickly from his wrist.

Her own wrist still ached from her turn with the butter. "Not on your life," she muttered.

"I didn't say this would be easy."

"You also didn't say it would break my arm."

"We'll take turns. I'll start."

He beat the eggs quickly, like it was effortless, until they began to thicken and turn white instead of clear.

"Looks like you're making seed," she observed.

"Seeds?"

"Seed. What shoots out of your cock when you—"

He shook his head. "Shame on me for falling into your trap."

She giggled.

"As your punishment for being crass, you can do the rest," he said, sliding the bowl of eggs over to her. "The goal is to whip them into stiff peaks."

"Making things stiff is—"

"Among your chief skills, yes, so you've implied. Show me."

She reached down for his crotch. He caught her hand before she could get a proper feel and put her fingers on the fork. "Whip."

She grumbled, but she did it. It made her wrist go numb, but she did like watching the slime turn into pretty little hilltops, not that she'd admit it to Eden.

While she worked, he stirred the yolks into a yellow froth, which he mixed into the larger bowl of butter and sugar.

"Am I done?" she asked, showing him her handiwork.

"Yes. Excellent work."

She smiled, pleased at the compliment. Baking was pure tedium, but she couldn't remember the last time she spent so much innocent time with a man—at least one who treated her with such kindness and good humor. It almost made her nerves act up. At least there were bawdy jokes to calm her. Nothing soothed the soul like a bawdy joke.

Eden showed her how to mix flour into the wet ingredients, then to carefully fold the egg whites into the batter, being sure not to stir too much and crush the fluff. Not that that would be a problem. She'd happily die having never stirred another thing again.

"I won't enjoy a cake for the rest of my days, knowing there's such misery in making it," she said.

He chuckled. "You'll be happy when you eat this one. Nothing like enjoying the fruits of your own labor."

She stuck her finger into the batter and licked a dollop of it. It was tasty. "Mighty good," she declared.

"I meant once it's *cooked*, Thaïs," he said.

She scooped up another dollop and held her finger to his mouth. "Taste."

His eyes went wide.

"Come on," she coaxed. "My hand won't bite you."

He tentatively leaned forward and put her finger to his mouth. He closed his eyes as he licked the batter off.

"Delicious," he said softly.

"Give me another taste," she said. And before he could react, she leaned up on her toes and kissed him.

She did not waste their time with one of his chaste pecks. She licked his lips, tasting the honey that lingered there, and urged his mouth open with her tongue. He stood rigid, like he'd come in half-frozen from a snowstorm.

But then—miracle of miracles—he kissed her back.

She took his head and pulled him down to get a better hold on him and guided his mouth with her lips. His teeth knocked into hers. Poor man clearly didn't know what to do, but to his credit, he didn't pull away, though she could tell it was his instinct.

He was trusting her with his clumsiness.

In a way, she felt honored that he was letting her see him awkward like this.

She felt something she rarely felt with a patron: affection. He was so nice, Lord Eden, and rather handsome, and charming in the bashfulness he'd revealed to her in this house—so unlike the stuffy lord she'd thought he was from knowing him before she came here.

She liked him, and she wanted him to like this. To like her.

Slowly, she could feel him get a sense for kissing. He relaxed a smidge, met her tongue with his ever so shyly.

She lowered her hands to his waist and urged him closer. And lo, but her joy at discovering hardness between his legs. She shifted to accommodate it, rubbing up against him.

Which apparently was more than he could take at this stage of his studies. He jerked away so suddenly he knocked the canister of flour on its side with his elbow. A cloud of flour flew into the air, getting all over both of them.

He looked at her, panting and embarrassed.

"I'm sorry," he said.

She took his dusty hand and kissed the back of it, leaving the imprint of her lips.

"Don't be. That's the most fun I've had since you dragged me here."

Chapter Fourteen

Eden excused himself from the kitchen to change his clothes, feeling so dazed it was like he'd been underwater, starved of breath.

So that was how a kiss was supposed to be.

Now he understood how lovers did it.

How *he* could do it.

How he might *want* to.

In the moment—relaxed by the cooking and the sparring with Thaïs—he'd somehow been able to overcome his apprehension and follow her lead. He'd been able to forget himself.

Perhaps Thaïs's dirty jokes were part of her master plan for educating him.

Or perhaps she was just incurably crude.

Either way, her vulgarity was growing on him.

She was growing on him. He'd liked her, of course, when he'd paid so handsomely for her services. But he had not realized quite how quick and clever she was. Likely, he'd been prejudiced. He had never thought of prostitutes as creatures of great intellect, when he'd thought of them at all.

But then, he had not known many prostitutes, and there was no reason to assume they were less endowed with natural gifts than the next person. He felt rather shameful for assuming Thaïs's chief characteristics were her skill at sex and her alluring body.

Not that he had lost interest in that body.

When she'd brought him close to her—God, the feeling of it. Her breasts were so pillowy and soft and bloody *big*, and she smelled so good and touched him so gently. He was still hard. So hard he'd love to satisfy himself. But this house was small, and he could hear her changing in the room across the hall. (She did nothing quietly or without cursing, including getting dressed.) He feared that she would hear him—*sense* him—touching himself, and the thought was mortifying.

Or . . . something. Tempting, almost, in a strange way, as much as it would be humiliating. The idea made him even more aroused, which made the problem worse. He would simply have to wait in his room until the trouble subsided.

Which, thankfully, it finally had ten minutes later, when Thaïs knocked on his door.

"Eden, come out," she demanded. "I'm bored."

He opened the door. She was standing in the hall in one of her new gowns, lit up by the sunlight through the landing window. Her dress was a shade of green that made her hair look even redder.

She was so beautiful he did not know how she did anything but admire her own reflection.

"Bored?" he asked. "How could that be possible? It's been a quarter hour since you were complaining about making a cake."

"A quarter hour since I was kissing you, I think you mean."

"I'm afraid I can't entertain you. I have work to do. I'm behind."

More to the point, he needed a respite from his attraction to her. If he spent more time with her just now, God knew what he might do.

She pouted. "You should hire me a friend to keep me company."

"I'm your friend, and I've been keeping you company. But every adult human must occasionally occupy themselves. And besides, don't you have your own work to do? Did you not say you would be ordering furnishings for the Institute?"

She'd mentioned it in passing over supper, though not with great enthusiasm.

She groaned. "All that reading hurts my eyes."

He softened. He supposed if he had trouble reading, he would find it far more difficult to entertain himself. It was his primary occupation.

Nevertheless, he had business he had to address. His secretary had been waiting on his response to a pile of inquiries for days. He needed to write a letter to his sister. He had a stack of reports on women to get through—

Ah. That was the solution.

"Here's what I propose. We can review a few of my potential brides before supper. But after we eat, I must work."

She smiled happily. "Yes. Let's find you a wife."

They did not find him a wife.

He read her the profiles of eight young ladies, and each was summarily rejected. Too young, too bright, too ignorant, too thin, too bookish, too musical. Her reasoning was arguably fatuous, but he shared her lack of enthusiasm for the descriptions of the ladies he'd been provided. They all sounded dull.

But that was unfair. Anyone would sound uninteresting when reduced to a few paragraphs of their physical traits and accomplishments, would they not? He could only imagine how unlikable he'd sound if described in such a way.

Lord Alastair Eden is a polite and serious aristocrat with a family seat in Cumbria and seventy thousand guineas a year. He read geography at Oxford and is fluent in Greek, Latin, and French, as well as an accomplished horseman with a stable twenty-thoroughbreds strong. Considered radical in his political views, he has written several treatises on the reform of government and economics. He has also authored papers on agriculture and ovine husbandry . . .

And that wouldn't even disclose the fact that he had a tragic family history and did not know how to bed a woman.

He made a simple supper of sausages and small potatoes, which Thaïs called Cock and Balls, arranging her portion into an approximation of the male anatomy.

"Oh, just eat it," he groaned.

"Well, I'd better, as it's the only prick my mouth is getting near."

He did not react, though it was a struggle as he could scarcely swallow at the thought of her mouth on his prick.

"Where's my cake?" she asked as soon as they were finished.

"Come with me to the kitchen. I'll show you how to serve it."

The cake was cooling on a rack. He found a serving plate for it and showed her how to use a knife to loosen the edges.

"Now turn it over gently to release it," he instructed.

She did so very, very carefully; her eyes closed like she was horrified she'd ruin it.

"Perfect!" he said as it slid whole and golden onto the platter. "Well done."

She opened her eyes and grinned delightedly. "Pretty lass, isn't she?"

"Beautiful. Before we serve it, the final touches."

He took a bowl of berries he'd collected that morning and scattered them over the cake. "Now we'll drizzle it in honey," he said.

He gave her the honeypot, and she did the honors, happy as a child.

"Let's have a taste," she said. Without bothering to slice it, she stuck a fork directly into the cake, broke off a hunk, speared a berry to go with it, and lifted it to his mouth.

He shook his head. "You first." He took the fork from her hand and held it out to her.

She took a bite and rolled her eyes in ecstasy, moaning.

"What heaven," she said, through a mouthful. "Here."

She prepared another bite and fed it to him. It was moist and light, sticky with the honey, the sweetness offset by the tartness of the fruit.

She watched him as he ate it. "Gorgeous, isn't it?" she asked.

"Utterly," he said. But he did not mean the cake. He meant this woman, smiling at him with pride in her eyes.

They ate a slab of it together, sharing the fork. When he could eat no more, he waved the fork away. "All yours."

"No, I'm stuffed."

An errant crumb clung to her top lip. On an impulse, he reached up and wiped it away.

She looked down at his hand, and then his lips.

She was doing it, he realized. Giving him the invitation to kiss her, just like she'd shown him during their lesson.

He wanted to do it. To show he understood. To put his lips to the sweet remnants of the honey.

But he'd be helpless if he did so. He was still shaken from their kiss this afternoon. He didn't know what would become of him if he allowed himself another one.

He stepped away and busied himself wiping crumbs off the table. He could sense she was disappointed in him and didn't look at her.

"You're a wonderful chef, Thaïs," he said. "You can make all of our desserts."

She didn't smile. "Not a chance."

"Well, time for me to work."

He left the room before she could call him out for avoiding kissing her.

He sequestered himself in his study for the remainder of the evening, leaving Thaïs in the parlor to sift through the catalogs of furnishings and decorations she'd brought with her. He resolved to work late, get ahead of his responsibilities, and help her write down her decisions in the morning.

She had retired by the time he finished his work at half past eleven. Evidently, she found country life dull enough to sleep through half the day. He felt guilty she was bored. Her principal occupation, after all, was to entertain him erotically. He'd erected—he smiled to himself, knowing how she'd cackle at the turn of phrase—enough barriers to lust that, at this point, a month might not be long enough for her to give him the education he had hired her to provide.

He would have to let down his defenses. Be more like the man he'd been licking cake batter off Thaïs's finger—letting his chest drift against her breasts—and less like the one who had dodged her lips when her eyes had beckoned him to kiss her.

A faint flicker of candlelight shone beneath Thaïs's door, and he imagined how she would react if he stopped and knocked. Asked for a chance to make it up to her.

He knew she would eagerly oblige him. Be proud of him for asking.

But he was tired. He rarely stayed up this late, especially in the country, where he tended to rise at dawn. And he'd so enjoyed their time today that he wanted to savor the memory, just for tonight, so he could enjoy it in the morning.

And he woke up very ready to commence such an activity. His cock was so hard it ached. It only took a moment to bring himself off in such a state, but the act of doing so did not beget the usual satisfaction. It brought a sharp rush of pleasure, to be sure. But not enough to linger over.

He never did this, but he was tempted to have himself again.

He lay back in bed, eyes closed, imagining the feeling of Thaïs against him. The slight softening he'd experienced quickly reversed itself as he began to stroke. He took his time, ignoring the glare of the rising sun coming through the window and the roosters that had begun to crow outside.

He thought of her breasts—those luscious, luscious breasts—exposed to him a few mornings ago. The thatch of flaming red hair he'd glimpsed above her womanhood. Of her hips, flaring like the contours of a cello. His breath caught, and he strained to be quiet, despite the fact that Thaïs would sleep for six more hours if he let her and Hattie would not arrive until seven.

He leaned his head back against the wall and let out a silent moan. He was close, and the feeling was almost perfect, if he just gripped a little tighter now—

His door flew open.

"Eden!" Thaïs cried. "If your damned birds don't stop that squawking, I'm going to go outside and wring their—"

She trailed off, realizing what he was doing. Horror rushed through him. But it didn't stop the cresting tide of his desire in time.

He came.

Not just that, he came with a deep groan, spending in great ribbons all over his bare belly.

Thaïs clapped a hand over her mouth.

"Go away!" he shouted at her, still spasming.

"I—do you need any help?" she asked softly.

"Get out, Thaïs," he yelled more forcefully. *"Get out."*

Eyes wide, she backed away and shut the door.

Chapter Fifteen

Thaïs softly closed the door and walked back across the hallway to her room.

She had the oddest feeling in her chest.

She was . . . hurt.

Eden had *yelled* at her. When, very well, she'd invaded his room without knocking and caught him having a go at himself—but still. Eden, shouting.

Eden shouting even as he was coming, which apparently he did without her help, despite the fact that he was paying her for just that service. Was that a slight? Did he find her unattractive? Did he not want her, and was being polite about it?

The thought of it made her sad, and the sadness made her angry, because a patron should not have the power to make her feel so small.

And it didn't help that the sun was burning her eyes and those damned cocks were still crowing their bloody heads off.

She took the nearest heavy object in hand—a Bible someone had left on top of the dresser—and hurled it out the window toward the henhouse. "Shut your beaks before I smash your heads," she yelled down.

Not that they paid her words, or the Lord's, any mind.

She heard Eden's footsteps outside her door and wondered if he'd stop to scold her once again. She squinted at the door, just in case he opened it, but heard him going down the stairs.

She returned to bed and dug her eye mask from the sheets. She'd go back to sleep, as there was nothing else to do in this godforsaken place.

But the damned benighted birds kept up their squawking, and the light was still too bright despite the mask, and then someone was pounding at the door.

"Who is it?" she asked, even though she knew there was only one person it could be.

"Alastair," Eden said.

She'd never called him by his given name, and he'd never invited her to. It was odd to hear him say it. So odd, it softened her a little, even if she didn't feel like being soft on his account just now.

"What do you want?" she asked.

"May I come in?"

"If you must."

The door cracked open, and he appeared, fully dressed for the day, carrying a tray of tea and milk.

"Hattie hasn't come yet," he said, "so there's no breakfast. But I can make you something if you're hungry."

She nodded without smiling. "Leave it on the dressing table."

He set it down and paused, like he was unsure whether to stay or go.

"Thaïs," he said, "I'm sorry."

Sorry? He was apologizing?

That was certainly a first.

She'd expected him to stay angry with her. To treat her like a misbehaving servant.

"I consider that act a very private one," he said quietly. Gravely. "And I was embarrassed that you witnessed it. I'm *still* embarrassed."

How frank. The men she dealt with weren't usually so honest about how they felt. She could understand, feeling as he did, why he'd yelled at her.

He hadn't been angry. He'd been ashamed.

"I understand," she said. "I should have knocked."

"Yes. I'd appreciate if you did so in the future."

"But you know," she said, "there's nothing shameful about frigging yourself. Most everyone does it."

"Be that as it may," he said stiffly, "being caught doing it is an undesirable consequence of satisfying the urge."

"Some people like being watched."

He blushed. "I'll leave them to their preference."

"Here's the question in my mind, milord," she said. If he could be honest, nothing was stopping her from being that way too. "When you have these urges, why not use me for them? Isn't that why I'm here?"

He clenched his jaw, looking unhappy. "You know that it is."

They stared at each other for a moment, neither speaking, both frustrated.

"What are you scared of?" she asked.

He sighed and ran a hand through his hair. "To be honest, Thaïs, I'm not quite sure."

"Don't you want me?"

His eyes widened. "Of course! It was you I was thinking of when I . . ."

She grinned at him. "Oh?"

He nodded solemnly. "Oh."

"Well, how about this. If you don't want me to touch you yet, let me watch you when you touch yourself. As a start."

He shook his head so hard it was like to come right off his neck. "No," he said. "Never."

"You could watch *me*," she offered.

His eyes nearly bulged out of his skull.

"Not possible," he said. "The sight might drive me mad."

"Isn't that the aim?"

"The aim," he said, "is to be a perfect husband. And making my wife perform such a thing for me would be—"

She knew his implication, and she didn't like it.

"Treating her like a whore?" she interrupted.

He looked surprised. "I was going to say *selfish*."

Oh. She felt a bit bad for snapping at him.

Still, his instincts were based on assumptions about what polite women liked. She needed to teach him not to assume.

"What if she enjoys it? You watching her?"

He cocked his head. "*Do* women enjoy that?"

"Some women do. Not every woman is the same."

"Well, if she did, then, of course, I would, er . . ."

"You would, er, what?"

"Accommodate her," he said, meeting her eye. "I would accommodate her."

With that, he bowed his head politely and left the room before she could say more. Leaving her to plot how she might change her strategy for his lessons.

She should try to make him feel he was doing her a favor by learning what she ought to teach him. Let him think he was giving *her* pleasure, as a means of getting him to take his own.

She was thoroughly awake, despite the wretched early hour, and her tea had gone cold. She dressed in her new yellow sprigged dress—quite fresh and pretty she looked in it, even if it did not expose enough of her bosoms for her taste—and went down to the kitchen to see if Eden could be persuaded to make her a new pot.

But he wasn't there.

Instead, a broad-faced young woman with pale blond hair and ruddy cheeks was standing over the washing tub, scrubbing something.

The woman turned around at the sound of the door opening and grinned.

"Why, you must be Miss Smith."

Thaïs nodded, though she had nearly forgotten she was supposed to go by a false name. Bless that she hadn't introduced herself first.

"And you must be Hattie," Thaïs said. "I've been meaning to come down and meet you. When I'm on holiday I tend to catch up on my rest. No little ones to look after at the crack of dawn."

Hattie smiled. "Nice, to sleep in. Though, I don't know how you do it with those cocks a-crowing like they do."

The roosters had quieted a bit, but they were still screeching at least once a minute.

"They're terrible this morning," Thaïs said. "I'm tempted to end their lives early."

"Won't have much in the way of eggs if you do,"

Hattie said, gesturing at a basket she must have just collected.

"I might like sleep more than eggs."

"Would you like some for breakfast, since you've made such a sacrifice to get them?"

Thaïs snorted. Hattie was a wit, it seemed.

"No, but I might like some of that honey cake with butter," she said. "And a fresh pot of tea."

Hattie nodded. "Shall I take it to you in the parlor?"

"No. I'll wait. Nice to have a woman for company after no one to talk to but my brother all week. And Sophie, of course, the dressmaker. Do you know her?"

"Of course. I know everyone in town. It's a small place, but it has its charms. Have you gone into the village yet?"

"No. I'm going to Sophie's shop on Friday. I'm looking forward to it. I haven't done much while I've been here, except resting and reading."

She had not done any reading, of course. Heaven forfend. But she assumed Hattie would think this was a great treat for a holidaying governess.

"And walking, of course," she added. "Lots of walking."

"Beautiful scenery about these parts," Hattie said. "Have you gone over to the Fellowes' yet?"

Thaïs had no idea what this meant. "Pardon?"

"The Fellowes," Hattie said. "Your neighbors just down the road."

"Ah, of course. No, I haven't had the pleasure of meeting them."

Nor did she have any intention to if it required

tromping down the dusty lane. She did enough sneezing just staying inside the cottage.

"Oh, you should pay a visit," Hattie said, slicing into the cake and smearing it with a generous helping of butter. "Their barn cat had kittens a few mornings ago. Precious, wee little things."

"Awww! Perhaps I will." She did love kittens. She loved baby anythings.

The kettle was boiling, and Hattie retrieved it from the grate and poured the water into a pretty flowered teapot. "Do you take milk?"

"Please."

"Take your cake and have a seat in the parlor. I'll bring your tea once it's brewed."

"Thank you," Thaïs said, though she'd rather have stayed in the kitchen. She could see Hattie was busy and would likely want to get on with her work, but she was rather lonely, after days of playing patience and rifling through furniture brochures while Eden did his work in the study. In London she was always occupied and rarely alone. She walked miles a day seeing to her errands and shopping, visiting her friends, looking after her charity. Some days, she looked after Seraphina's baby, which was always a treat.

More than ever, she wished for a baby of her own. Something about being in this little house made her broody, perfect as it was for a new couple with a baby.

She imagined sitting in the sunshine in the parlor, cooing at an infant. How the sweet baby smell of milk would mix with the scent of roses drifting through the windows.

But who would she be if she had such a life?

She couldn't expect to be a harlot *and* a wife. And more to the truth of it, she wouldn't want such an arrangement. She had a yen to be married to a man who loved her and wanted her for his alone.

But where to find such a man? She wasn't ashamed of her lot in life, but she had no illusions about the way the world looked at a whore. They saw her as a dirtied thing. Immoral and unclean. You swived her. You didn't care for her. You didn't cherish her.

Even men who had no qualms about putting babies in their mistresses didn't *marry* them. At most, they patted their bastards on the heads from time to time and paid for schooling.

That wasn't what she wanted for her child.

She'd never had a family, and she wanted to give one to her baby. To herself.

Odds were it wouldn't happen.

The whole thing made her sad.

Hattie brought in the tea and wished her a good day, as she was going back to town.

This left a glum stretch of empty hours ahead of her. She drank her tea in silence, staring out the window. The minutes ticked by slowly.

Eden emerged from the study and looked startled to see her.

"Good morning, again," she said.

"Good morning. I would have thought you'd have gone back to sleep."

"Not for lack of trying. Damn your cock."

He blushed. "Cocks," he corrected.

"Both."

He walked past her toward the kitchen.

"Care for a game of cards?" she called after him.

"I'm sorry. I need to work."

"All day?"

"All day."

He came back in, carrying an apple. "If you'd like, I'll join you for luncheon in a few hours," he said.

She wrinkled her nose. A cold lunch was not exactly a treat in the best of circumstances, and especially not while one was still eating breakfast.

"How droll," she said.

He shrugged. "Entirely your decision. For now, excuse me."

He retreated to his study and shut the door.

She sighed. Her legs were beginning to vibrate with the effects of the tea. She had too much vim to sit around like this day after day, especially when she was used to being so quick on her feet.

She decided it was time to venture outside, hay fever be damned.

She was going to go look at the kittens.

She put on her boots, found a straw hat in the kitchen, and went off in the direction Hattie had pointed toward the Fellowes'.

It was a beautiful day, and the sun felt nice on her back, even if the road was still muddy from the rain a few days before. Her sneezing was unpleasant, but not as violent as it had been when she and Eden had walked through the field. It was better than sitting alone in the house.

In what she reckoned was about a mile, she came upon a cottage not unlike the one she shared with

Eden. It must belong to the Fellowes, as there were no other houses in sight.

She went up the path through the garden and knocked on the door.

An older man answered; she'd guess he was in his sixties. He was Black with a bald head and a trim silver beard. Quite handsome, she thought.

"Good afternoon," she said. "Are you Mr. Fellowes?"

"I am."

"I'm Miss Smith. I'm on holiday at the cottage down the way, with my brother."

He smiled. "Oh, yes. I heard there were visitors. How do you do?"

"Very well. Hattie Hart mentioned to me this morning that you had a litter of kittens. I hope I'm not imposing, but I was wondering if I might take a look."

"Of course!" he said. "They're in the barn. Tiny little creatures. I'll show you."

He stepped out into the sunshine. "Just this way."

They walked together toward a barn to the side of the house, making companionable conversation. Mr. Fellowes was a retired tailor who'd moved out to the countryside after passing his shop in the village down to his son.

He led her past a milk cow, two horses, and a cart toward a hay bale in the corner. There, nestled in the straw, was a mama cat and six tiny babies barely bigger than mice. Several of them were nursing. A few were cuddled together, their eyes not even open yet.

Her heart went sweet and sticky as a pool of honey.

"May I touch them?" she asked, dropping to her knees on the dirt floor.

"Of course," Mr. Fellowes said.

She picked up the largest kitten. He mewled ever so quietly as she pressed him into her neck. So warm and soft. She rubbed her cheek against his fur and murmured nonsense to him. She then put him back and proceeded to do the same to every kitten who wasn't at its mother's teat. They were so sweet and limp and lovely. She wanted to take them all back to Eden's.

"So precious," she said to Mr. Fellowes, who was watching her with a smile.

"They are. I'd offer you one, once it's old enough to leave its mama. But you're not staying long, is that right?"

"No," she said sadly. "Just until the end of the month." She resolved to get a kitten of her own as soon as she returned to London.

She bade farewell to Mr. Fellowes, who encouraged her to come back anytime she wanted, and set out down the road.

She was in a good mood, humming as she walked. Perhaps short walks in the country were tolerable, especially if she got to pass the time with nice old men and kittens.

She was just in sight of Eden's cottage when she slid on a slick patch of muck and went barreling on her arse directly into a hedgerow.

Chapter Sixteen

Eden had grown accustomed to hearing Thaïs grumbling and swearing, but usually it came from the parlor, not through the open window. And usually, she did not do it in a screech.

He jumped up and looked outside.

She was limping toward the house, covered from neck to feet in mud.

He bolted out the door and into the garden just as she kicked open the gate.

"What happened?" he cried, rushing toward her.

"What does it look like happened?" she said.

And then she began to cry. "Shit," she wailed. "Shit, shit, shitting *fuck*."

He winced, but could not blame her in this instance for the expletives. Shitting fuck, indeed.

"Stop gawping at me," she said. She used one of her knuckles to wipe her tears away, and it left a smear of mud on her face. She wailed, and then sneezed, and then wailed louder. "I hate it here!"

He had no idea what to do. He rummaged in his pocket and produced his handkerchief.

"Hold still," he said, wiping the mud off her cheek.

"Some good that'll do." She sniffled.

"Poor thing," he said and sucked in a breath through clenched teeth, rapidly searching for some way to handle this.

The dress.

First, she needed to remove the muddy dress. And then she could wash. Which meant he should pump water from the well. And it would be more comfortable for her to wash up if it were warm, so he should light a fire.

"Stop bloody *gawping* at me," she said again, with more emphasis.

"Sorry," he said. "Come. Let's get you clean."

"How? You don't have a tub."

"I'll warm some water for you."

"It's in my bloody *hair*," she said. "You'll have to wash it for me."

He had no idea how to do so, but he did not wish to upset her further. "Of course. Come with me to the back garden."

She limped behind him. He slowed his pace and offered her his arm. "Lean against me."

She refused the gesture. "No use in you getting filthy too."

"I don't mind," he said. "I want to help you."

"I can walk on me damned own," she said in her most alley-child accent.

She was still crying. He wanted to press her to his chest and hold her . . . though, ideally, when she was clean.

They reached the terrace outside the kitchen door. "You'll need to undress before going inside," he said. "Or else we'll coat the kitchen in mud."

She glared at him. "Oh, how awful for the kitchen." She began clawing at the laces of her bodice.

"Oh, uh . . ." he said. "Shall I give you some privacy? I'll go find you something clean to wear."

"No use in wearing something clean when I'll just get it dirty. Stay here and help me."

"Help you . . . undress?"

She was untying her bodice, taking care not to get mud on her undergarments.

"Yes," she said. "Are my stays dirty?"

He had no idea, because he had averted his eyes to avoid the sight of her bosoms covered by so little.

"Eden!" she snapped. "Now is not the time for modesty. Are my stays muddy?"

He forced himself to look.

She was resplendent. Utterly resplendent.

And, miraculously, her undergarments were clean.

"No, they're not muddy," he said.

"Then unlace them for me. My hands are dirty."

The laces were in front, below her breasts. He would have to touch her intimately to help her.

"I'm not sure that's appropriate," he objected.

"I'm your bloody *mistress*," she snapped. "It's about time you undress me. Will you insist your wife stay dressed up to the neck while you rut away at her?"

He objected to the idea he would *rut away at* anyone, but Thaïs was right. He could not continue to flinch from nudity.

Or from touching her, for that matter.

But he needed a moment to prepare himself. He held up a finger. "First, let me pump water for you and put it on the fire. Stay put."

"Where do you think I'm going to go? To the damned butcher shop with me arse covered in mud and my tits out?"

"Right," he said, knowing he was absurd. "I'll be quick."

He hastened over to the well, pumped two buckets of water and lugged them back to the terrace, where Thaïs was standing with her arms out so as not to get her stays dirty.

"Hurry," she said.

"I'll be back in a moment. Apologies, I know you're uncomfortable."

He dashed inside and poured the water into an assortment of smaller pots, so that they'd heat up as quickly as possible.

When he went back outside, Thaïs had, thankfully, stopped crying.

"There," he said. "All done. May I—?" He gestured at her stays.

"Of course you bloody may. Get them off me."

He approached her, trying not to reveal his trepidation. She sighed. "It's not complicated, Your Lordship. Just untie the damn laces."

There was no way for his hands not to brush her breasts as he did so. Soft and full and heavy. He longed to cup them in his palms.

That he could—that she was impatient for him to—embarrassed him. His fingers shook a bit, making him clumsy.

He could feel her breathing, and the intimacy of it made him blush.

"I'm sorry," he said, instinctively.

"Oh stop," she said. "You're doing nothing wrong, just get it done."

He worked his way down, drawing the strings out of one loop, then the next. It had never occurred to him how complicated women's clothing was.

Finally, the garment was unlaced. Thaïs held up her arms so he could take it off her.

Which left her standing in her shift.

It was nearly transparent in the sunlight. He could make out her nipples, which were hard. She was cold. He needed to be faster, for her comfort.

"Now untie my skirt," she said, gesturing at the hidden ribbons tucked against her waist.

This task was at least less finicky. He undid the strings and helped pull the skirt over her hips, so she could step out of it. Which left her standing in her stockings, boots, and shift—all of it dirty from her shins down to the soles of her feet.

"I'll have to strip down to my bare skin," she grumbled.

She leaned down to unlace her dirty boots, giving him an inviting view of her buttocks. He'd never noticed a woman's rear before, but Thaïs's, which was broad and round, set off by her generous hips, made an uproar of his loins. Her curves were absolutely luscious. So luscious he was going to become visibly aroused if he did not collect himself.

"The water should be warm enough to wash your hands and arms," he said. "I'll go inside and get some for you."

She grumbled her assent, still attempting to kick off her boots. He went into the kitchen to collect a pot, a cloth, and a bar of soap.

When he went back outside, she was standing in the garden completely nude.

"Thaïs," he yelped. "What in God's name? Someone will see you."

"No one can see me over the hedges," she said. "Except you."

He was not entirely certain this was true, and he could not bring himself to even fathom the calamity that would befall him if rumors that his so-called sister was prancing about naked out of doors reached the tiny village.

"Come in at once," he hissed.

She rolled her eyes but did as he asked, leaving a pile of dirty clothes in a heap on the terrace.

"Wash your hands," he said. "I'll go get you something to wear."

He darted out of the room, went upstairs to her bedchamber, and pawed through the garments in her wardrobe. Of course, there was nothing suitable for her to change into except her one clean dress, which would not do until she'd bathed. He would not give her the satisfaction of bringing her one of her transparent robes. He went across the hall and retrieved a clean nightshirt of his own.

When he got back into the kitchen, she was bent over naked, that gorgeous rump up in the air as she scrubbed dirt off her legs. He tossed the shirt on the table, averting his eyes.

"You can put this on while you dry off, so you're not cold. I'll give you privacy."

She let out a very long, very frustrated sigh.

"I need help, not privacy. There's mud in my hair."

She popped up and tossed her long mane of red curls, which was indeed caked here and there with clumps of drying mud.

"I can't wash my own hair without a tub. You'll have to help me. And I'm not putting on a damned shirt just to get it filthy with muddy water."

This was reasonable.

It was also impossible.

He stared at the table trying to find the words to explain that he *could not* help her when she walked over to him and took him by the chin with her damp hand. She tilted up his face, forcing his eyes to meet hers.

"I need your help, love."

She *needed* him. It was his duty to help a woman in need.

Especially her.

He was being an arse.

"Of course," he said instantly. "I'm sorry, I'm just . . ."

"Nervous," she finished.

He nodded.

She put her hands on his shoulders. "Don't be. It's just a naked woman. And she doesn't mind your eyes on her."

She took his hands and put them on her bare shoulders. "Or you touching her."

It felt so wonderful to touch her skin, so warm, so intimate. He stroked her with his thumbs, nodding.

She smiled. "Care to touch me lower?"

God, he wanted to. But if he did, he would become indecent. He was *already* becoming indecent. And if anyone was going to notice, comment, and take advantage of that, it would be Thaïs.

He almost, *almost* wanted her to.

But there was still that sliver of . . . What *was* it? Not fear, per se, but an anxiety that he would reveal himself to be inadequate. That he'd hurt her, or be clumsy, or in some way disappoint her.

That he would fail.

Nothing diminished his arousal like that fear.

"Let's wash your hair," he said. "Tell me what to do."

"It's not hard. Just bend me over the sink and pour water over my head to get my hair wet. Then wash out the muddy bits with soap, and rinse it out."

Bend me over the sink. Good Lord.

"Very well. Let's see if the water is a comfortable temperature."

He picked up the largest of the pots he'd warmed and brought it to the sink for her to test. She dipped her finger in it. "Perfect."

"Good to hear it."

Good to hear it? Why had he said that? Why was he being so bloody unnatural?

"Ready?" he asked.

Thaïs nodded and leaned over the sink, so that her rump was spread out before him like a heart. Her cascade of hair fell down into the basin.

The only way to wash it was to stand close behind her, so his groin lined up directly with the small of her back.

He got as close to her as he could without brushing against her and was thankful he had long arms so he could reach her hair without leaning into her.

Carefully, he poured water out of the pot and over her head.

"Is that all right?" he asked.

"It's getting in my nose," she said with a snort.

"Sorry. Here, I'll just work on getting out the dirt."

He took the bar of soap and rubbed a lather into one of the clumps of mud. He had to massage it with his fingers to break it up.

"I'm going to rinse it out," he said. "Close your eyes."

She nodded, and he poured water over the strands, letting mud rain down into the sink until it ran clean.

Fine. That wasn't so hard. He just had to do it . . . eight more times.

"I'm afraid this might take a while. You're very dirty."

"Damn right I am," she said in a flirtatious tone, waggling her arse. Obviously, her mood was improving.

The waggling closed the distance between them. Her buttocks brushed against the front of his breeches. The decent thing to do would be step away, but bending over at such an angle was beginning to hurt his lower back. He gritted his teeth and took the next clump of hair to wash it out. He worked methodically, scrubbing, rinsing, scrubbing, until all the mud was gone.

"There you are," he said. "All clean."

"Give it a final rinse," she said. "To get out all the soap."

He poured the remaining water in the pot over her head, making sure he rinsed out all her curls.

Thaïs sighed. "Feels good."

He smiled. He liked making her feel good. Instinctively, he took her hair in both his hands and gently wrung out the water.

"Mmm," she murmured. "I like that. Rub my head, would you?"

That he actually knew how to do. He'd often done it for his sister when she was a child, to soothe her when she was upset.

Though, soothing his sister and massaging Thaïs's scalp to bring her pleasure were two entirely different concepts.

Still, he wanted to show her that he could, at least, do this one small thing to please her.

He ran his fingers through her damp curls and put his hands just over her ears.

"Heaven," she said.

He smiled to himself. He bent closer and massaged her from her temples to her crown to the nape of her neck, enjoying her sighs of contentment.

And then, he felt himself stir.

He had been so focused on the pleasure of his task that he had not been aware he was on the verge of hardening.

And now, with her nude form bent in front of him in the most suggestive pose he could devise, he was suddenly conscious of the eroticism.

His cock surged.

He quickly untangled his hands and backed away, but they both knew she had felt it.

She turned around, confronting him with the full vision of her. The breasts that made him so uncontrollably aroused, the bright red hair at the junction of her thighs, the soft belly and swell of hips. A woman so perfectly made by God to arouse his wanton instincts that he let out a gasp.

He looked at her. He *really* looked at her.

"You are so beautiful," he whispered, looking up into her eyes. "I can't believe you're real."

She stepped forward and put a hand above his heart. "Feel that? I'm plenty real."

He sucked in his breath at her touch. He wanted more.

"I'm gripped with desire," he confessed.

"Good."

She put her arms around his neck and kissed him. It was soft and yet so thorough he felt like she was melting into him, and he was melting into her, and his entire body was alive with the sensation of her nearness, his skin prickling and tender, his heart beating like the reverberations of a drum.

She moved her hands up, ruffling his hair, caressing his scalp the way he'd held hers, and it was so sweet and kind and felt so good and she was so close, her belly pressed against his bulging, rock-hard cock, and he kissed her more deeply, and then suddenly—

He spasmed and cried out and had to brace himself against the table with both hands as an unexpected orgasm coursed through him so powerfully his knees went weak.

Very slowly, Thaïs parted her lips from his. There was a gentle expression in her eyes.

"There we are," she whispered.

His seed was seeping through the fabric of his breeches like the shame seeping from his entire soul.

"I'm *so* sorry," he gasped out, his voice hoarse from the force of his passion, his embarrassment, his shock.

Thaïs leaned forward and kissed his cheek. "Nothing to apologize for, love. It's a compliment."

No. It was a humiliation.

"Please excuse me," he said.

He untwined himself from her and walked away, toward his room and privacy and a basin of water to wash away the evidence of his forever overeager cock, as fast as he could without running.

Chapter Seventeen

Eden hid in his study for the rest of the day, emerging only to tell her he was going to bed early, claiming he had a headache. (A lie, she was certain.) This left Thaïs to be the most bored woman in the world, except when she remembered falling in the mud and became the most irritated one, or when she remembered making Eden come with nothing but a kiss and was the most smug.

She scavenged in the kitchen for bread and cheese and apples, muttering that she wasn't a damned mouse. Unfortunately, the house was not built in such a way that there was hope her muttering would disturb Eden in his bedchamber, so her display was entirely for her own benefit, which seemed a waste of ire, as part of the pleasure of cursing was shocking the people who heard you.

And Eden was so easy to needle, it was hard not to enjoy it.

But she'd learned something else about him this afternoon in the kitchen: he was a pleaser. Appealing to his kindness got him to do things he otherwise wouldn't dream of.

And he liked tenderness. She'd called him *love*, and

his eyes had gone soft with emotion. He must not have had enough affection in his life.

She knew how that was.

Maybe she didn't need to shock him into learning how to fuck. Maybe she needed to seduce him.

But not the usual way.

She could tell he was already sick with lust for her. No man would pop like that from just a little kissing if he wasn't half-mad. No, she didn't need to tempt his passions. She needed to tempt his heart.

Be sweet to him.

It wasn't really in her nature, sweetness, but she could always rise to a performance when required. She was, after all, the best in her trade.

She'd begin her assault in the morning.

For now, she occupied herself by looking through her leaflets and making notes in her special code for what she wanted to buy. She'd ask Eden to help her with a letter and to check the sums tomorrow. He liked to assist her.

Squinting at drawings and tiny letters by the dim flickering of the candle made her tired, and she was a bit sore from falling in the mud. So at nine—nine!—she went to bed.

The trouble with going to bed at nine was that she was more apt to wake up with the bloody cocks.

"Shut your beaks," she groaned in the general direction of the window. "Shut up, shut up, shut up."

She wanted to go outside and make rooster stew of every last bloody fowl, but with her luck, they'd peck her, and she'd fall into the chicken coop, and Eden would have to wash bird shit from her hair.

She suspected this was not how to seduce an earl, even one who liked to help.

So rather than storming into Eden's room yelling about poultry poison, she dressed and went downstairs.

Eden was in the kitchen, drinking tea as Hattie fried up eggs for breakfast.

"Good morning," he said to her. "You're up early."

She glared out the door toward the roosters. "'Tis difficult to sleep through that, I'm afraid," she said in her governess voice.

"I'm sorry they disturb your rest. I know you don't get much of it. If there was anything I could do to quiet them, I would."

"Well, I know one way," Hattie said, making a gesture like wringing a bird's neck, and winked at Thaïs.

"Please don't encourage her," Eden said. "She's being polite in front of company, but she might very well murder them yet."

Hattie laughed. "Mr. Smith said you had a spill yesterday," she said to Thaïs. "I'll take your dress home to launder it. Pretty gown. Shame to see it covered in mud, and you with so few things to wear."

"Well, seeing the kittens was worth it," Thaïs lied. "And anyway, I have an appointment to visit Sophie's shop Friday to pick up two more gowns. That should be enough to suit me until it's time to leave."

"Glad to hear it," Hattie said. "Breakfast?"

"Please," Thaïs said. She was ravenous from her rodent's meal the night before.

Hattie chatted with them about the weather while she served them, and then Thaïs went upstairs to take a nap, now that the crowing had stopped. When she went back downstairs, Hattie was gone, and Eden was in his study, reading.

"Milord, I need your help," she said, hoping those words would do their magic. "I don't suppose you could spare a quarter hour?"

"Of course," he said, rising. "How can I be of assistance?"

"You can help me carry all my things into your bedchamber."

He squinted at her, looking far less inclined to be useful.

"Why?" he asked.

"Because Elinor is arriving tomorrow, and she'll need somewhere to sleep."

"I was assuming she would sleep with you."

"Won't she think that's odd? You keeping me as your mistress, but not wanting to touch me?"

He considered this. "If she does, surely it's better than what she might think of us sharing a bed."

She felt like beating her head against the doorframe. He was so stubborn, and he'd ruin his chances of learning if she couldn't speed him up.

"I'd feel a bit shameful if she thought I wasn't doing my job," Thaïs said. It was a lie. Elinor was the least judgmental person she knew. But appealing to Eden's emotions seemed more effective than appealing to his loins.

He ran a hand through his hair, looking like he couldn't make up his mind.

"Besides, love," she said, "it's getting time for us to move on with your lessons, if we're going to teach you how to please your lady before we have to leave."

He nodded, slowly. "I suppose you're right."

"So you'll help?"

"Yes. Shall we do it now?"

"If you don't mind."

"No, I could use a chance to stretch my legs."

He followed her up the stairs and into her room.

"It's the contents of your wardrobe you wish me to move?" he asked.

"Yes," she said. "You take those, and I'll take my bits and bobs."

They set about transferring her things across the hall. When they were done, he had laid out all her clothing on his bed.

"You can hang them in here," he said, gesturing at his wardrobe. "And the bottom two drawers of that bureau are empty. I didn't bring much here."

He turned to leave.

"Before you go," she said, "would you like to pick out something nice for me to wear tonight?"

His usual reply—*no*—flashed across his face.

But then something new happened.

A bit of color bloomed on his cheeks, beneath those distinct bones that made him look so handsome.

He nodded. "Yes," he said. "I would."

Delight fluttered in her chest. She was pleased with herself and proud of him and a bit excited to see what he would choose.

She gestured at the open wardrobe. "Dress me, milord."

He winced. "Please stop calling me that."

"Very well, Your Earlship."

"That's not even a word."

"Pardon me, Your Highness."

"Could you just call me Alastair? This formality between us seems a bit absurd, given the circumstances."

That flutter happened again, and this time she was less sure why. But it made her not want to make any more cracks at him.

She nodded. "Alastair it is."

He quirked up a lip. "I like how you say it."

The flutter turned into a flash of hurt. Was he making fun of her accent? Lord knew she could use a nicer one, but it was still mean of him to mock the way she spoke.

"How do I say it?" she asked.

He smiled. "As though you like forming the word."

She let out her breath, surprised by the look on his face. Like it brought him genuine joy that she liked his name.

"Well, I do," she admitted. "Sounds nice. A bit like music."

"Thank you. Though I must admit, I didn't pick it out myself."

"Would've been awfully clever for a newborn if you had."

"I would imagine I was only clever at crying, sleeping, and securing milk."

"And shitting," she added.

He winced. "How detailed of you."

She grinned at him. She very much enjoyed making him wince. It was almost as good as making him cringe. Though, the best was when he closed his eyes and said "Thaïs!" in that voice that sounded like he wanted to laugh and cry at the same time.

He was quite vivid, in his own way, her stiff Alastair.

Stiff. A reminder of the task at hand.

"Enough stalling, now," she said. "Choose what I'll be wearing for you."

"Right."

He turned to the wardrobe and began rifling through her things. He paused here and there to look at something closer, then kept rummaging until he pulled out a long, lace, ivory-colored dressing gown. It was one of her scantiest robes: you could see her whole body through the delicate lace, unless she wore a chemise beneath it.

Which she wouldn't.

He flushed as he held it out to her. "This is rather nice," he said bashfully.

"Oh, I look delectable in that," she agreed.

He blushed brighter, looking at the floor, and cleared his throat.

"Well, off to work for me."

Chapter Eighteen

Concentrating on one's latest article on agricultural advancement was not an ideal—nay, not a possible—occupation for a man preoccupied with visions of Thaïs Magdalene wearing nothing but lace.

In one's *bed* wearing nothing but lace.

Eden turned his attention—whatever shreds of it he could summon—to the latest broadsheets, making notes on developments pertaining to political issues he intended to take up in the next session of Parliament.

Still, he thought of lace. Pink nipples beneath lace. Red hair beneath lace. Creamy skin beneath lace.

The anticipation made a thrum of pressure tingle in his groin. He kept finding himself hard, daydreaming of the night to come. Were he guaranteed any privacy, he'd succumb to it, relieve himself. But Thaïs had caught him attending to this urge once before, and it had been embarrassing enough. He did not need her barging into his study to find him with his cock in hand. Or to hear him gasping through the door.

And there was something rather pleasant about the wanting itself. It was languid, enlivening. He was aware of his body and his skin in a way he could not recall being in the recent past.

He took a walk; Thaïs, of course, refused to join him. He cooked supper: roast beef with carrots and onions braised in the jus, and a simple cheese and pear tart.

He summarized his latest batch of reports on marriage candidates to Thaïs as they ate, listening to her reasons for rejecting every woman on the list.

He read a book in the parlor, or pretended to, as he watched her play patience, grumbling as she shuffled around the cards and, he suspected, cheating.

Darkness fell, and they sat companionably in silence until he yawned.

Thaïs looked up from her game.

"Shall we go upstairs?"

His instinct was to come up with an excuse. But why was it that he wanted to delay the thing he'd been imagining all day?

No. He needed to stop doing this. He needed to force himself to learn, even if it meant more slips of his control. Even if it meant her seeing him fumbling his way through something he had no practice at, and no inherent skill for.

He hated the idea of it, and yet he craved her. He *wanted* to see her in that lace, and by God, he would let himself.

"Yes," he said. "Let's."

She flounced her hair and stood up, looking pleased. "Me first. To don my finery. Come up in a quarter hour."

He took a deep breath as soon as she was gone.

This will be fine, he assured himself, not at all believing it.

He tried to read, but all he could think about was what he was about to see and how he would react.

He watched the clock as the minutes ticked past.

"Alastair?" Thaïs called down the stairs. "I'm ready for you."

And he was ready for her. So ready that he wanted to bring his book upstairs with him to hide the unmistakable bulge in his breeches.

Thaïs was waiting on the landing of the staircase, holding a candle, absolutely resplendent in lace. It stretched across the peaks and valleys of her body in some miracle of tailoring, nipping in at the waist below her breasts and flaring out at the hips. Her hair was swept over one shoulder in a loose plait, exposing her long neck. Her nipples were so pink beneath the ivory that he wondered if she had rouged them. He'd heard courtesans did such things. The idea that she might do it for him made him tremble.

"My God," he said. "You're so beautiful."

She smiled, put down the candle, and ran her hands down her body, stopping at her hips, which drew his eyes down to the fiery patch of curls between her legs—just as red as the dazzling hair on her head. He wanted to do as he'd seen in his erotic books: put his mouth there.

He wanted to put his mouth everywhere.

"Touch me," she said.

He stepped forward, tentatively, and put his hand on her shoulder. He wanted to drag it down, feel the rest of her.

Listen to your body, she had told him.

And so, he did. He put his hands on her breasts and

lightly stroked their contours. He had to hold back a groan at the sensation.

"Would you like to see them?" she asked.

Not here, on the landing, like an animal.

"Let's go to the bedchamber," he rasped out.

She nodded solemnly. "Yes. Take me to bed."

Take me to bed.

He took her hand and led her to his room. She'd lit every lamp and candle she could find, giving it a golden glow. In that flickering light, her lacy gown was even prettier. She looked like a fairy, glimmering.

She shivered.

"Are you cold?" he asked.

"A little," she said. "But I won't be if you hold me."

Hold me.

He knew she was saying these things because he responded to them. He knew that she was performing, doing what he paid her for. But by God, it was working.

He walked toward her and opened his arms. She stepped into them. He wrapped himself around her.

So soft. So plump and ripe, like a perfect, juicy summer peach. And so much more petite and delicate than she seemed in daylight. Her mouth and carriage gave her the illusion of a stature she did not actually possess. He wanted to bend down and kiss the top of her head.

So he did.

"Oh, Alastair," she murmured. "You're so sweet."

She looked up at him, and he bent down and kissed her mouth. She murmured and pulled him closer, deepening the kiss. When she put her tongue in his mouth, he met it. He didn't know what to do, yet somehow, he also *did*.

His hand slid down to the small of her back, just over the cleft of her arse, and then he was cupping her bottom, reverently tracing its generous contours, hardly believing he had the privilege of feeling her soft skin. He belatedly realized what he was doing was forward and rude, and he dropped his hands down by his sides. He broke apart from her, breathing raggedly.

"I'm sorry," he said. "I shouldn't have—"

"You needn't stop," she said. "I like to be touched. It feels wonderful."

He wanted to believe her, wanted to resume what he was doing. But embarrassment was descending upon him once again.

He'd misjudged, cocked it up. His instincts were constantly the opposite of what they should be. It was alarming how bad he was at this.

Thaïs clearly saw his disappointment in himself. His bewilderment at what to do next. His shame.

"Let me show you," she said.

"Show me how to touch you?"

"In good time," she said with a smile. "But first, I think it might be better to show you how good it feels to be touched. So you stop doubting yourself and feeling guilty."

The idea of it was unnerving. But he was paying for her tutelage, and if this was the lesson she recommended, he would defer to her superior knowledge.

"I, er . . . Yes. If you think so."

She nodded. "I do think so."

He stood slack, clenching his jaw, waiting to see what she would do. But she didn't move any closer to him. Instead, she walked over to an armchair in the corner and sat down.

"Before I begin, take off your clothes," she said.

"Pardon?"

"Undress, Alastair."

"Why?"

"You like seeing my body, do you not?"

"I do," he admitted. "Very much."

"Well, your lady will want to see you the same way you want to see her. And it's important to know your lover's body—by sight and by touch. How will you please each other if your skin is a mystery?"

He could not imagine why a woman would want to look upon him nude. The female body struck him as a work of art, all smooth curves one wanted to caress. The male form was stark and straight by comparison, except for the rude protuberance in the middle. Nothing to stir the blood.

Well, not *his* blood, he reasoned. But he supposed it did follow that there might be a parallel pleasure for the opposite sex.

Regardless, Thaïs had told him to undress, and so he would. He quickly removed his coat, hanging it neatly in the closet, and then his cravat, and then his shirt. He was about to fold them when Thaïs cleared her throat.

"That can wait until we're finished. Never interrupt passion for tidying the house. Keep going."

He nodded and kicked off his boots, then slid off his stockings.

Which left only his breeches, which were tented by the silhouette of his erection.

Her eyes were trained softly on exactly that part of him. His nipples hardened, and he could not say if it was from his exposed skin in the cool night air or the idea of her looking at his cock.

He took a deep breath, closed his eyes, and undid the falls, kicking his breeches down and over his ankles.

There. He'd bloody done it.

He stood up slowly and felt her eyes tracing him as he exposed his full nude body to her gaze.

"Oh, Alastair," she said. "You're even more splendid than I imagined."

This was heartening to hear, though he was not sure if she was saying it to be kind or if she really liked the looks of him.

"Thank you," he said, to be polite.

"Let's get in bed, love," she said softly.

It was foolish, but his heart hitched every time she called him that. *Love*.

He obeyed her, feeling sheepish with his cock sticking straight up in the air. He sat down on the edge of the bed and waited for Thaïs to join him.

"Lie back," she said.

As he did, resting his shoulders against the feather pillows, she stretched out beside him.

"Now, then," she said. "Can I put my itching little fingers on that chest of yours?"

He nodded.

"So strong," she said, rubbing her hand over his breast. "But then, since you do the work of ten servants, I shouldn't be surprised."

He couldn't reply, because his breath hitched at her

nearness, her spicy scent, her hair brushing his bicep. Her hand on his abdomen, lightly stroking.

My God. If this was what it felt like to be touched in such a way, then he should have been touching her like this for days.

Her thumbs found his nipples, and he gasped. She sighed happily in response.

"Feels good, doesn't it?" she murmured, stroking them in circles. "I like that too."

Her fingers traced lower, to his rib cage and his waist. And then she landed on his stomach, just below his navel, and just above the place where all the desire was churning inside him, making his skin feel hot and strained. She lightly grazed him with her nails, going lower and lower ever so slowly until her thumbs rested on his hip bones and her fingers played with the trail of hair leading to his groin.

His cock jumped at this sensation, which felt like she was manipulating some chord deep inside him. She traced up and down, back and forth, teasing the skin above his pubic bone until he shook.

"Darling boy," she said, "you look like you want me to go a little lower."

If she went any lower he was going to black out.

"Oh, uh, maybe not just yet, because, you see—"

"Let's just try, and if you don't like it, only say the word, and I'll stop, aye?"

"Uh, very well, yes, if you don't—"

She slid her hand down. Right down *past* his cock and to his balls, which she held in her palm, stroking with her thumbs.

"Is that where you want it?" she asked innocently.

And he did—he truly did—but more than that, he wanted her hands up higher, on his erection, so badly that it was torture.

And she knew it, the wicked girl. A teasing smile curved over her lips, and her eyes danced with mischief.

"Is there anywhere else you might like me to venture?"

She was going to make him say it.

And he would. He had to. He couldn't stand it any longer.

"My cock," he groaned. "Please, Thaïs."

With no further preamble she gripped his shaft in one hand and rubbed her thumb over his bellend.

He cried out. He wanted this, he wanted this, he wanted this, and she gripped him tighter, caressing the head of his prick, rubbing the wetness there around, and his stomach seized and his hips shot up and he moaned her name as he erupted all over her hand.

Fuck, fuck, fucking fuck.

The French called this *the little death*.

And it was true. He wanted to die.

Chapter Nineteen

She was beginning to understand.

All this time, it wasn't that Eden didn't want to swive her. It was that he wanted to swive her too much.

It didn't have to be a problem, spilling quickly. She could certainly help make him last or at least find ways to make his eagerness erotic. But convincing him of it might take a bit of vigor, by the looks of him. He was standing over the washbasin wiping away his seed with his shoulders slumped and his head bowed. When he turned around, he kept his eyes trained on the floor.

It took a lot of self-disgust to make an earl stand in shame before a whore.

Poor man.

"Alastair," she said gently, "is this what happens when you're with a woman? You spurt before you want to?"

He nodded.

"It's quite normal, you know," she said. "To get overexcited."

"For a twelve-year-old," he muttered.

"For all sorts," she said. "I would know better than you, I reckon."

"You don't have to comfort me. The pity makes it worse."

"It's not pity," she said. "It's fact."

"The fact," he said in a correcting voice, "is that I'll never be able to make love to my wife, because I can't last half a minute."

"That's why I'm here. To teach you. And I will."

"Some things can't be taught." He gestured between them. "This was a mistake."

"No. Hiring me was smart of you. Stop pacing. Come back to bed and talk to me." She patted the sheets next to her.

"We've talked enough," he said, collapsing down beside her. "Let's go to sleep."

She propped herself up on her elbow and frowned down at him. "Afraid not, milord. You hired me to give you lessons, and I have an important one to teach you."

He pulled the covers up to his chin and closed his eyes. "Teach me in the morning."

"In front of Hattie? Very well, if you insist."

"Fine," he said, opening his eyes. "What is it you wish to impart?"

"First of all, when was the last time you were with a woman?"

He shook his head. "I told you. About a decade. I can't quite recall."

"So you've got ten years of randiness burning up inside you."

"No. I see to my own needs regularly. As you were kind enough to witness when you barged in on me in the act."

She ignored this.

"Does it happen when you're alone? Spilling so quick?"

"No."

"Well, any person who hasn't been touched in ten years—who hasn't gotten to kiss or hold a woman he wants—is bound to be a little more eager with a girl than he is with his own hand."

"That accounts for a fraction of it, maybe. But most men can fuck without humiliating themselves. I can't."

"I'll be deciding that. You're my lowly pupil."

He closed his eyes again. "Good night, Thaïs."

She poked him in the ribs.

"You know," she said, "when you want someone very badly, you get more excited. And you want me very badly, don't you?"

She might have said this boastfully if she was in another mood, but she wasn't trying to needle him. She just wanted to make him see the truth of what was happening to him without the haze of shame.

Thaïs did not believe in shame.

"Well, of course I want you," he said. "I would think that's quite obvious, given the circumstances. I devised an elaborate scheme to hire you. I paid a fortune for your time. I can't look at you without—" He gestured at his cock, which was half-stiffened even despite his ill temper and the fact that he'd spilled his seed not ten minutes ago.

"And I *like* all that," she said. "I see the way you look at me, and where your eyes are always glancing. I know how much you love my breasts and arse, how much you like to feel them. And when you let yourself touch me, I see how it affects you. How you tremble and swell for me, treat me like I'm precious. And I *love* it, Alastair. And your wife will too, if you pick her right."

He was quiet.

"Even if all that is true," he finally said, "it doesn't change the fact of my affliction. I can't have children if I can't stay erect long enough to spill inside a woman. I can't give my wife a family, nor have the chance to be a father. As it is, it would be unfair of me to marry at all. If I can't provide children, and I can't provide pleasure, I won't wed."

Her heart squeezed for him.

She knew that fear so well—the longing for a family, and the worry that you'll never be the right kind of person to have one.

But Eden was wrong.

He *could* have it. She would give that to him.

"Well, giving pleasure needn't be a matter of rutting," she said. "You can make a woman sweat with your hands and mouth, if you know how. And I'm going to teach you that too. But first, we're going to work on making you last, so you don't feel so bloody terrible."

"Good luck with the impossible."

"Oh, don't you test me. When I'm done with you, you'll be fucking for hours. Your ballocks will be so hard and full you'll wish you'd never met me."

"I don't see how."

"Well, that's what you have me for. And look—you're nearly hard again, and you're in a miserable bloody temper and I haven't even touched you. I'd wager that if we go again, you won't reach your peak so fast."

"I doubt it," he said. "You excite me tremendously, Thaïs. You're at least right about that."

"Well, let's try it and find out."

He shook his head. "I can't tonight. It's been too much."

She understood this, though she wished he'd be a bit more willing to try things, even if they might not go perfectly the first time.

"You could also see to yourself alone, before you're with your lover. To make yourself less lusty. Or let her watch you have yourself. Or help you."

He laughed darkly. "I can't imagine anyone would want to do either of those things."

"You have a piss-poor imagination."

"Thank you. May I sleep now?"

She sighed. He was awfully stubborn for a man who claimed to want to learn.

"You needn't be so gruff with me. I'm only trying to give you what you paid for."

He let out a long breath. "You're right. I'm sorry, Thaïs."

He was sincere, she could tell. Her men didn't usually apologize for their ill temper—or if they did, it was only to mollify her to get another frig. She'd never been with a man like Eden, who was so nice even at his worst.

She wanted—truly wanted—to help him.

And the only way to help was to get him used to her. Make him feel manly about himself, if that's what he needed.

"I'm cold," she lied, feigning a shiver. "Will you hold me until I fall asleep?"

"Hold you?"

He wasn't being ornery. He seemed not to know what she meant.

She picked up one of his arms and draped it over her body. "Like that, see? But use both of them to cuddle me up."

"I want to make you comfortable," he said. "But if I touch you that way, I might . . ."

"And who cares if you do? You're here to practice. And women like sweetness."

"Very well," he said. "If you're certain."

He put his arm around her, and she snuggled into his side.

It felt surprisingly nice. She was fibbing about women wanting to be held—certainly not all of them did, and she wasn't often one of them. Too much of a man made her feel trapped.

But not Eden.

"Put your other arm around me," she whispered.

He did.

His body was tense. He held his hips apart from her, so her skin wouldn't brush his prick, now fully hard again. He was trying to please her, despite his roiling feelings and bad mood and—she suspected—the agony of craving another orgasm and denying himself.

She closed her eyes and tried to fall asleep, but Eden's tension made it hard to drift away. She felt him straining, his muscles rigid, his heart beating hard and fast.

She couldn't take it. Neither of them would get a wink tonight if this went on.

"Alastair?" she said.

"Yes?"

"You're dying. Let me help you."

And he must have been more desperate than even

she knew, because he trembled at the mere words and grazed his cock against her leg. It was slick. His body was weeping with desire for her.

It made her own loins quicken.

Slowly, lightly, she brushed his belly with the tips of her fingers. He moaned and shook, pressing himself more firmly against her bare leg.

"Make yourself feel good," she whispered.

He groaned and thrust himself against her leg again.

That was all it took. He cried out, clutching at her so desperately she knew he was not aware he was doing it. He buried his face in her neck as he yelled out his pleasure, squeezing her like she was the only thing between himself and sanity.

Blessed boy, he'd *needed* that. She'd never been so happy to cause a man to come.

She leaned over and kissed his brow. "Now sleep," she said.

Chapter Twenty

When Eden had imagined sleeping beside a woman, he'd pictured her snuggled in his arms, using his chest as a pillow, pretty and peaceful as an angel.

This was not the tableau that greeted him at five in the morning, when he awoke with a stiff neck, nearly dangling off his side of the bed.

Thaïs was no angel. She was a thief.

One who was sprawled on her stomach across the mattress like a climbing vine taking over a wall, with one leg flung over his calf, the other scissoring off the bed, and her arm nearly crushing his neck.

And she snored.

Loudly.

It was so absurd he might laugh were her arm not pressing down painfully on his windpipe.

He wriggled out from under her, trying not to rouse her but also not so committed to her sleep that he was willing to suffocate.

She stirred, mumbled some incoherent curse, stretched out even wider to fully colonize the space he'd wriggled out of, and promptly went back to snoring.

It was reassuring to see her in so ungainly a pose. A reminder that as alluring as he found her, she was a human being, not a goddess. Which was heartening, after the way he'd humbled himself before her last night.

Through no fault of her own, of course.

She'd been so kind in the face of his mortification and so confident in her belief she could alleviate his affliction. And when she'd urged him—helped him—to release before he slept, it had felt like an invitation to surrender.

He didn't have to hide from her. He could come to her for mercy.

He wished he had not resisted her for so long. He'd wasted a week hiding his hindrance. Now that his problem was in the open, he felt lighter—grateful that he had a woman like Thaïs who knew how to help him, and eager to try the remedies she'd suggested.

He was most intrigued by her assertion that he could *make a woman sweat* using his mouth and fingers. He imagined a woman—Thaïs—as desperate for his touch as he was for hers. God, how proud he'd be of himself if he could accomplish that. *This* was what he wanted to be able to give his wife.

And to learn how, he had to face his fear of failing and ask Thaïs for help.

He would stop hiding behind chaste lessons in courtship—lessons that, if he were honest, he didn't really need—and summon the bravery to trust Thaïs with his body and his fears. To teach him how to be the lover he wanted to be to his woman.

He left Thaïs to sleep and went downstairs.

As Elinor would be arriving in a few hours, he went around the house and tidied up. Thaïs had left her playing cards and furniture brochures and letters scattered about the parlor. With any other person this messiness would annoy him, but he felt oddly charmed by it. Thaïs's chaos was like her complaining and her cursing: things he shouldn't like but did.

He changed the sheets in Thaïs's room so Elinor would have fresh linens and left a note for Hattie to dust and sweep the parlor. Then he retreated with his tea to his study, enjoying the peace of the sunrise.

Until the cocks began to crow.

Thaïs was not wrong about the roosters here. They seemed louder and redder and more truculent than was typical of their kind, crowing deep into the morning and pecking ankles whenever they had the chance. They reminded him a bit of Thaïs.

He heard stomping upstairs, then heavy footsteps on the staircase. "Alastair!" Thaïs called. "Go outside and kill those birds."

He rose and stuck his head out the study door. She was wearing his nightshirt and nothing else.

"Go upstairs and dress, please, before Hattie sees you."

"Legs aren't anything Hattie hasn't seen before. She has a pair of her own, if you hadn't noticed."

"Yes, but I doubt she's seen many sisters wearing their brother's nightshirt. Let alone half-dressed ones."

"I will if you come upstairs with me," she said.

"I'm busy."

"You haven't had your morning session."

"What session?"

She made a crude gesture at her groin. "That session."

"Absolutely not. Hattie will be here any moment."

"Then you'll have to be quiet."

"You're being ridiculous. Go get dressed."

"Would you rather do it tonight, with Elinor in the next room?"

He'd rather sleep in the henhouse.

"Elinor is not to know we're . . ."

"What else do you suppose Elinor will think is happening here? You paid twenty-five thousand pounds for my services cleaning your fire grate? Driving your coach? Teaching you Latin? Of course she'll know."

He reckoned it had been unrealistic of him to think he could avoid the truth. Thaïs would be sleeping in his bed, after all. And after last night, he preferred it that way. He didn't want to sleep without her.

"You're right," he said. "I'm being foolish."

"Come upstairs, love. You'll be wanting a bit of satisfaction before you have to spend two nights beside me depriving yourself of my favors."

Given he had skipped his morning ceremony, perhaps there was merit in this idea. He would certainly not engage in any sexual activity with Elinor under his roof. Though, with Thaïs in his bed, it would be a form of light torture to keep his appetites in check.

"You're indulgent with me," he said.

"You get what you pay for."

He followed her back up the stairs and to his room, where she had left the bed a nest of tumbled sheets and blankets.

She closed the door behind him, locked it, pulled his nightshirt off and dropped it on the floor.

His nerves instantly gave way to desire.

So much desire.

It made him pant just to look at her.

"Let's play a game," she said. "No touching me, or me you. You can gaze upon me all you like while you touch yourself. I want to see how you do it."

This, at least, he was an expert at. But the act was so personal. He'd never once imagined, before her, that there could be anything but embarrassment in letting someone watch.

Trust her, he reminded himself. She's here to help.

And looking at her, naked and beautiful, he wanted a frig powerfully.

He slid his breeches to his thighs and pulled his cock out.

"Nice staff you have there," Thaïs said. "I like them thick like that. Hits the cunny good. Though, you'll have to be careful with your virgin. Make sure she's nice and ready so you don't make her sore with what you're swinging."

The idea of Thaïs liking the shape of his penis made him even harder. He could scarcely make sense of what she said about a bride because all he could think about was what it would be like to be inside Thaïs. My God, her *cunny*.

The word sent desire crashing through him. His cock trembled, and he mindlessly reached down and gave it a blessed tug. He was already close.

"Oh, that's lovely," Thaïs said. "But do you usually do it with your breeches still on?"

He snapped back to attention. "Er, no. Usually in bed, when I wake up."

"Then let's have you do it that way."

He stripped and sat on the bed. She continued to stand where she was.

"You aren't joining me?"

"Better view from here. For both of us."

God, she was really going to watch this. He was really going to let her.

He sat back against the headboard to get comfortable, then slid his hand up and down his shaft with a loose grip, not taking his eyes off Thaïs.

Thaïs's breasts, specifically.

He fought the urge to yank his cock in a few firm grips and let the peak rip through him there and then. But no. He would control himself, enjoy this view for as long as he could last.

Seeing where his eyes were, Thaïs ran her hands over her breasts, tracing the shape of them.

"Feels good," she said. "It will feel better when it's you touching them."

He stopped moving his hand, knowing that if he didn't take a break he'd burst.

"Don't torment me," he said. He closed his eyes and took a deep breath to steady himself.

When he reopened them, she was smiling at him indulgently. "You're awfully handsome, Eden," she said. "I like to look at you."

He didn't much think about his appearance, but it was gratifying to hear that she didn't find him wanting. "Thank you," he said.

"Back to it," she said. "It's all right if it's quick. This is purely for my education."

"I want to enjoy it," he admitted.

"I want you to as well. But you can't enjoy it if you don't do it at all. Have a stroke."

He positioned his hand in the way that he liked—

the way that was so familiar—and tightened the grip. Keeping his eyes on her, he began to have himself in earnest.

He focused on the up-and-down motion, letting the anticipation flow through his belly, his nipples, his limbs.

"That's it," Thaïs murmured. "You like a long, slow stroke, aye?"

"Yes," he said.

"Would you do it faster, if I weren't here?"

"I might. Depending on my mood. Some days I—" he stopped talking for a second to catch his breath "—some days I prefer to linger. Like now."

Despite this desire, the sensations were becoming more urgent. And he was dying to touch under his balls.

Fuck it, he would.

He gripped them with his left hand and used a finger to put pressure between his thighs and gasped at the heightened sensation.

"Ah, yes," Thaïs whispered. "You like that, indeed. I'll keep it in mind when I have my way with you."

At the idea of her fingers providing this pressure for him, he nearly choked.

He quickened his pace, gripping harder. He was moments away, and he'd dragged it out as long as he could stand to and—

He heard the door open downstairs.

Hattie.

He dropped his cock, horrified that if she'd come a few seconds later she might have heard him.

Thaïs shook her head. "Don't stop," she whispered. "You need this."

He *did* need it. Without the stimulation of his hand his cock pulsed painfully in the air, screaming for relief.

He had to finish.

He just had to be utterly, utterly silent.

He put his hand back to his dick and squeezed his balls. He felt it deep behind his groin.

"That's it," Thaïs coaxed, so quietly her words were barely perceptible.

He yanked the bloody hell out of his cock and felt a bolt of something so powerful he nearly screamed.

But he couldn't.

And the effort not to make a sound made it even more intense.

He shook and rocked as wave after wave of pleasure gripped him. He felt almost attacked by it. The bed creaked as his hips bucked, but he couldn't help it. He took a pillow, buried his face in it, and groaned as softly as he could.

It took a full minute until he was fully spent.

He lay sprawled and limp and exhausted. Thaïs was smiling at him, looking downright *proud*.

Silently, she brought him a cloth to wipe himself clean.

And then she bent over and kissed him on the lips.

"That made me hot between my legs," she whispered. "I can't wait for you to touch me."

He reached out to cup her arse, but she stepped away.

"Not yet, Alastair. I can't promise I can be as quiet as you can."

Chapter Twenty-One

Thaïs was used to being leered at so lewdly it felt like being pawed. She didn't mind it. It was her livelihood to make men horny, and horny men were not apt to be polite about their lust, especially to harlots.

But Eden's gaze on her—while lusty to be sure—was different from those leers. He looked at her like her body was a miracle he couldn't quite believe.

It was not her bent to get excited over the men she swived for money. It was *better* not to, as the job was to notice how to please them, and a muddled mind made a girl unsafe. Even when she liked her patrons, the lust she showed for them was to whet their appetites. Sex was a performance, and her body was her stage.

So it was odd how hot she felt when she watched Eden. Maybe it was because he was so earnest about sex. Maybe because he was so kind a person. She liked plenty of the men she fucked, but Eden was her friend. She wanted to do right by him.

And that caused a part of her she usually kept cold to thaw.

Which was not good.

She was here to service him. Getting slick between the legs would only frustrate her when it was time to send him off to his bride.

Eden dressed and went downstairs to greet Hattie while Thaïs readied herself for the day. Getting up so early was beginning to feel less numbing. In fact, it might be good for her complexion, as she had a rosy glow.

She went downstairs and munched on toast while Hattie tidied, chatting with her about the weather, then took her brochures outside and sat on the terrace circling things she wished to buy.

Time moved slowly as she waited for the telltale clop of horses on the gravel drive.

She had missed Elinor horribly these past few months. It seemed that all her friends were busy in their own lives. Seraphina was writing a new book and had a baby and two stepchildren to raise. Cornelia was spending half her time in the country with her husband, helping reform the estate he'd inherited to benefit the whole community. Elinor was plagued by the loss of her children and had been on the road for months trying to find them. And when she was in London, she spent most her time with Jack, her lover and the leader of the Equalist Society.

Her dearest friends had all found love—except Thaïs. It was less than two years ago that the four of them had spent all their time together, more like a family than friends. And she still loved her girls like sisters, and Elinor like a mother. But deep down, beneath the busy pace of her life in London, she was lonely. And being in the country only made it worse.

Another vehicle approached. Thaïs prayed it would turn right.

When it did, she hooted and ran inside the house.

"Eden," she called. "She's here!"

She raced out the front door and hopped from foot to foot as she waited for Elinor to get out of the cart that Eden had hired to meet her at the coaching inn in town. As soon as Elinor's feet were on the ground, Thaïs went flying toward her, arms open, beaming.

"El! Come here, you quacker."

"*Quacker*?" Elinor said. "That's a new endearment. Or, at least, I assume it's an endearment?"

Thaïs kissed her cheek. "You know that you're my dear. My *dearest*."

Elinor wrapped her arms around Thaïs and squeezed. "And you're mine."

They turned toward the house. Eden was standing awkwardly beside the door, redder than the roosters that she so longed to kill.

He bowed to Elinor. "Lady Bell."

Elinor paused for a moment to take him in. Thaïs had warned her that she was here with a mutual acquaintance but had not revealed his name in her letter.

"Lord Eden," Elinor said smoothly. "What a pleasure."

"Indeed," he said with visible effort not to grimace. "Welcome."

"No need to *Lord* and *Lady* each other," Thaïs said. "Around here he's plain old Mr. Smith, and God help you if you curtsy to him. He'd just as soon you kick him in the shins."

"I would prefer a curtsy to being assaulted, actually."

"Just a turn of phrase."

"How vivid," he said.

"You know me!"

"I'm certainly beginning to."

"I promise not to curtsy," Elinor said. "And I'll do anything you ask to maintain your privacy. I'm so very grateful you have opened your home to me . . . Mr. Smith."

"I'm pleased to help, and so glad you may soon be reunited with your daughter."

"Thank you," Elinor said. "It's such a fortuitous co-incidence."

"Although—" Eden bit his lip "—I hope you won't think ill of me for the circumstances under which we're here."

Elinor shook her head. "I would never think ill of anyone for enjoying the company of my dear Thaïs."

Ah, she was a gracious one, that Elinor.

"That's right," Thaïs said. "Methinks I'm quite a fine companion."

"Of course," Eden said. "I just meant . . . well, Elinor, I'm not here for lascivious purposes. Or, that is I suppose I *am*, but not—erm, excuse me." He coughed. Thaïs tried not to laugh.

"What the poor dear means is I'm here to help him study up husbanding a woman. If you know what I mean."

"I see," Elinor said with a smile.

"Yes. That is, I asked Thaïs to help me prepare to marry soon. And I'd hate for whoever I wed to think of me in a poor light, so if you would not mind keeping our arrangement a secret, I'd be most grateful."

"Eden," Elinor said, "you have my word. And I think that's one of the most romantic things I've ever heard."

Thaïs hadn't thought of it that way. It had seemed

practical to her. Even a bit fussy. But Elinor was right. Behind Eden's wish to be perfect was a desire to bring someone joy and contentment in her life.

Any man who valued such a thing would be a wonderful husband.

"Me too," Thaïs said. "You're a good type, Mr. Smith."

Eden looked at her oddly. "I am?"

"Well, don't go about thumping your chest about it, but aye, you'll do."

"Thank you," he said, flushing. "Elinor, I'll take your bag up to your room."

"Fancy a rest after your journey?" Thaïs asked her.

"Actually, I'd love to stretch my legs after that long carriage ride. Might we take a stroll?"

These aristos and their damned strolls.

"Fine," she said, trying not to groan. "But we can't fall in any mud. This is my last clean dress."

"I wasn't planning on it, dear."

"Sneaks up on you here, plans or no plans. You should have seen me yesterday. Filthy from head to toe. And not—"

"In the good way?" Elinor finished drily.

"Don't steal my jokes."

"Why don't you have clean clothes?" Elinor asked. "Did you not pack your usual fifteen trunks?"

"Five trunks, thank you. But I thought I would be dressing for the boudoir, not the barnyard. Eden won't let me wear my lovely whorish finery. He's afraid someone will discover who we really are and his reputation will be ruined."

"The two of you aren't getting along?"

"We get along splendid," Thaïs said, realizing it was true. "But Mr. Perfect only deigns to entertain me when he's not doing his never-ending work, and there's nothing to do out here but fall in mud and get pecked by geese."

"Well, it's only for a few more weeks. Then you'll be back in our pristine London, with no mud in sight."

"You think you're funny, don't you, milady?"

"You bring it out in me, my dear. You're a delight to tease. One gets an immediate reaction."

"Have you heard from the girls?" Thaïs asked. They didn't write her unless they had to, knowing her hatred of letters.

"Sera wrote me last week," Elinor said. "She and Cornelia have been consumed with preparing the Institute to open. I feel guilty that I'm not able to be of more help."

"Those two can manage anything. Me, on the other hand? Barely done a lick of work. At the rate I'm going, there won't be any beds or chairs."

"What's stopping you?"

"I've picked out what I want to buy, but I need to send in the orders. It takes me ages."

"Shall I help you, when we return?"

Blessed relief, the idea of that.

"Please. Otherwise Eden will be looking over my shoulder every minute, pestering me to let him write them for me."

Elinor looked surprised. "He helps you with your correspondence?"

"Loves to. It's embarrassing. Makes me look like a numbskull."

"Thaïs, no one who spends a quarter hour with you would think you're anything but brilliant. I'm sure Eden recognizes your intelligence."

She hoped so. For some reason, she cared very much about him thinking she was smart.

After a stop at the Fellowes' barn to cuddle the kittens, they returned to the cottage to spend the afternoon munching biscuits and working on Thaïs's letters. With Elinor at the quill, it went quickly and pleasantly.

But as the stack of work waiting to be done shrank, she felt a slight pang of disappointment. For the more that Elinor helped her, the less there would be for Eden to do.

And maybe she liked him helping her after all.

Chapter Twenty-Two

Eden found himself grateful that Elinor was here. Thaïs was happier with her company. He wished he had thought more about Thaïs's happiness before bringing her here. He should have known she'd get lonely. She was accustomed to a life of revelry, parties, entertainment, and charity work. He was the worst possible companion for her. It was amazing that they got along at all, considering their opposite dispositions. Eden liked revelry about as much as he liked headaches. Less, as at least headaches gave one an excuse to be quiet and alone.

At five he emerged from his study to begin preparing supper and found the ladies in the parlor, working on Thaïs's correspondence.

"You've made progress," he observed, seeing the tall stack of letters that had replaced the messy pile of brochures.

"Elinor's a better secretary than you are," Thaïs said.

"I'm sure she is. But does she match me in taste for candlesticks and china?"

He had come to enjoy teasing Thaïs about her selections to purchase, debating such things as whether oak or cherry were best for dining chairs and what type of cutlery best suited a dining hall for one hundred.

"Elinor has a better eye than you do, but I doubt she's as good at cookery."

"I am not good at cookery at all," Elinor said. "But I would love to watch the *chef de cuisine* prepare our meal."

They followed him to the kitchen and sat at the table drinking wine while he prepared a chicken to roast.

"He is astonishing," Elinor commented to Thaïs as he made a fragrant sauce with onions, butter, herbs, and wine.

He wanted to make them something indulgent and delicious. He knew Elinor was having a terrible year. He'd do what little he could to give her a bit of pleasure.

"I can hear you, you know," he said.

"Forgive me for marveling. But an earl preparing a meal? You must know this is a remarkable occurrence."

"Once in a lifetime, I reckon," Thaïs said. "We should charge admission. Make a bloody fortune."

"Thaïs isn't a bad cook," he said. "Did you know she can make a sponge cake light as air?"

"I did not," Elinor said. "I'm surprised to learn she enjoys baking."

"I don't," Thaïs said.

"Oh, she does," he assured Elinor. "She's especially fond of beating the eggs."

Thaïs snorted. "This man tortured me with stirring for two hours. Thought my wrists would break clean off my arms. And that would rightly—"

"Destroy your livelihood?" Eden asked blandly.

"Now you're stealing my lines too?"

"You'll have to think of cleverer ones."

"I'm plenty clever. Is that ready?" She pointed at the steaming food. "I'm starving to death."

"It is," he said. "It seems you will live to see another day. It's lovely outside. Shall we dine on the terrace?"

They took plates of food outside and lingered there, enjoying the mild evening. Elinor's presence made him feel more assured. He might not know how to be a lover, but he knew how to be an excellent host.

"It's good to see you, Elinor," he said. "Though, I wish it were under better circumstances."

"If I see my daughter tomorrow, the circumstances will be fine, indeed."

"How long has it been?"

"Nearly two years."

Awful. He couldn't imagine if Anna had been taken away from him when she was growing up, let alone for so long.

"Unconscionable," he said, "depriving children of their mother."

"My estranged husband is not known for his commitment to compassion. Nor ethics."

"Dare I ask about the divorce?" he said. He knew that it was looming over everything in Elinor's life. She stood to lose anything Bell had not yet managed to take away—any hope of seeing her children until they came of age, any money she'd brought to the marriage, and even the right to marry again, which he suspected she'd have liked to do, given her obvious love for Jack Willow. He knew she would get through it—she seemed as strong as iron—but she'd already been through so much. She deserved happiness, family, and peace.

"Bell's petition will be heard in the first few weeks of Parliament, I'm told," she said. "And we have every reason to believe it will pass. Which is why I am so desperate to find the children now, so I can see them before I'm not allowed to as a provision of the law."

"At least you'll be rid of the bastard," Thaïs said. "Small mercies."

"And he'll be rid of me," Elinor said. "Do you know he has already begun planning to court a new wife? I'm told by Sylvia Coulter he has his eye on a very young woman—Miss Emily Clark. The ward of some old gentleman—I can't recall his name."

Thaïs whistled. "Pity the poor girl who gets tossed off to the likes of him."

Pity, indeed. Eden wondered if Bell was courting any of the ladies in his dossiers. The idea disgusted him. He'd marry a girl just to spare her a lifetime with that bastard.

"Let's speak of something more pleasant," Elinor said.

"I'll leave you two to catch up," Eden said, rising. He wanted to give them privacy, since their time together was limited.

He took their plates inside and began to clean the kitchen. Their voices floated through the open windows as they spoke about their friends. He didn't want to eavesdrop, but it was impossible not to hear as he scrubbed the pots and pans.

And then he caught his name.

"Eden's very gracious," Elinor said. "And more relaxed than he seemed when we were all together at Gardencourt last year. It's nice how comfortable the two of you are together."

But *were* they comfortable? They enjoyed each other's company during the day, but he felt so nervous around her when it came time for his lessons that sometimes it made him lightheaded.

"We're just like man and wife," Thaïs quipped.

That would be the day. He doubted he'd ever be so unnerved around another woman. Well-bred young ladies would not dare to display such verve, and he doubted any of the girls he'd read about would possess Thaïs's confidence and enthusiasm for lovemaking.

"Man and wife, eh?" Elinor said. "How sad I wasn't invited to your wedding."

"My wedding, ha! That'll be the same day I finally learn my Latin."

"Why do you say that?" Elinor asked.

Thaïs snorted. "Who would marry me? No secret I'm a harlot. Not many gents clamoring for my hand."

She said this lightly, but he wondered if he detected a note of sadness in her tone. If so, it was a pity. He could imagine her warm, funny energy at the center of a home. She would certainly not be a tranquil helpmeet, but she'd be the soul of the family.

"You have the biggest heart, Thaïs," Elinor said.

"No. That's just my bosom."

"Don't make a joke. Marriage isn't necessary for love to take hold—look at Sera. Look at me and Jack. You deserve someone to cherish you."

Eden nodded to himself.

She did.

She truly did.

Chapter Twenty~Three

When Thaïs climbed in bed with Eden, he was already asleep. Or at least pretending to be, to avoid any chance that she'd go after him with her wanton ways.

Not that she would.

She knew the very idea of it made him squirm, and she didn't want to torment him when he'd been so nice to let Elinor stay.

The covers were warm from Eden's body, a comforting feeling. It was nice to lie beside him, listening to him breathe.

She'd never shared a bed chastely with a man before.

Well, chastely enough. When the devil roosters woke her up, she was wrapped around him like a monkey.

"Ah. You're awake," he said in a whisper.

"And how could I be asleep with all that racket?" she whispered back. "It's about time you made me rooster pie for supper."

"You wouldn't like it. Might I trouble you to release me?"

She squeezed him tighter. "I don't know. You're awfully nice to cuddle."

"Well, I'm glad I have at least one talent in the bed."

She did not care for the self-blame in his quip.

"You'll have a hundred when I'm through with you," she said.

His chest rumbled with a laugh. "That might be too many. Wouldn't want to injure anyone."

The idea of Eden doing any such thing made her snort.

He pried her arm off of him and wriggled out from under her legs. She watched him get dressed, which he did as neatly and precisely as he did everything.

"Looking handsome today, milord," she said.

"Don't call me *milord*. Hattie might hear you," he whispered. But he was smiling.

She dressed and knocked on Elinor's door. "You awake?"

Elinor opened it, fully dressed. "Of course I am. Who could sleep through the cacophony of those birds? Do they do that every day?"

"Yes, the infernal creatures. Never woken up so early in all my life."

They went downstairs for breakfast. Eden introduced Elinor to Hattie as their aunt, and Hattie didn't question it.

"I washed your gown for you," Hattie said, gesturing at a basket with a neatly folded garment. "Good as new."

"Oh, thank goodness," Thaïs said. "I thought I might have to start wandering around stark naked."

Hattie gave her an odd look, and Thaïs realized she'd said it in her normal accent, rather than her put-on governess voice.

"A joke," she said in her most genteel way of speech. "Can you imagine?"

Hattie laughed. "'Fraid not."

Thaïs and Elinor spent the morning finishing the last of Thaïs's letters so they could take them into town. At eleven Eden emerged from his study.

"Would you like me to drive you into the village or would you rather walk? It's a pretty stroll. About two miles."

Thaïs scowled. "You think the likes of me plans to walk, sneezing my damned head off? You'll be driving us, please and thank you."

Thaïs did not find the drive *pretty*. There was nothing to look at but grass, sheep, and hedgerows. Though, given Eden's famous love for sheep, she could understand why he found the view so breathtaking.

They arrived at the dress shop, and Eden bade them farewell, telling them to meet him at the pub across the street when they wished to return home.

Thaïs led the way inside. Sophie was on her knees, pinning up a dress for a girl with her back turned. Thaïs would have known her anywhere, with that upswept chestnut hair and delicate frame. She slapped a hand over her mouth.

"Maria," Elinor cried out in a strangled voice.

Maria turned around, eyes wide as sovereign coins. "Mama!"

She ran into Elinor's arms, pins in her hem be damned.

Sophie sat back on her haunches and stared at the scene in confusion. Then she shrugged at Thaïs and went over to the bassinet in the corner, where her baby was beginning to fuss.

"Oh, my darling girl," Elinor murmured, kissing Maria's hair over and over. "How I've missed you."

Thaïs watched them embrace. It was so beautiful a moment that it made her feel a little sad that she might never have this bond with a child of her own. Elinor carried so much pain from missing her children, but her love for them was powerful enough to make it worth the agony.

"How did you know I was here?" Maria asked, through tears. "They won't let me write to you. They read all my letters."

"*Miss Smith*," she said, pointing at Thaïs, "heard that your grandmother had a young lady staying, and we hoped that it was you. I rushed here as fast as I could."

Maria nodded, seeming to understand the implication that Thaïs was using a fake name.

"Thank you, Miss Smith," she said. "I'm so glad you took the chance."

Thaïs went up and threw her arms around the girl. "Anything for you, m'dear." She'd known Maria since she was a baby, and she'd worried about the poor child, trapped under her father's tyrannical control.

Maria looked nervously out the windows in the front of the shop.

"Mama, we can't be seen together. If Papa learns you've been here, he'll be so furious that . . . well, I'm frightened of what he might do. His temper has been mighty ever since he lost his case against you. The slightest thing can bring him to a rage."

"Oh, my darling. How I wish I could protect you

from him," Elinor said. "I wish I could take you with me. But under the law, you're his alone."

"That might be so, but in my heart I'm all yours."

Elinor clutched her daughter to her chest. "I love you, Maria. And I'll do everything I can to see that you're safe. As soon as you come of age, you can live with me."

Maria put her head on Elinor's shoulder. "I love you too, Mama. So much."

A tear slid down Thaïs's cheek. She stole a glance at Sophie Gerity, and the dressmaker was also tearing up. The feeling between mother and daughter was beautiful to see.

Thaïs longed for such a connection.

"How is your brother?" Elinor asked her daughter. "Do you know where he is?"

"Scotland," Maria said. "At Lord Young's shooting estate. He hates it there and wants desperately to go back to school, but Papa has forbidden it. He told Charles you might abduct him."

"If only I could."

Maria glanced at the window again. "My coachman has instructions to return at half past."

"Oh, darling. We'll have to leave. I won't risk endangering you. But I wish I could stay. I wish I could take you with me."

They held each other for a long while. And then Elinor wiped away her tears and turned to Thaïs. "Shall we make our way, Miss Smith?"

"Don't leave without your gowns," Sophie said. She went behind the counter and pulled out two boxes wrapped in brown paper. "Tell Hattie if they need any adjustments, and I'll come and do them for you."

"I appreciate that," Thaïs said. "I'm sure they're beautiful."

"Mrs. Gerity, can I ask that you keep our confidence about my visit here?" Elinor said. "There is no telling what Maria's father might do to her if he finds out she's seen me."

Sophie put a hand on Elinor's shoulder. "You have my word. Mother to mother."

"Thank you," Elinor said.

Elinor wept openly on the street as they made their way to the pub. "My heart is broken," she said. "Utterly broken."

Thaïs took her hand and kissed it. "You'll get them back. They love you fiercely. Between the three of you, you'll find a way."

"I couldn't say this to Maria, but their father will be able to keep control of them even after they come of age. They depend on him financially until Colin inherits. Maria will already have enough trouble finding a husband because of me. Oh God, Thaïs, sometimes I think I should have stayed with him."

Thaïs stopped her and looked right into her eyes.

"He would have *killed* you, Elinor. And I would wager your babes'd rather have you than Bell's accursed money."

Elinor took a shaky breath. "Thank you, my sweet girl. I don't know what I would do without you and Seraphina and Cornelia. You're the daughters of my heart."

They walked holding hands into the pub and found Eden at a table by the window, sipping a dark ale.

His face tightened at the sight of Elinor's tears.

"What happened?" he asked in a low voice, glancing at the barkeep whose back, thankfully, was turned.

"We should leave," Thaïs whispered. "Can't have El spotted."

He nodded, put a coin on the bar, and escorted them through a side door to the mews where he'd left his cart.

"Did you find Maria?" he asked as soon as they were outside.

"We did," Thaïs said. "She looks well, but she's lonely. Terrified of her bloody father."

"I'm sorry, Elinor," he said.

"I feel that it's my fault my children are suffering."

"Oh no it's not," Eden said firmly. He knew the story, as did most of the country after the scandal Bell's criminal conversation trial against Elinor had caused. "If Bell had not abducted you out of your home in the middle of the night and put you in a mental institution, you would still be with him. He's the one to blame, not you. You'd do anything for those children."

Elinor wiped away her tears with the back of her hand. "I would," she said. "I would. It's only that there are so few things I *can* do, aside from seeing them in secret."

"Will you try to visit your boy?" Thaïs asked.

"Of course. I'll travel to Scotland immediately. Is there a coach heading north in this town?"

"I believe so," Eden said. "Stay here. I'll stop and check at the post office."

He returned a few minutes later. "The coach comes at four in the afternoon. We can take you there tomorrow."

Elinor checked her timepiece. "If we return home

now, there would be just enough time for me to collect my things and make today's coach. Would you mind very much if we rushed back?"

"No, of course not," Eden said.

They quickly returned home, and Thaïs helped Elinor pack up her belongings and carry them downstairs. Eden was waiting in the parlor to drive Elinor back to town. Elinor wrapped Thaïs in her arms.

"I love you fiercely, my darling," she said.

"And I you," Thaïs said back, squeezing Elinor as tight as she could.

"Take care of our girl, Mr. Smith," Elinor said to Eden over Thaïs's shoulder.

"That I will."

As they left, Thaïs wondered at those words, *our girl*.

What would it be like to be Eden's girl? To be taken care of by him?

It was just a turn of phrase.

She could take care of herself.

But it made her imagine an entirely different life.

Chapter Twenty-Four

As much as Eden had enjoyed Elinor's visit, now that it was dusk, he was glad that she'd left early.

Dusk was beginning to have a witching effect on him, transforming him from the capable man he was under normal circumstances into a wreck of nerves. His entire body tingled in anticipation of what Thaïs might teach him, but his mind recoiled at the humbling nature of his overeagerness and lack of skill.

Half of him wanted to touch her, to be caressed by her. His other half wanted to excuse her from her duties and consign himself to a life of bachelorhood.

He wanted, more than anything, to be competent. To transform into the perfect lover he so longed to be.

But his chaste night in bed with Thaïs had done nothing to ease the overeagerness that plagued him. He already felt lusty, and she'd done nothing more suggestive than eat the leftover chicken he'd served for supper.

He decided to try her suggestion of relieving himself before she joined him in bed, so as to lessen his excitement. It sounded unseemly, but he was increasingly willing to try anything if it helped to make him last.

He excused himself from the parlor and asked

Thaïs to wait twenty minutes before joining him upstairs.

She grinned at him wickedly. "Aye. Go have your torrid way with yourself. I won't sneak a peek, much as I'd enjoy it."

He walked upstairs conscious of his visible erection and dispatched his errand without much preamble, trembling with the thought of her knowing what he was doing. *Enjoying* the idea of it. He was in bed, calmer if still amorous, by the time she knocked.

"Schoolmistress is here," she said. "May I come in?"

"Please," he said.

"Are you ready to return to your lessons, my pupil?" she asked, waltzing in.

"I hope I shall be a better student than the last time."

"Practice makes perfect."

She was undressing as she spoke, and he began to stir as the layers came off her body and landed on the floor. The flickering of the candles in the room made dappled light across her creamy skin.

"You're so beautiful," he said.

"Don't sound so unhappy about it."

"I'm not, believe me. A gentleman should never ogle, but I can't take my eyes off you. I'm sorry to be so rude."

"A gentleman had better ogle at his woman." She did a little twirl. "What's your favorite part?"

"Come here," he said, patting the bed beside him.

She did, and he put a finger to her nose. "I love your freckles," he said. He took a curl and wrapped it around his finger. "And the way your hair falls right down to—"

"Me luscious arse?"

He blushed. "Yes," he whispered.

"Go on," she said. "Admire me all you want."

"I love your breasts," he confessed, venturing to touch them. He traced their shape and stopped at her nipples, tweaking them with his thumbs.

"That feels nice," she sighed. He had no idea if she was being genuine or trying to improve his confidence, but he hoped she was sincere.

"I want to make you feel good," he said. "Very much."

"Kiss me, then."

He pulled her into his arms and did as she asked. This time, he didn't stumble. He wanted her too badly to hesitate or think. They went on like that until he thought he couldn't stand it. He broke away from her, panting.

"You're doing well," she said.

He realized it had been ten minutes of having her against his body, and he hadn't spilled. Perhaps the trick had worked.

"I think for tonight's lesson, I'll touch your cock," she said. "Lie back."

"This shouldn't take long," he said, but he obeyed her.

He braced himself for the inevitable as she stroked his lower belly. He willed himself not to get too wrapped up in the sensation.

Her touch felt good, but something strange was happening. He was going soft.

She lowered her hand to his cock and stroked it.

He looked down in consternation as what remained of his erection withered at her touch.

"A bit shy tonight," she said. She moved her hand to his balls, but it did not have a livening effect. To be sure, it felt wonderful. But he was so bemused by his failure to rise to the occasion he could not enjoy it.

"I don't know what's wrong," he said, hearing the distress in his own voice.

"Hush," she whispered. She lowered herself down, so her mouth was poised just above his cock. "You just need a bit of love to rouse you." She put her lips to the inside of his thighs, teasing him with the gentle brushing of her lips.

He'd imagined her doing this when he'd perused his erotic books. He'd looked forward to it.

But no matter what she did, he stayed limp.

She looked up at him. "Are you not in the mood for this, Alastair? It's all right if you're not. No need to force it."

"But I *am*," he said. "This has never happened before. I shouldn't have touched myself before you came up. I was just so worried about . . ."

"You're too wrapped up in your thoughts," she said. "We need you thinking with your body, not your mind."

"When I think with my body, I don't last two seconds."

"That's the trouble. You're being hard on yourself for that, and it's making your cock soft."

"Well, it's embarrassing. As is this. God, how could I be so bad at something barnyard animals can do without a second thought?"

"You're not bad at anything. You're just nervous. Let's try more kissing."

She got on top of him and took his mouth with hers. But all he could think about was the softness between his legs. He broke off the kiss.

"Thaïs, I don't think this is going to work. Would you mind very much if we went to sleep?"

She stroked his hair. "That's fine, love. You'll be raring to go again in the morning."

But in the morning, despite waking up with an erection, it happened again. He went soft as soon as she took him in her hand.

After ten humiliating minutes, he ended the lesson.

Thaïs looked unperturbed, but he suspected she was keeping her dismay hidden for his benefit.

"I don't know what to do," he said. "This is hopeless."

"Of course it's not hopeless. It's just nerves. We need to get you past them. And I have an idea."

He certainly hoped so. He was despondent.

"What is it?" he asked.

"I won't be touching you this evening. You'll be touching me. You want to learn how to give a lady pleasure. You don't need a hard cock for that."

At the idea of it, he felt himself stiffen. Just a bit, but enough to give him hope.

He'd think about it all day. And then tonight—

Well. Perhaps there was hope for him after all.

Chapter Twenty-Five

When Hattie arrived, it was with an especially fat stack of letters for Eden. Thaïs silently cursed the sight of them. Every page was another quarter hour he'd spend locked up in his study. She wished he were not so busy during the day, and not just because the isolation bored her. By saving all her lessons for nighttime and early morning, he wasn't learning fast enough.

Their time together was waning, and he needed to practice fucking to gain the cocksureness he lacked. His soft prick was yet another sign that his silly desire to be perfect was ruining his ability to learn, let alone enjoy himself. If he couldn't last or stay hard, he was right: it would be difficult for him to conceive a child.

She knew that if she could break through his defenses, he would have the makings of an excellent lover. He was watchful and kind. He'd study his woman and learn how to please her like he was mastering a new language. And he was eager, when he let himself be. Nothing wrong with his appetites. He'd be even lustier once he was sure of himself.

He emerged from his study at lunchtime and seemed surprised to find her at the table, surrounded by her own papers. She felt more comfortable with her work after Elinor had helped her, willing to read the last of the pamphlets without fear. And she was bored enough to do anything to keep her mind busy. She'd played so much patience that her eyes twitched at the very sight of her deck of cards.

"I was going to have lunch outside, given how nice it is," he said. "Care to join me?"

She all but flew out of her seat. "I'll join with you anytime."

"What a fresh new vein of humor. Wildly unpredictable."

"I charge extra for originality."

She noticed he had a letter in his hand and wrinkled her nose. "You won't be working and eating, will you?"

"It's a report on a young lady. I thought you might want to share your opinion."

"That I do."

She enjoyed this game. It was fun to hear about all the young maidens who'd swirl about London's dance floors this season. Thaïs was not welcome at the kind of balls such girls went to, and she was curious.

Eden gathered the assortment of cold foods Hattie had left for them and arranged them on a tray. They stepped out into the warm day, and the air was so nice—soft, and smelling of roses—that Thaïs didn't even mind the immediate fit of sneezing.

"Had I known you were so sensitive to the blooms of the countryside, I would have arranged for us to go to a city," he said apologetically. "I truly am sorry to see you suffer."

"Where'd you have taken me?"

"Hmm. Perhaps Manchester. I've never been to Manchester."

"Manchester!" she cried. "Am I not worth Paris?"

"We both know too many people in Paris. We'd be recognized."

"Edinburgh then, at least."

"I'm afraid I have Scottish holdings nearby."

"Where don't you people have holdings?"

"*You people*?"

"Lords. Seems like you all have ten houses at least. And me, just the measly one."

"What's your home like?"

"Wouldn't you like to know."

"Yes, I would. That's why I asked."

"You'd think it small as a snuffbox."

"Smaller than this cottage?"

"Three rooms. Big, airy ones, all fixed up for lounging. It's decorated with pink silks and flowers and Cornelia's art—mostly nude portraits, of course. And I've got the largest bed you could imagine."

"Unlikely," he said. "My own bed is quite large."

"Really? Why, when you sleep there alone?"

"Earls tend to have enormous furniture, along with their multiple holdings."

"Wouldn't know. Earls don't usually bring the likes of me to their family homes."

"Pity the earls. They're missing out on a lovely experience."

That was such a nice thing for him to say that she smiled and patted his hand. "And here I thought you were sore with me."

"You did?" he asked with concern. "Why is that?"

"All the harassing you to come to bed with me."

"I treasure your eagerness to share a bed with me.

I only wish I were better at proving myself capable there."

"We'll get you proven. Now, read me your letter. Let's see if this is the right woman to sprawl out in your big bed."

He used his finger to break the wax seal and unfolded the paper. His brow tensed as he scanned it.

"What's wrong. What does it say?"

"Another young one."

"Read it."

"Miss Emily Clark has just turned eighteen. An orphan, she resides with her guardian, Lord Hoover. An heiress, Miss Clark will bring with her to marriage a fortune of—"

"Wait a minute," Thaïs interrupted. *"Emily Clark,* you said?"

"Yes."

"That's the name of the girl Elinor said Lord Bell is courting."

"Ah, you're right. I knew the name sounded familiar. Eighteen, though? Bell is courting an eighteen-year-old maiden? Isn't he in his sixties?"

He sounded horrified.

"Don't act surprised. You know he's a frog-rutting turd."

"Surely Lord Hoover wouldn't allow his ward to make such a match."

"You know him?"

"In passing. He's a bit odd. Never married and dedicated his life to amassing one of the largest collections of antique daggers in the country. He's rather elderly himself. Perhaps the inappropriateness of the match has not occurred to him."

"Or perhaps he just wants her off his hands."

"He always seemed like a decent fellow, if a bit eccentric."

"You should write to him. Warn him off Bell."

"Men don't take kindly to hearing other men tell them their business."

"Who cares if he takes it kindly. At least he'll not be ignorant. Poor girl shouldn't be delivered to that monster. Especially with no mother to help her handle him."

"You think that matters? Her not having a mother?"

She was bloody certain of it. Her own past was the proof.

"Of course," Thaïs said. "Women may lack power to protect their daughters, but they at least have information they can give their girls. And love, of course. Love makes a difference."

Eden nodded. "Of course. I hadn't thought of that. I wish my sister had been blessed with a living mother."

"Anna's fine. She had you to love her."

"An older brother is not the same as a mother, no matter how much I care for her. I often found myself flummoxed by how to raise her. Especially once she came of age."

"It's not just daughters who need their mother's love, you know. Sons need it too. I'm sorry you lost your mama so young."

"And I'm sorry you lost yours."

"Me too. Likely would have quite a different life if I'd known my family."

"You didn't know them at all?" he asked.

"I have foggy memories of my ma. Mostly her being sick. But we had a roof over our heads. And I remember her hugging me."

"My mother gave the most glorious hugs," Eden said. "I'd like to marry a woman who can hug like that. Someone with such a great capacity for affection, especially for children."

The wistful way he said it sent a pang of affection through her. He was such a good man. A sweet one. She wished he knew that better.

"I bet your mother would be giving you so many hugs you'd have to push her away, seeing how you've grown up into such a fine person. Doting on Anna as you do. Not to mention how much you love your sheep."

He laughed. "Yes. She'd be even more proud of my relationship with the pigs. We have two potbellied ones at the abbey. They're more spoiled than the horses."

"And here the only pigs I know are the grown-man kind."

He looked at her with alarm. "They treat you badly? Your patrons?"

"Oh no," she assured him. "Most of them don't. Occasionally you get a bad seed."

"I hate to think of you in danger."

"I look after myself. I have a bell to pull that rings downstairs and a strong man I pay to sit by it on the nights I entertain. I haven't had much trouble. Doesn't stop the bad eggs from being prigs, though. Thinking they own you, just because they've paid for a night of your time."

"You always make it seem like you enjoy your work. Is that merely a pretense?"

"No. I do enjoy it, for the most part," she said honestly. "Doesn't make it perfect. But then, what work is?"

"Thaïs," he said. "I think your mother would be very proud of what you've made of yourself."

She rather thought so too. But she was shocked that *he* would think so. Shocked and flattered.

She grinned at him. "Now, that's a rare thought. Most men wouldn't expect a woman to be proud that her daughter's a whore."

"You're an independent woman of great kindness and skill. You're brave, and you take care of yourself. And you fight for what you believe in, and to help people. Even this young girl you don't know." He pointed at the letter.

Now he was making her emotional. She rarely had such compliments from people outside her close circle, unless they were praising her bosoms or her arse.

She stood up and walked over to him.

"Come here," she said, holding out her arms.

He stood up and let her wrap herself around him. She squeezed him, this motherless boy just like herself in so many ways, for all she was worth.

And she'd be damned if he didn't squeeze her back just as tight.

"Thaïs?" he said, when they broke apart.

"Aye?"

"You give wonderful hugs too."

Chapter Twenty-Six

Eden spent the rest of the day awash in contentment. Thaïs's embrace had filled his heart.

Christ, but he liked her. Her insistence on candor made her so easy to talk to, and she was a surprisingly soft person, underneath all her sexual bravado and brazen jokes. He had not been able to speak so openly of his feelings about his family to anyone, even Anna. He protected his sister from his own pain, so that he could be a strong shoulder for her sadness about losing her parents so young.

He would miss his friendship with Thaïs when they parted. He knew that once he was married it would no longer be appropriate for him to have a relationship with a woman of her reputation. When they said goodbye, it would be for good.

The thought made him rather melancholy.

He should drag himself away from his work and spend more time with her while he had the opportunity. Not only because he needed to learn everything he could while he had the chance but also because he enjoyed her. He could not remember liking anyone's company quite so much in ages.

So he made a simpler supper than usual—a spring

soup with vegetables Hattie had brought from her garden—and did not return to his study after they ate.

"Shall we retire early?" he asked Thaïs when he joined her in the parlor after tidying the kitchen.

She brightened. "Are you eager for your lesson?"

"I'm a bit apprehensive," he admitted. "But I trust you to look after me."

She looked pleased. "Thank you, Alastair. Look after you I shall."

They went to the bedroom, and she asked him to help her undress.

"You could do this for your wife," she said. "It's more intimate than leaving it to a lady's maid. And certainly more pleasant for a girl than struggling to get out of a gown and stays all alone."

"I'll keep that in mind," he said. He had a feeling that a woman with a greater sense of modesty might not be as eager as Thaïs to let a man untie her ribbons and look upon her in her stockings. But he wouldn't argue. Now that he knew how to do it, he enjoyed undressing Thaïs. It was like unwrapping a gift. Or perhaps more like peeling an orange. You knew what would be under the rind, but the fruit was so soft and round and fragrant and juicy that it was a heady pleasure each time.

Once Thaïs was nude she twirled around for him. "Like what you see?" she asked.

"So much," he answered, for if she could stand here naked without a care in the world, he could at least be honest.

"Enough to give us a hug?"

He smiled at the reference to their moment in the garden. "I've been thinking about hugging you since the last time."

She opened her arms, and he stepped into them. She wrapped her hands beneath his shoulders and rested her head on his chest, above his heart. He hesitated for a moment—it was all so much—but then wrapped his own arms around her, letting his hands fall to her waist.

She sighed contentedly. "I love how tall you are," she said. "You make me feel like a tiny, little thing."

He kissed the top of her head. "You are a tiny, little thing."

She snorted. "I'm an ample, buxom woman. Not even short."

"You're short to me."

"What else am I to you?" She stepped back, so he could have a look.

"Beautiful," he said. "Perfect."

"Well, that goes without saying. Be more descriptive."

"Curvaceous. Pale and peachy, but with the most striking red hair I've ever seen."

"You like my ginger locks, eh?"

"I *love* your ginger locks."

Especially, he did not say aloud, the thatch between her legs.

"What else do you love?" she asked.

"Your breasts."

She gently lifted them and squeezed them together, making a feast out of her cleavage. "These old things?"

"How dare you call them that? They're magnificent."

"Touch them, if you like them so much."

He stepped toward her and cupped the sides of them, gently, as she had done. She sighed. "Your touch feels good."

He took her at her word and caressed every contour of them. He'd never touched a woman this way—exploring her, looking at her, taking his time.

He noticed that her nipples had gone hard, and he brought his thumbs to them.

"That's the best part," she said. "The nips go straight to the pussy."

He froze at the coarseness of her language and also at the idea of touching her most private feminine part. But then he relaxed. He was here to be talked to like this. To imagine such things.

"Is that so?" he murmured, stroking her nipples with more pressure.

"Mmm," she said. "Would I lie to you?"

He hoped she wouldn't. It sometimes felt like in her bluntness she was the first person who had ever been completely honest with him. Granted, her honesty sometimes veered into unpleasant truths, but few people ventured to deal so candidly with men as rich and powerful as himself. It was as refreshing as it was unnerving.

"You can pinch them a little," Thaïs said. "Not hard, mind."

"I don't want to hurt you."

"Then be gentle."

He pinched her nipples as delicately as he could, and she sighed.

"Harder than that, if you please."

He increased the pressure. "Ah, that's nice. But do you know what would be even nicer?"

He shook his head.

"Your mouth on them."

Oh dear God, the effect those words had on him.

He lowered his head, lifted one of her breasts, and kissed it. "Like that?"

"Yes. Good lad."

He did the same to the other breast.

"Let's go to bed," she said. "So you can take your time and explore me all you want."

She spread herself out in the center of the bed and beckoned him with nothing more than her eyes.

"Your assignment," she said, "is to learn my body. Study me like you would a map. Use your eyes and hands and mouth. Let your wants guide you. And if you aren't sure if I'll like something, just ask me."

He nodded, and she closed her eyes.

Without her gaze on him, he felt a bit more confident.

He returned his attention to her breasts, lowering his mouth to kiss one. Up close, she smelled even more of that spicy scent. He wanted to burrow his head into her neck and inhale her. Which, he supposed, was reason enough to do it. He put his nose to the hollow of her throat.

"You smell so good," he said.

"So do you."

"Me? What do I smell like?"

"Yourself. And there's a lesson there."

"What do you mean?"

"You should like the way your lady smells. And not

just her perfume. Her skin. It's a sign that you'll be good in bed together."

"Well, there's no way of knowing that until I'm *in* bed with her. I can't just go around sniffing necks."

"You can kiss her wrist."

"Men have been shot for less."

"Don't do it in range of a pistol."

"I'm serious. There is no way of knowing what my wife will smell like until we're married."

"If you can't find a way to be close enough to get a good whiff of her, you probably don't want her badly enough to wed her. Let that be a warning to you."

He was not going to argue this point. Thaïs was here to teach him about sex; the intricacies of interacting with perfectly bred young ladies was more his province than hers. He went back to kissing her breasts instead.

It was remarkably enjoyable. He took his time, tasting her skin. Basking in her heat. Letting his hands roam. He ventured his way back to her nipples.

"I want to kiss them. Is that . . . Would you like that?"

"Yes," she said. "I like it all."

He put the pink peak into his mouth and laved it with his tongue. When she sighed a bit, he ventured to lick, then suck.

"You're doing wonderfully," she said softly. The encouragement was heady. He moved his attention to the other breast.

"Do you know what would be nice?" she asked after a fashion. "If you went lower with that mouth of yours."

Obediently, he allowed himself to wander to her stomach, kissing his way down, down, down until he reached her hip.

"Why'd you stop?" she asked when he hesitated. She put her hand to the skin just above the hair guarding her womanhood. "This bit is quite sensitive. It wants a bit of love."

He mirrored her fingers with his own, stroking her softly. She shivered under his touch.

He loved that shiver.

"Now your mouth," she said.

He kissed her there, and she shivered again.

"Do the same thing to my thighs," she said.

He put his lips to the soft, soft skin. Her smell was stronger here. It drove him mad. Madder still when she opened her legs a bit, to give him access to her inner thighs.

"When you kiss me there, it's a tease," Thaïs said. "Gets a girl imagining your mouth between her legs."

He'd been imagining just that and feeling like a cad for it.

"That's something a woman wants? A man's mouth between her legs?"

"Not all women want the same thing. And your wife might be shy at first. But if you know how to eat a pussy, it's among the finest skills you can have. Drives a girl wild. Numbs her bloody brains."

He wasn't sure about numbed brains, but the idea of driving Thaïs wild was deeply appealing. He was already hard as a rock, and his loins clenched right in that place Thaïs had said was sensitive.

Which was good information. If the sensations in

her body paralleled his, then perhaps he could use his own desires as a guide.

"How would I . . ." He could not bring himself to say the words *kiss your pussy*, and he did not want to be japed at for calling it something more formal, like *labia*.

Luckily, she knew what he meant.

She always knew what he meant.

"Have you ever seen a pussy?"

"Well, yes. I've had sex."

"You've been inside one. But have you *looked* at one?"

"Not . . . closely," he admitted. He had books on anatomy and had ventured to pore over the female parts. But that was not the same as . . . this.

"Well, let's have a look, shall we?" Thaïs said. "I'll teach you how they work."

She spread her legs wider, and the thatch of hair parted to reveal something more beautiful than he could have imagined. It was a much pinker color than her skin, richly toned like her nipples, except glistening. Her folds reminded him of orchids.

"The most important part to know about is this," she said, putting her hand to the nub at the center of herself, between her lips. "It's a lady's precious pearl. And if you touch it in a way she likes, she'll come until she cries."

She took his hand and placed it there. "Rub it a bit," she said. "Get a sense for it."

He massaged her lightly. "That's nice," she said. "Perhaps a bit firmer with the pressure."

"How much firmer?"

"Hmm. Push gently until I stop you, and we'll see."

He did as instructed, using his first two fingers. After a second or two of going very, very slowly, she sighed. "Ah, right there. Just like that."

He froze in place, not wanting to ruin whatever she was feeling.

"Now, if you wanted to make me come, you'd have to move your fingers back and forth to find a rhythm."

"If I wanted to? Now?"

"Have a go."

He began to move his fingers.

"Side to side, then up and down, like you're drawing a circle," she said.

He fumbled a bit, and her hand came on top of his to demonstrate the motion she desired.

"Ah, there we are," she sighed. "Like that."

He kept at it, watching her intently, wondering how long it might take to make her orgasm and what that might look and feel like. The idea of it made *him* want to come. Which was a relief, after his last two failed attempts.

"Once you have her in a rhythm, try going a little faster. See if she likes that."

He sped up the motion, and she gasped.

"A bit too fast, love. Try halfway."

He did and she sighed. "Ah, that's it."

She undulated her hips a bit, subtly meeting his movements.

"Now, she might want a little more," she said breathily. "For you to slide down a little, toward her slit."

"Like this?" he asked, moving his hand lower. She breathed in sharply.

"A girl might like that, yes. A finger moving in her pussy while you play with her pearl."

He found this complicated, initially. "I'm not sure I understand."

"Watch me," she said.

She put her own hand to her womanhood and demonstrated how to move around her folds, inside and out.

"Now you try," she said.

He noticed she had grown more slick. "You're wetter," he said.

"Aye. The more a girl is wanting, the wetter she becomes."

He slid his fingers in her juices reverently. It slayed him that he could help make this transformation in her body. That there was empirical evidence he was doing something right. "I love this," he said.

"So will your woman."

He wished she had said *So do I*. She was the only woman he wanted to do this to.

And he wanted to do more.

"You said it would feel good if I used my mouth," he said. "Should I . . . try that?"

"Ah, he wants to be an advanced pupil," she said.

Really, he just wanted to taste her wetness, lick her pearl, trace her slit with his tongue. He could imagine it now, the heat of a mouth on an inflamed place. He could imagine her doing it to him.

He *wanted* her to do it to him.

But he wanted this more.

"How should I start?" he asked.

She lifted her knees up and widened her legs even more, so she was completely open to him.

"Lick her the way she liked you to touch her," she said.

He put his lips gingerly to her flesh. She was hot, tasting of salt and something fresh and sweet, like grass.

The best thing he'd ever tasted.

"Oh, *fuck*," he said, without meaning to. He hated to curse.

But maybe this *fucking* warranted it.

"You like that?" she asked breathily.

"Thaïs. This is . . . I don't . . . It's shocking. It's the nicest thing I've ever felt."

She ran her fingers through his hair.

"You're going to have a very happy wife, if that's the case."

"Can I . . . can I kiss you there?"

"You may kiss me all you like."

He pressed his mouth fully to her wet flesh and slid his tongue up and down. He kissed her pearl like it was her tongue, passionately, moaning into her. He was conscious of the pressure of the bed against his cock, and he had to shift his hips away from it because he was likely to burst with just the slightest stimulation, and he didn't want to stop this.

Especially because she was rocking her hips with him, making heart-stopping little noises, murmuring his name.

Remembering his lessons with his fingers, he gave her more pressure. And then he remembered she'd liked it when he lightly sucked her nipples and decided to try that, very gently with her pearl.

She cried out when he did it.

"I'm sorry," he said.

"That was the good kind of noise," she said. "Do that again."

He did, and she closed her legs around his head and began to pulse beneath his mouth, crying out, "Oh Christ."

He kept doing it as she bucked against him, making the most delicious noises, noises he could not mistake for pain now that he knew what her pleasure sounded like.

As she shook, he began to tremble, his cock seizing. He desperately pressed it down onto the bed and made a rutting motion, too overcome to care that he was fucking a counterpane, and as he came he moaned her name into her pussy.

Thaïs. Thaïs. Thaïs.

Chapter Twenty-Seven

"I'm sorry," Eden groaned, his face still so close to her cunt she could feel his breath. "I'm so sorry."

If Thaïs had not been so thoroughly exhausted from feigning that orgasm, she might have laughed.

But that would hurt him, and he should be bloody proud of himself for what he'd just achieved. He'd taken to instruction like a right genius. By the end of the month he'd be as adept as men who'd been happily lapping away at cunnies for decades. For a moment she'd been tempted to go with it and let herself orgasm for real.

But that would not be clever of her. She'd already let herself enjoy Eden's hugs. Enjoying him in bed would be taking it too far.

"You fool," she told him, sitting up. "How could you be sorry after doing that to me? You should be crowing like one of your deranged roosters. Did you see what you just made me do?"

He stood up and gestured down at the wet front of his breeches. "Yes. I was so moved by it I spilled in my bloody smalls."

"My poor boy," she said. "I'll take that as a compliment. My quim is such a dream you don't even need to be inside of it to drain your balls."

He looked so miserable you'd think he'd just dropped a hammer on his prick instead of shot a merry load with it.

"Oh, come now, Alastair," she said. "Yesterday you couldn't stay hard, and today you're virile as a bull again. Besides, now that you've come once, we'll see if you repeat the trick a little later."

"You're very kind to assuage my feelings," he said. "But imagine if I did this in front of my wife on our wedding night. I'll be *forty* in six days, Thaïs, and I perform like I'm fourteen."

"Well, say you do. Say you're incurable. I'd think your wife would be a virgin. So it won't be a problem."

"Why's that?"

"Because she won't know what's what. She'll be expecting you to guide her. For all she knows it's normal for a man to want her so badly he fucks his own breeches."

"It was the bed I rutted," he said. "At least grant me that dignity."

"Stop moping and clean up," she said. "Then you can come and have a kiss. You deserve one, for being my prized pupil."

Eden peeled off his clothing and was cleaning himself off roughly, like his own seed was poison.

"Don't chafe it," she said. "I have plans for that cock. Now, come back to bed."

He lay down beside her, his body about as relaxed as a plank of oak and his face like a bust of an angry old man in a museum.

"Oy," she said, turning over to face him and throwing a leg around his thigh. "You listening to me?"

"Yes," he said darkly. "It's difficult not to when you shout like that."

She threw her arms around his chest before he could protest and snuggled her head under his chin. "Give us a hug."

She could feel him hesitating, his muscles tense beneath her body.

"Please, love," she coaxed, burrowing even closer. "Hold me."

He put his arms around her stiffly, but after a few seconds his body softened. His hand came to her shoulder blade, and he stroked her back.

"This is nice," she said.

He murmured an assent and held her tighter.

He really *was* good at giving hugs.

It was sad he'd spent so many years not giving any. Or getting any back. He was so sensitive to touch—even innocent touch like this—that it seemed like he was starved for it.

"You have perfect arms for loving on a girl, Alastair. If you feel off in bed or out of it, you can always return to this, you know. Plenty of girls would rather be held by a sweet, adoring husband than ravished by some master swordsman."

She would know.

"That's kind of you to say," he said into her hair. "But I thought the lesson was over."

"Oh no, sir, we're only halfway through. We haven't got to your bit yet."

He kissed her shoulder. "What's my bit?"

"I'm going to do to you what you did to me."

His whole body went rigid again. He stopped rubbing her back.

She broke their embrace and propped herself up on her elbow to look at him. "What's wrong? You don't want me to suck your—"

He let out a ragged sigh. "I, erm . . . I don't know if my heart can take it."

"Your heart doesn't have to," she whispered to him like they had a secret. "I'm talking about your *cock*."

He laughed and shook his head. "You truly delight in being a vulgar wench, don't you?"

"*Vulgar wench*. Put it on my headstone. Now, are you ready for me to give you the best pleasure of your life?"

"Can we wait a little? I need to gather myself."

She was not one to push. She wanted him to let himself go further tonight, but they could take their time.

"Of course," she said. "What shall we do in the meantime?"

"Can I just hug you?"

The man wanted another hug. A *hug*. And God help her, she wanted it too.

"You can do whatever you like with me," she said, lying back down beside him and curling up against his side.

"Thaïs," he said in a serious tone.

"Mmm?"

"I *hate* it when you say that."

"Say what? That you can do what you want?"

"Yes. It reminds me you're only doing this because I'm making you."

"Well, that's rich, since I'm the one always making *you* do things."

"Yes, but you'd not be here had I not bought your time. And I know it's foolish, but I suppose I wish you were *choosing* this. Choosing me."

He said this to her cheekbone, so she couldn't see his face. But she could hear the brooding in his voice.

"Alastair?"

"Yes?"

"I can't think of a man I'd rather be spending this month with than you. And I haven't done a single thing I haven't liked. Well, except waking at dawn. And making that damned cake. And sneezing my face off on your bloody stroll."

He laughed wryly. "Yes. The month of your dreams, clearly."

"Hear this. The things we've done in bed have all been to my liking. If I had my druthers, we'd be doing a lot more of them."

"I know. I've been distracted by my work. And perhaps using it as an excuse not to practice my lessons, like a naughty student. But I'll be better. There's nothing more important than this in the next fortnight. I want to be perfect."

This tripe again.

"Alastair, my dear," she said, "*perfect* is a myth outside the sheets and certainly doesn't exist between them. You need to know this, or you'll always find yourself wanting."

He was silent. He obviously didn't believe her.

"I'm not just saying this to make you feel better," she said. "I swear."

"Well, there's no harm in trying to achieve greatness. And I vow to make it—you—my priority."

She was awfully glad to hear it.

"Good. Because I like playing with your cock far better than playing patience. Not to mention writing blasted letters about carpets."

He squeezed her tighter. "I'm sorry you've had to play so much patience."

"I'm sorry you've made yourself read so many papers about sheep."

He laughed, then they were quiet.

For a few minutes, they lay in silence, their bodies entwined, listening to each other's breath. It was so cozy Thaïs could fall asleep.

And then, she must have done so. Because cocks were crowing, and there was light peeking through the windows.

Eden's body was still wrapped around hers, but he was awake.

And he was hard.

"You let me sleep away the night, you weasel," she said with a yawn. "Should have woken me up when I dozed off."

"It's nice to watch you sleep. It's the only time you're peaceful."

"You like me well enough when I'm awake, by the feel of it," she said, waggling her arse against his erection.

"I think we're far enough along here that that's hard to deny."

"Good. I have plans for you."

He looked at her longingly. "God, I want you."

She almost said, *Lucky for you I'm a sure thing.* But then she thought of what he'd said last night. How he worried she didn't want to be here. And it felt so good, the way he was touching her. She *did* want to be here.

So she said, "I want you too."

His mouth quirked up. "You're only saying that to flatter me."

"No. I'm saying it because it's true."

"What lesson did you have in mind?" he asked, grazing her nipples in his soft way. "I'd like to know what I'll be failing at before we commence."

"You can't fail at this one," she said. "Here, scoot down to the end of the bed."

"Must I let go of you?"

"Believe me, you'll be glad you have when I get done with you."

She scampered away from him and stood. He scooted to the end of the bed and put his feet on the floor. His cock stood in the air.

She knelt between his legs.

"There are many ways to do this," she said. "But some of them can hurt a lady's neck. So when you teach your girl what I'm about to show you—"

"I suspect I will never teach anyone what you're about to show me."

"Once you see how good it feels, you'll want to teach everyone to do it to you. You'll be teaching Hattie, Sophie, your footman, everyone."

Before he could reply, she took his cock in her fist and licked the head.

Usually she would lead up to this by touching him, playing with his balls and arse, kissing his stomach.

But she didn't want to give him cause to come too quickly, so she limited herself to toying with the tip of his prick with her tongue.

She glanced at him, and he was looking down at her with half-closed eyes. He seemed to like it well enough, so she took him fully in her mouth.

"Thaïs," he said in a strangled voice, "you don't have to do this. It looks . . . uncomfortable."

She released him from her mouth. "You don't like it?"

"It's nice, but I feel guilty."

"Well, don't. I like doing it." Or, at least, she liked doing it to him.

"Are you certain?"

"Close your eyes and let yourself enjoy it."

"If you're certain."

He sat up straighter and adjusted his weight onto his haunches, like he was about to ride a horse.

"You can relax," she said.

He nodded but did not relax at all. Were he not very, very hard she might have abandoned this altogether.

She returned her mouth to him, and he leaned back on his hands, his stomach muscles rippling. She could tell he was resisting the pleasure. Trying not to spill.

She stopped.

"Catch your breath," she said. "We're not in a rush."

He was biting his lip, clenching his jaw, but he nodded. His eyes were still closed.

"When you feel you're about to pop off too fast, you can take a moment. Breathe."

He took a deep breath, then another.

"Better?" she asked.

He nodded. "Better."

She took him in her mouth again and used her tongue to play with his bellend. She felt him seize and braced for him to spill, but he put his hand on her shoulder. "I need a moment," he ground out.

She released him. His cock pulsed in her hand, angry for its fix, but he breathed through it.

Oh, she was so proud of him. He was learning his own body, sensing when pleasure was about to overwhelm him, steadying himself to keep control.

"Tell me when you're ready," she said.

"I'm ready," he said breathlessly.

This time, when she put him in her mouth, she took him deeper.

"Oh God," he uttered, shaking. She stopped, waited for him to calm, and did it again only when he nodded. She went slowly, slowly, until they found a stop–start rhythm they could both predict without having to speak.

His breath was ragged, coming out in gasps, and his hands had wandered to her hair, which he stroked when she paused. Not urging her to take him in, as other men did—plenty of men liked to fuck her face as though she weren't there—but touching her tenderly, just for the sake of the way it felt.

She took him deep into the back of her throat—a trick that she was good at—and he began to moan in a way she knew he could not control. His pleasure now was more intense than she'd seen him feel before—not frantic but gut-deep.

Which meant he was ready for his climax. The well-earned kind that built up so long it curled your toes.

She swallowed, pulling sounds from him so filthy

they made her own loins tingle. His body began to jerk.

"Thaïs," he cried, "I'm—" and he began to come. His seed pulsed into her mouth, and she knew he would be horrified, poor man, but he was past the point of reason, lost to his release. She continued to suck him as he came and came and came, racked with spasms powerful as sobs.

Only when he stopped shaking did she gently release him from her mouth. He collapsed backward onto the bed, his breath coming in great gasps. She got off her knees and smiled—until she realized he was wiping away tears.

"Christ, Alastair. What is it?"

"I'm sorry. It's only . . . it's never felt . . . that is, until now I haven't understood why people enjoy it quite so much."

She lay down next to him and cupped his head to her bosom.

"God, I'm sorry," he sniffled, half laughing at himself. "Look at me. I've gone mad. And here I utterly defiled you and haven't even apologized for spending in your mouth—"

She kissed his eyes, left, then right. "Darling man, you don't have to apologize. I'm so happy you fancied what we did."

He laughed roughly. "*Fancied*. Thaïs, I loved it. It was unlike anything I've ever felt. Thank you. For understanding my ailment and giving me this gift."

"For the ninetieth time, you don't have an ailment. You have enthusiasm. And soon you'll have the skills to give that to whatever girl you like."

"You're the girl I like," he murmured.

Her heart clenched.

She knew he was sex-sated—that he meant *right now, in bed*—but the words made her throat ache all the same. She'd never liked any of her lovers quite so much. She wanted to give this man all that he needed, arm him with the confidence and skill to fuck the way she knew he could. Not *perfectly*, but joyfully and sensuously, with his whole mind and body.

She was excited about what they had ahead of them.

"You know, Eden," she said.

"Alastair," he corrected her.

"*Alastair.* I think you're ready for your next lesson."

"We don't have time for another one," he said. "Hattie will be here soon. We should dress."

"I don't mean right this instant. But methinks you're ready to be inside me."

He was quiet for a second, and she waited to hear what his objection was.

"I'm dying to feel that," he said, in the most shocking words she'd ever heard from him. "Can we try this afternoon?"

Chapter Twenty~Eight

Eden went directly from the bedroom to his study, eschewing his usual morning conversation with Hattie. He was too unsteady to chat, too abuzz for tea.

All he could think about was Thaïs. It was like she'd made the sun rise over the horizon and illuminated perimeters of the world that hadn't been visible in nighttime.

His skin was tight, his nipples ached, he felt fluttery behind his loins.

And he could not wait for Hattie to leave.

He fiddled with his papers, but reading about husbandry was hopeless when he felt like this, and reviewing finances was worse. The only thing he wanted to think about was the weight of a breast in his palm. How a woman tasted. How it would feel to be inside Thaïs.

He retrieved one of his erotic books and perused it for positions, wondering which ones Thaïs would start with. It made him so hard that he needed to touch himself right now.

He locked the door, hoping no one would hear the turning of the latch, and took out his cock. He worked it slowly, as Thaïs had done, pausing when desire threatened to overtake him, resuming when he'd caught his breath.

He lasted six glorious minutes.

Granted, he was far less aroused by his own touch than he was by Thaïs's, but he was still satisfied that with practice at controlling himself, he'd be able to deflower his wife.

But that wasn't, in this moment, what he cared about.

He didn't want to imagine some faceless woman he had not met—some perfectly bred virgin with demure manners who'd defer to him on every matter. He wanted the crass, louche, defiant woman in this house, who was currently gabbing away with Hattie in the kitchen.

He wanted only Thaïs.

He was gratified when he heard her say goodbye to Hattie. He found her in the kitchen standing in front of a window, enjoying the warmth of the sun. She had a slight smile on her face, and the light gleamed off her hair. She looked like a goddess hewn in fire.

He walked behind her and put his arms around her, placing a long kiss on her neck.

She put her hands over his arms, letting him hold her.

"What are you looking at?" he asked her.

"There's a pretty bird out there, on the rosebush by the trellis. See it? With the yellow on its breast?"

"I do. It's a great tit."

"A great tit! Are you the one making the bawdy jokes now?"

"No," he said with grave seriousness. "That's what the bird is called."

She laughed. "Well, no wonder I like it."

He moved his hands up to her breasts. "I like it too."

She turned around, glowing with a smile. "Mind you don't get too wicked with that mouth. You'll have your wife sobbing to her mother she's married a rake."

"I think my mouth is incurably wicked after last night."

"Well, let's see what other parts of you we can make wicked."

"All of them, given how I feel this morning." He lowered his voice. "I had to satisfy myself once already, just thinking about what we'll do next."

He pressed against her. She reached down and rubbed his erection through his breeches.

"Look at you, becoming a lech."

"Am I too wanton?"

"Not at all," she said, stroking him. "I like you in rut."

He removed her hand from his prick and kissed her knuckle.

"I like it too. But beyond the physical pleasure, I want you to know how grateful I am for what you're teaching me."

"Keep sweet-talking me like that and you'll swell my head, when we're here to swell your—"

"My cock. Yes. Very good. Though, right now, that's not a problem. Let's go to bed."

"Thought you'd never ask."

He walked behind her up the staircase, giving himself permission to enjoy the swaying of her arse. He'd lavished so much attention on her breasts that he'd let her magnificent hips and buttocks go without proper admiration.

He'd have to right that in the next two weeks.

Two weeks. What a blessing, to have such a length of time to spend with her. And what a fool he was for squandering that same amount of time out of fear. She'd been right to be salty with him for avoiding his lessons. He wished he could start over, relive that first day, when she'd offered to crawl under the desk.

But no. That wasn't right.

Had they not spent so much time talking and pretending to court, he would not feel so at ease with her. So able to show her his foibles. To trust her.

He'd have to remember this lesson for when he married: giving oneself over to sex was a question of trust. This feeling of safety was something he needed to give his future wife.

In the bedroom, Thaïs pulled open one of the drawers she'd claimed and removed a jar of condoms. She held it up to him.

"You know what these are?"

"Yes. For disease."

"We'll use them. I don't think I'm afflicted with anything—I'm very careful. But it's good to guard yourself. And if you should take lovers who aren't your wife, you should use these—"

"I would never do that," he interrupted her. "Ever."

He said it more sharply than he'd intended. The idea of it violated the ethics he strove to live by. He'd not make a vow to a woman and then break it. Which brought home the fact that once he was married, he'd never again be with Thaïs.

"I didn't think you would," she said appeasingly. "But I'm here to teach you, aren't I?"

"Yes. You're right. I'm sorry for interrupting. What else do I need to know?"

"Well, do you know how to put one on?"

"You slide it around your prick and tie the string? I've done it before, though of course it was years ago."

"That's right. I'll help you practice."

Normally sticking his prick in sheep innards would not be an arousing prospect. But Thaïs applying the sheath to him was strangely appealing. He loved the ministrations of her small, soft hands and nimble fingers.

"Is there anything else I need to know before we begin?" he asked her.

"Yes. This is very important. If you don't want to make a woman pregnant, don't spill in her."

He was aware of this but had not considered the practical implications. A horrifying thought occurred to him.

"That might be difficult for me," he said. "With us. Given I spill so easily."

He did not want to make Thaïs pregnant. He could not leave her with a child to raise alone, nor hurt his future wife with the knowledge he had a baby outside their family.

Besides, after overhearing her conversation with Elinor about marriage, he highly doubted Thaïs wanted to be a mother.

"We'll go slowly, to start, and you'll do your best," she said.

He was not sure what his best would solve if he accidentally spent before withdrawing. But there was no getting around it. In order to complete his education, he needed to become better versed in sex.

And if he did not get to make love with Thaïs, he might die of disappointment. He would just have to use what he'd learned this morning and take care to protect her from his seed.

"How should we start?" he asked.

"You want your lady to be wet and ready for you before you stick your cock in her. So you'll want to bring her pleasure before you get aswiving."

"Aswiving? What a pleasant concept."

"Before you fuck her. Is that better?"

"It does have a vulgar ring to it."

"I knew I was corrupting you."

"I'm hopelessly despoiled."

"Let's not tell your wife until you know her better."

"So you're saying I need to seduce her," he said, returning to the matter at hand.

"Yes."

"And to do that I should . . ."

"Say nice things to her. Tell her how much you want her. Then you can practice your other lessons—kiss her, embrace her, caress her, tease her with your fingers and your mouth."

In other words, do the things he'd longed to do all morning.

"Thaïs," he said, "I've never wanted anyone as much as I want you."

"There you go. That's the kind of thing to say.

Though, with your bride, you might not want to remind her you've had other women."

"Ah. Right. Let me try again. Thaïs, you are the most alluring woman in the world. I'm honored that you're mine."

"Thank you, my lord," she said, using her cultivated accent. "You're rather handsome yourself."

He stepped toward her, and she crossed her arms over her breasts and regarded him nervously.

"I'm frightened, dear husband. My mother told me this was painful."

"I'll be gentle with you, darling. I want you to enjoy our time in bed. I hope this will be the beginning of many pleasurable nights."

"That's good," Thaïs said in her normal voice. "But you'll want to reassure her. Take her into your arms and hold her."

He stepped toward Thaïs and drew her close. She was stiff, rather than her usual pliant self.

"I'll never hurt you, darling," he whispered. "I love you."

They both started at those words.

He was only playacting, of course.

The idea of falling in love with Thaïs was laughable. Gentlemen did not *love* their mistresses, no matter how infatuated they were with their charms. And even if *they* did, *he* couldn't. It was antithetical to everything he wanted.

Still, when Thaïs said, "I love you too, my husband," it was painful to hear those words and know that they weren't true.

He didn't like this. It was making him confused. He did not want to pretend he was buttering up a theoretical wife. He wanted this first time to be about the two of them.

"Thaïs," he said, "let's not pretend that I'm deflowering you. I'd rather practice the niceties of it later, once I'm better skilled."

"As you wish," she said in her normal voice. "Let's get ourselves naked. You have a fine physique. Your lady will be pleased."

Her words were like cold water on hot skin. *She* was not emotional or wistful. *She* had not forgotten she was here only because he'd paid her to be.

If he were wise, he'd get a hold of himself.

But he didn't want to. He wanted the memory of this day to be about the two of them and no one else. And he wanted her to know that.

"I don't want to talk of other ladies," he said. "Today, the only one I want is *you.*"

At the sincerity in his voice, she stopped undressing.

She stepped toward him. "You know what, Alastair? I want you too."

She gazed at his mouth, biting her lip—the signal, he knew, to kiss her.

He put his lips to hers. Softly, he finished undressing her, kissing the bare skin he uncovered.

"How is this?" he asked. "Do you like it?"

"It's lovely," she said. "You're lovely."

"Can I touch you between your legs?"

"I thought you'd never ask."

He lifted her onto the bed, and she spread herself

for him. He put his fingers to her pearl the way she'd taught him.

"This is all right?" he asked. "You like it?"

"You're doing wonderful. Keep going."

He went a little faster. He kept his gaze trained on her face, hoping to read her expression for clues. She sighed, relaxing deep into the mattress.

He spread his fingers into the wetness at her slit and groaned. It was intoxicating, the evidence of a woman's arousal. Knowing he had caused it.

She whimpered as he explored her. He wanted more of that. He loved her sounds.

"Would you like it if I put my mouth on you?" he asked.

"Yes," she murmured.

He bent his head and kissed her lavishly, using the techniques she'd taught him and trying a few others that he sensed might please her. She wriggled beneath him in a way that drove him mad.

"I'm ready for your cock," she gasped out, putting a hand on his head to stop him.

"You haven't reached your peak yet," he objected.

"There's more than one way to do that. It's enjoyable to have a man inside you, if he knows what he's doing."

He did not know what he was doing, in point of fact, and he wanted to ensure she was not dissatisfied. He wanted her to thrash wantonly around, the way she had the first time he'd kissed between her legs.

"Let me bring you to pleasure," he said. "I want to."

"Go right ahead, then. You're doing very well."

He buried his face exuberantly in her folds until her

hips bucked and she spasmed and he knew he'd given her what she needed.

It made him deeply contented. He could do that to her all day.

"I want more of you," she said.

"Me too."

"Are you ready to fuck me?"

"Yes."

She took his prick in her hand. It jumped at her touch.

"There are many ways to do this," she said. "But let's start with the simplest. You on top of me. Aye?"

"Yes," he agreed. This is how he'd bedded his other women, so he'd at least know the basic motions.

"Are you ready?" she asked.

"Yes," he said. "But I'm nervous. I don't want to spend inside you."

"Go slowly. Stop when you need to. Pull out when you feel it coming. You'll be fine."

He wanted to be a lot better than *fine*.

She parted her legs and guided him inside her. The walls of her pussy wrapped around him, tight and wet and hot. He felt like a virgin on his wedding night. He had to withdraw so he wouldn't faint.

"So good," Thaïs murmured. "Now, take a deeper thrust, when you're ready. See how it feels."

He slid into her and paused there, reeling.

Heaven on earth.

Impossible not to do it again and again.

He felt pressure building in his ears, and his vision blurred. He stopped, his cock throbbing and pulsing inside her, and caught his breath.

"I love this," he said. "Being joined with you."

"Oh, I know. I know. I want you deeper."

She shifted underneath him, and he knew that he was done for. His hips moved of their own volition, driving out and in, and it took everything he had to rip himself out of her, just in time.

He came into the condom.

But he wished, as the orgasm ripped through him, that he was still in her body.

Tearing himself away was the hardest thing he'd ever done.

Chapter Twenty-Nine

*I*t was delicious to watch Alastair Eden fall in love with sex.

He was like a little boy who'd just discovered sweets and didn't want to eat his supper.

They fucked four times that day, until they were both sore. He lasted longer with each session, needing to stop less frequently.

She put on a great show to encourage him. The orgasms were fake, but the pleasure she took wasn't an act.

She *could* have peaked if she let herself.

But she was becoming too attached to him. She had to keep reminding herself it wasn't real.

In the next few days, she began to teach him other postures. She got on top. She knelt so he could take her from behind. They did it standing up and sitting down—on the desk in his study, on the dining table, on the floor. The night before, when Alastair was certain they wouldn't be spotted by a neighbor, they did it in the garden. It rained just as they were finishing, and she got soaked down to her bones, but it was worth it to see him in the moonlight, taking rapture in her body.

He was exploring what his body was capable of—what *he* was capable of.

And he was becoming very capable, indeed.

He wanted her all the time. She was happy that he'd found this part of himself. That he was feeling confident in his skills in bed.

The trouble was that she wanted him all the time too. She no longer minded her early morning wake-ups, as they meant there was ample time to be with Alastair in bed before Hattie arrived. She joined him in the kitchen while he cooked, so that they could steal kisses—or more. She liked watching the stack of letters on his desk grow taller every day, because he was ignoring everything but her.

It was nice to be the center of his life.

It was nice to know he craved her body the way that she craved his.

She wished she could fully give herself to him—to take pleasure in him the way that he took it in her. But she knew the truth: she was his mistress. And soon, he would replace her with his wife.

She wondered if he would let himself behave this way with the woman he would give himself to permanently. Would he spend the first weeks of their marriage besotted? Learning her body and teaching her his own? Would he fuck *her* in his garden by moonlight?

Thaïs began to hate this phantom woman. He did not read her more reports on girls—perhaps because he hadn't opened them, or perhaps because discussing them ruined the fantasy of their own closeness. Reminded him that soon, they would both go home, never to be with each other this way again.

They had seven days left, and her heart was already breaking at the thought of their goodbye.

But today she would not think of that. Today was about Alastair.

It was his birthday.

He'd made no mention of it since he'd let slip that it was coming, but she'd not forgotten. Forty years alive was something to celebrate, and he was here without Anna or his friends. She had no gift to give him, and she doubted there was anything he'd want in town even if she snuck off to go.

But she had another idea.

Granted, it would require her to make a sacrifice not unlike that made by the Lord himself in healing the world's sins. But for Alastair, she'd do it anyway.

When Hattie left, she told Eden they would not be practicing this afternoon.

"Why?" he asked.

"Because you kept me up all night rutting in the rain, and I'm tired."

He looked disturbed. "Oh, of *course*. My God, I've been awful. Yes, you should rest. Is there anything I can do for you?"

"Yes," she said, "you can take one of your walks. A big, bloody long one. Leave me in the house alone to get some peace."

"Of course. I'm so sorry, Thaïs—"

She did not want him so lit up with guilt he backslid, so she put her finger over his lips. "None of that. Let's not flagellate ourselves unless it's for fun, aye? You haven't injured me, and a little waiting can make things sweeter later. A lesson for you to remember."

"I've been meaning to walk over and ask Mr. Fellowes about his flock. Hattie brought that cheese from his ewes' milk, and it had an exceptional flavor. I'd like to see what grasses—"

"Yes. What fun. You do that. I don't need to know the sordid details."

He laughed. "I'll take a book and do some reading by the lake. You can have the whole day to yourself."

"Good boy. Now, arse off."

She made a show of taking herself up to bed and put an eye mask on. She waited until long after she'd heard the front door close, then went down to the kitchen.

An apron hung there, like a red shirt waving at a bull.

"Don't get bloody used to this," she said to the garment as she grabbed it off the hook. "Once-in-a-lifetime occasion."

She had watched Alastair in the kitchen enough times that she knew where he kept all the ingredients. She gathered them onto the table—flour, butter, honey, salt—and of course, the dreaded eggs. She knew that he liked fruit, so she went outside and plucked some peaches off a tree.

And then she went to war.

When she was done, both of her arms throbbed from fingertips to shoulders. She was so tired she felt like she *was* getting ill.

But it wasn't fever that ailed her.

It was baking.

For her efforts, a cake sat on the windowsill, cooling. It was not as pretty as the one Alastair had made, and when she flipped it to remove it from the pan, it came out in four clumps with burned chunks on the bottom. This was why she was a harlot, not a cook.

She arranged the pieces like a puzzle on a plate, smooshed them together until they passed for something edible, and covered the cake with enough peach slices that you couldn't see the cracks.

Then she hid it in the sideboard in the parlor and set about her next great tragedy of the afternoon: cleaning the kitchen.

By the time she had it back to rights, she really did need a nap and took herself upstairs to bed. By the time she awoke the light was fading, and she smelled roasting meat.

Alastair was in the kitchen stirring something in a pot.

"Smells good," she said.

"There you are. Feeling any better? You look flushed."

She yawned. "Just my coloring improving from my little nap. How were the sheep?"

She let him prattle on about grass seeds and litter sizes while she nursed the glass of wine he poured for her. When the roast was ready, they ate it in the parlor with a sauce he made from Mr. Fellowes' plums.

The delectability of the food made her nervous. It was one thing to make a man a cake, but to make Alastair Eden a cake was like a seaman warbling an old fishing ballad to an opera singer.

"You still look tired," Alastair said. "Why don't you go to bed while I clean up. We needn't make love tonight."

"Of course we'll be making love," she said. "But first, I'm in the mood for something sweet."

"Oh. I didn't make dessert, but there's fresh cream I

brought back from the Fellowes' that will be delicious with the rest of the strawberries. I'll just go—" He rose but she shot up and stopped him.

"You sit down. I have a surprise for you."

He sat, looking perplexed, as she knelt down and retrieved her cake from the sideboard. It was sunken, and the peaches had dried out more than she liked.

It was a bit pitiful.

Well, nothing she could do about that now.

She stood up and held it out to him.

"Happy birthday, Alastair."

His mouth fell open.

"How did you know?"

"You said last week it was coming. The girl may not be a genius, but she can count to six."

"You *baked*?"

She looked down at the atrocious cake. "Can't you tell?"

He was up on his feet, laughing and beaming. He took the cake from her hands and put his arms around her tight.

"I cannot *believe* you."

"The cake's not *that* bad."

He pulled back and looked at her in wonder. "Thank you. I'm—" he cleared his throat "—touched, Thaïs."

Good God. He was laughing, but his eyes were also misting over.

"Eden!" she squawked. "At least *try* the damn thing before you *cry* over it."

He wiped his eyes, his shoulders shaking with mirth. "I'm sorry," he gasped out. "This is just . . . incredibly sweet. And also very funny. The idea of you in there all day, whipping butter and beating eggs . . ."

She swatted his shoulder and he caught her hand and pulled her close and gave her the longest, deepest hug.

"Thank you," he whispered in her ear. "This is the best birthday gift I've ever received."

"Unless I poisoned it."

"Did you?"

"Not intentionally."

They took the cake out onto the terrace with two forks and sat in the fading light. Eden speared a bite and put it in his mouth.

He chewed for a suspiciously long time.

"Delicious," he pronounced.

He was obviously lying.

She tasted her own slice.

She immediately spit it back out. "It tastes like a burned omelet."

Eden took another bite and chewed thoughtfully. "Yes. But with peaches."

She snorted and grabbed his fork. "Don't eat that."

He snatched the fork back and plunged it into the cake. "Is that . . ." he said, pulling up a hunk ". . . a peach stone?"

She put her head in her hands.

"You can choke on these, you know. Were you hoping my fortieth year would be my last?"

She giggled. "Didn't mean to put that in there."

"I think it complements the texture."

"Don't clown on me."

"Oh, she can mock him all she wants for weeks,

but he must solemnly respect her sacred baking skills?"

"I have other skills," she said.

He took her hand and pulled her to her feet. "That, my girl, you do."

She took him by the hips and pressed him closer. "Care to sample them?"

"I do. But first, I want to thank you."

"You already did."

"No, not enough," he said, moving apart from her. "And not just for tonight. For this month. For being such delightful company. And so, so very kind."

It was almost . . . romantic, the husky way he was talking. The earnest look in his eyes.

Like they were two old lovers laughing on a special night, holding each other as they began to think of making love.

It felt real.

And the first rule of mistressing was remembering what was fake.

She was Eden's paid performer, not his lover.

She could flatter and flirt and beguile and seduce. She could writhe and moan and contort herself in ways he would remember on his deathbed. She could feign raptures of pleasure.

And the act of pretending made her safe. It reminded her this was her job.

It was time to remind Eden of that too.

"We should start practicing for you to take your wife's virginity."

He looked at her oddly. *"Tonight?"*

"We only have a week."

He shook his head and took her hands. "Let's do it tomorrow. Right now I don't want to pretend. I want *you*, Thaïs."

How could she resist that?

And what would one more day hurt? It was his birthday, and if he wanted to spend it in this fantasy, well—he was paying for that too.

They went upstairs and got in bed and didn't bother with undressing.

He pinned her on the bed and kissed her hungrily, already hard. She loved how vast his appetite for her was.

"I need to be inside you," he said raggedly. "Can I—" He took her legs and pulled them open and slid into her, all the way. He fit her perfectly. So perfectly that it was torture not to simply give in to the pleasure of him and let herself fall apart.

She wanted to. She had to dig her nails into the bed to resist it, she wanted to so badly.

He cupped her arse and lifted her up to get even deeper.

Once there, he stopped moving.

"I love this," he said. "It's the best feeling in the world."

And it was, it was.

With him, it was.

He reached down to her cunt. "I want to touch you while I fuck you. Is that done?"

She was grateful for the question, as it gave her a moment to get her senses back.

"Anything can be done if you have a mind to try it," she said, ignoring how good his thickness felt, pulsing at her core.

"Then can I try it on you?"

"Of course."

"I need a better angle. Here." He rolled off her and got on his side. "Lie next to me."

She pressed her back against his front, so she was embraced by his whole body, and helped guide him back inside her pussy.

She'd never done it this way before. Shocking, given she'd had sex on horseback, on a ship's bow, and on a swing made for fucking by an enterprising glass merchant.

It was sweet, this position. Like being in one of Alastair's perfect hugs.

He kissed her neck and put his fingers over her cunt. "That's better," he said. "Now I can touch you and fuck you at the same time."

And he did. Achingly slowly, while fingering her just the way she liked it best. She tried to distract herself from the heady pleasure by saying filthy things to him, but she kept getting too distracted to talk. His arms around her, his cock inside her, his hands driving her insane, his lips kissing her neck in a way she knew would leave marks.

She should stop him, as she'd have to wear scarves to hide herself from Hattie, and because it was blinding her and making her tremble, but she wanted just another moment of it, just another taste.

She closed her eyes, just for a second, to let all of it wash over her. To really *feel* it.

All of a sudden, she was blind.

Alastair was pounding into her while his fingers stroked urgently on her pearl, and the world was rolling, just the two of them in it, and she couldn't help it, it was all too late, because he had her. He had her.

She spasmed around his cock as liquid squirted out of her.

Wave after wave came, and she soaked the sheets, gasping and shaking, as fervid with pleasure as she was, already, with regret.

When it was over, she and Alastair were both completely still.

He pulled out of her without finishing and stared at her in wonder.

"What just happened?" he asked.

"I . . . uh . . . spent."

She did not like her lovers to know her body did this, because then they'd be suspicious when it didn't happen.

"I didn't know women did that," he said.

"Some do, some don't. It doesn't happen every time."

"But you never have before. Not once."

She shrugged.

"Thaïs, look at me."

Reluctantly, she met his eyes.

"That was different, wasn't it? For you."

She nodded. She couldn't deny it, lying in wet sheets.

"Have you been holding back? Pretending?"

She sighed. "I . . . don't usually let myself get so carried away."

He looked hurt. "So all these nights, when you told me I was giving you pleasure, you were lying?"

"No. You were giving me a great deal of pleasure. You always do. But it's not my job to take it."

"You're here to let me learn to pleasure a woman. If you're not being honest about what brings you to bliss, how will I learn?"

He had a point. "I'm sorry, Alastair. If you truly wish for me to let go, I will."

But even as she said it, she was vowing never to let it happen again.

"I do wish for that," he said. "I wish for it most fervently." He propped himself up on one elbow. "Tell me what you like. Be honest."

"I like it all," she said, truthfully. It was not a problem to *like* what she did. It was a problem to let herself relax. When you did—especially if you also *liked* the person in your bed—you were in danger of believing it was real.

And she already *liked* Alastair Eden far too much.

"Let me change the sheets," she said. "They're damp."

"No," he said firmly. "I want to make you do that again. Tonight. Right now. Tell me what to do."

She held back a sigh. Now she would have to let herself get lost in it, just to please him. She would have to hold back in her mind, without holding back in her body.

And so, quickly as she could, she invented a scheme so far outside of how she pictured Alastair that she couldn't possibly confuse the acts with those they practiced honestly.

"I like to be tied up," she said. "Blindfolded. Spanked. Called filthy names."

He looked at her with deep concern. "That doesn't sound very nice for you."

"When a lady tells you what she likes, believe her."

He nodded slowly. "So I'll tie you up. If that's truly what you wish for."

"Alastair, if *you* don't like it, then we won't. It's important for both people to like what they do."

"I can try it. Perhaps I *will* like it."

At first he was tentative, as he used corset strings to bind her wrists to the bedposts and a scarf to blind her. But then he found his domineering side—the lordly aspect of his personality.

When he was like this, it was easier to picture him as another of her other clients. As someone like Camberwell, who saw sex as a game.

Her want for Eden did not diminish, and she let herself orgasm when he took her. But she insisted on the blindfold. It was easier to keep herself safe when she could not see the genuine care and hunger in his eyes.

And when he held her afterward, she kept her eyes clamped shut.

Chapter Thirty

Eden knew he was many things—some good, some less so—but one thing he'd never been was blind.

Now that he had a better understanding of sex, and of Thaïs, he could see his lover clearly. And he knew that when he'd tied her up she'd been pretending not to be pretending.

It was true that she let herself orgasm again, as she'd promised she would.

He felt the difference when her quim contracted tight around his cock as she peaked. He could see and feel the utterly erotic liquid she produced when he brought her particularly intense pleasure. But it did not escape him that she had not been fully *there* when this happened. Her eyes were blindfolded, her hands were bound, and her spirit was far away.

He didn't confront her about it. He'd paid for her body, after all, not her soul. Their agreement was that she'd teach him how to bring a woman pleasure, and she had. He was not entitled to demand more of her if she didn't wish to give it freely.

But it broke his heart.

She'd transformed him by teaching him to let sex carry him away. To let his body feed his soul. She

was so generous and giving as a lover, so percep-
tive as a teacher, so sensitive to his needs and wants
and fears, for all her raucous bluster. She gave so
much of herself. To think that she did not let herself
receive pleasure and care in kind—and that, worse,
she worked so hard to perform as though she did—
made him ache for her.

She said she liked her work, and part of him believed her. But the fact that her physical enjoyment
was a pretense made him realize there was something
personal she was protecting.

Of course, her caution made sense. They'd part in
less than a week. If he were wiser, *he* might be more
cautious in pouring his feelings into their coupling,
knowing that it—she—would be a memory.

But her distance pained him. He wanted her to lose
herself not just in pleasure and desire but in the deep
connection that he felt with her.

He wanted to make love to the woman who had remembered his birthday and made him a terrible cake.
To the one who'd reminded him what a real hug felt
like. To the one who cursed at roosters and cooed at
turtles and wrote in pictograms and bribed dressmak-
ers to help her friends.

He opened his eyes and reached for her and found
her body hot to the touch.

"Thaïs?" he said, pressing the back of his hand to
her forehead. She was dewy with sweat, but she shivered. She opened her eyes, and their usual vivid green
was dull.

"Darling, do you feel ill?"

"I'm so cold," she murmured. "It hurts."

He pulled her close to him and wrapped his body around hers, rubbing her skin gently with his hands. She shivered again—her teeth were chattering—and he damned himself for not seeing the signs of this last night when she'd seemed flushed.

This was his fault. He shouldn't have made love to her outside in the rain.

He would make her tea and broth. And then he would have Hattie send for a physician. But first he must move Thaïs to her own bed. The thought made him feel a bit bereft. She had not slept there since before Elinor had visited.

He helped her put on her least revealing dressing gown, which she did sluggishly, fumbling to get her arms inside the sleeves. "Can you walk?" he asked.

"Yes," she said faintly. But when she stood, she instantly sat back down on the side of the bed, looking like she might collapse.

"I'll carry you," he said. He picked her up as he might a baby and found his throat catch at the weight of her, snuggled in his arms. He carefully walked her across the hall and tucked her into bed.

"Try to sleep," he said. "I'll bring you tea."

She closed her eyes, mumbling something, and fell instantly to sleep.

Downstairs, he set about boiling the kettle, then gathered some vegetables—onions and celery and a carrot—from the pantry. He was going to make Thaïs the chicken broth his mother had made him as a boy and he in turn had made for Anna when she'd been ill as a child. It was not a cure for fever, but sipping it seemed to help fortify the sick, even if it was only as a comfort.

When Hattie arrived he sent her immediately to town to summon the village doctor, then went up to Thaïs carrying tea with extra honey, in case her throat was sore.

He sat on the edge of the bed and helped her to sit up.

"Drink some of this," he said, putting the teacup to her lips.

Obediently, she took a few sips, then shivered and sank back into the pillows.

Poor thing. She was so wan that she seemed almost like a different person. Even her freckles were pale. He bent down and kissed her forehead.

"Can I bring you anything?" he asked.

She shook her head. "I'm just going to . . ." but she'd already closed her eyes.

He went downstairs to check on his broth, which was simmering on the stove. He stirred it a bit, then realized he had nothing to do except worry about Thaïs. He occupied himself pacing about the garden until the doctor and Hattie arrived.

"Your sister is ill, I'm told," the physician, Dr. Burwell, said.

"Yes. She woke up with a fever."

"Symptoms?"

"She said her body aches."

"How long has she felt this way?"

"She seemed well last night."

He desperately hoped that he had not contributed to her illness by fucking her three times the previous day. Oh God, what if his greediness, his constant need for her, had so exhausted her that she'd fallen ill?

He'd have to take more care. The way the days were ticking by so quickly was making him frantic with desire for her. Not just for her body, but to be near her, talk to her, spend time with her. Absorb as much of her as he could before he had to part from her.

"May I examine your sister?" the doctor said.

"Of course. Follow me."

He led the man upstairs. In her sleep, Thaïs had pushed the covers off, revealing her rather scanty nightdress, which was tangled about her hips.

The sight was so pitiful, and she was so dear to him, that it was Eden's impulse to rush up and fix her garments to restore her modesty. He nearly did so, until the doctor cleared his throat and Eden realized that, as her ostensible brother, he should turn around.

He also realized that the doctor might wonder why a supposed governess possessed such revealing garments, let alone wore them when she was ill. He hoped the man would be discreet, whatever the conclusions he might draw.

"I'll just be outside," Eden said.

He stood near the open door, not peering in, but not wanting to leave Thaïs alone with a strange man. He could hear the doctor asking quiet questions, and Thaïs mumbling weak answers.

He couldn't make out the accent she was using. He doubted she had the wherewithal to put on an educated diction when she was barely lucid.

The doctor came out into the hall. If he had suspicions about who Thaïs was to Eden, he didn't voice them.

"I'll have to leech her," he said.

Eden winced. He hated this practice, how it left the ill even weaker than they had been.

"Should we perhaps wait and see if the symptoms lessen on their own?"

The doctor scowled at him. "I think not. She's very feverish."

Eden relented. He puttered nervously outside the door while the doctor went back in, and waited in the hallway until he reemerged.

"Let her sleep," Burwell said. "I'll return tomorrow."

"Thank you."

Eden excused Hattie with the doctor and went inside. The cottage was fragrant with the scent of simmering broth. He hoped it would make Thaïs feel better.

He went upstairs to check on her and found her sleeping, pale as the sheets, with a sheen of sweat over her face. He dipped a cloth in cool water and dabbed it to her brow.

Her eyes fluttered open.

"Alastair," she whispered.

"Don't talk," he murmured. "Save your strength."

"I'm sorry," she said. "We don't have much time, and I'm—"

"Darling, no," he said. "That's not important. All I care about is you."

He spent the day taking care of her. He made her sip liquids every few hours, helped her to the necessary, and stroked her hair to soothe her back to sleep.

He tried to turn his attention to his long-neglected correspondence, but it made him nervous to be so far from Thaïs, where he couldn't hear her if she called for him. And it felt like too abrupt a return to the real world he so wished he could avoid for a while longer. He savored the idyll he had here with Thaïs. He hated how soon they'd have to leave it.

For two days, he sat in a chair beside her bed and read a book, making it his only purpose to care for her. He made a pallet on the floor and slept beside her, so he would hear her in the night if she needed him.

On the third day of her illness, to his immense relief, her fever ebbed a bit. She was still warm to the touch but not burning as she had been, and she was able to remain awake for short stretches, with no delirium.

When the doctor arrived he pronounced her on the path to recovery and did not let her blood. "Summon me if she gets worse," he said. "For now, continue to feed her broth, and see that she rests."

"I don't like that man," Thaïs said faintly when the doctor left.

"Neither do I," Eden said, thinking of how frighteningly wan Thaïs had looked after the leeches.

She shivered. "I'm so cold," she said in a small voice, more to herself than to him.

"I'll get you another blanket."

He fetched the quilt off his own bed and spread it over her, tucking it carefully around her all the way up to her neck.

"Is that any better?" he asked.

She shook her head. "Maybe if you got in with me? You're so nice and warm."

He would not deny her any small succor he could offer. And in truth, he missed the feeling of her tucked up beside him. He wanted to cuddle her in his arms.

But it would not do to climb into bed in his clothes.

He stripped to all but his lawn shirt and smalls and slid under the many blankets. Thaïs instantly melted into him. It was like being surrounded by flasks of hot water.

She shuddered in his arms.

"Poor girl," he murmured.

"Will I get you sick?"

"I could not care less."

She drifted off to sleep. Lulled by her heat and her heartbeat, he closed his eyes as well.

He awoke to the feeling of soft fingers on his lips. He opened his eyes, and Thaïs was staring at him, flushed with fever, her face full of affection.

"You're so handsome," she said, moving her fingers down to stroke his chin. "Like a prince."

"Just a lowly earl, I'm afraid."

"That will do."

"You are as pretty as a princess."

"Just a whore, I'm afraid."

"You are so much more than that," he said.

"No harm in whoring," she said faintly.

"Of course not," he said.

"And I'm so good at it," she said, closing her eyes.

He kissed her eyelids. "That you are. You're also burning up. Let me get you some tea."

She put a hand to his chest. "No. Not yet. Stay with me."

He held her for a while, until she drifted back to sleep. Then he went downstairs to gather tea and broth for her. He decided to give her a little bread as well, in case she was up to eating solid food.

She was whimpering in her sleep when he returned, so he woke her up.

"There, there," he said. "Have a little to drink, and then you can rest."

"I dreamed I had a baby," she said. "It was sad."

"You don't like babies?"

"I *love* babies," she whispered, like she was telling him a secret. "More than anything."

He had the sensation of learning something that *should* have been surprising but did not startle him at all. The idea of her as a mother seemed oddly right. She could be so soft and nurturing and understanding, beneath her bawdy bluster.

"Then what was sad about the dream?" he asked her.

"I want a family," she said softly. "You're lucky that you'll have one soon. A wife and sweet children. I want that more than anything. A little family of my own."

His throat clutched. He thought of himself and Thaïs with a tiny infant tucked between them in this bed, cooing. Nursing at her breast. Soothing the squirming little precious creature as Thaïs looked on, eyes brimming with love for both of them.

He didn't know what to say to her. Of course she could have children if she desired. Plenty of men had families with their mistresses, and some men married former courtesans, though none of his class.

But he did not want to think of her with another man.

"I think you'd be a wonderful mama," he said, honestly.

She laughed ruefully. "You don't have to tell me lies. But it's kind that you do. You'll be a perfect husband. You could send me home today, if you like."

"I don't *want* to send you home," he said. "I treasure

our remaining days together. And there are still things you can teach me."

"Like what?"

"Like how to care for the person you . . ." It was on his lips to say *the person you love* but he trailed off just in time. For of course he could not imply he *loved* Thaïs. It wasn't true. It could *never* be true, in this world where he was who he was, and she was who she was.

"How to care for one's wife," he said instead.

"You are very good at caring for all things, milord. Even your famous sheep. You don't need me to teach you that."

"Well, I like to practice on you," he said.

He brushed a kiss over her damp brow, and wished it wasn't practice.

Chapter Thirty-One

Time went in and out like the flickering of a candle. Thaïs lost track of the hours, the days, the nights. All she knew was that when she was awake, Alastair was with her. He brushed out her hair for her and braided it. He wiped the sweat from her brow with cool cloths soaked in orange water. He made her drink cold liquids when she was hot and warm ones when she was cold. He did not let the doctor draw her blood again.

She felt guilty for wasting the time that he had paid so much for. Terrible that she was too feverish to drill him on his pleasures.

But she also felt contented, like a cat. Because having his attention and his kindness trained on her was among the nicest things she'd ever felt. No man had ever treated her this way. Her friends had nursed her lovingly through illnesses, but it hadn't felt like this. Like Eden's entire being was trained on her every comfort. Like her sickroom was the only place in an exceedingly small world made up of just the two of them.

It had felt that way since the night before she'd gotten ill. Since that moment she'd let down her guard and admitted—if only to herself—the way she really felt for him.

She was so stupid to let herself be so besotted, and so sick she didn't care.

When she asked him to, Alastair lay in bed with her and rubbed her aching muscles. He squeezed her tight against him to warm her shivering body. Even through the discomfort of her fever, it brought her pleasure and well-being.

She found herself confessing things to him. Secrets only Elinor, Cornelia, and Seraphina knew. She told him about her childhood, cleaning and serving in the brothel. About how terrified she'd been when she realized the patrons her elders fucked and flattered would eventually become hers too. How she'd hated when her breasts came in because she felt like a price tag had been placed upon her head, and it got fatter with every expanding inch of her bust.

She told him of the first man who had taken her, how she'd trained for months and been prepared for pain, but he'd been kind. That she was lucky—so very, very lucky. She told him how she'd hated those few years when she'd been kept as a mistress. How she felt that her time was never hers, that her body was on loan. How she liked it better to perform for a single night, then say farewell forever. How her skill at that work, and her ability to make a name for herself, delighted her.

She told him about the girls she helped and how she longed to keep them safe and healthy. How sometimes it wasn't enough. How girls like her could suffer and how guilty she sometimes felt for her good fortune. She'd been found beautiful enough for special treatment. Fallen into the right hands. Met Elinor and the girls, who had shaped her into a woman who could traverse many kinds of worlds.

He listened and listened and listened. He listened to her like she was the most fascinating person in the land. He asked all sorts of questions about her life. The things she'd seen, the men she'd known, the good nights and the bad.

He asked her what her dreams were, and she was ill enough to tell him. Three children, maybe four. A brood, the older ones doting on the babies.

"You'll be such a wonderful mother," Eden had whispered, filling her with warmth.

"I worry I won't, having no ma myself," she confessed.

"You'll love your babies," he'd replied. "That's what matters."

"I'll love them more than life itself."

"Can I ask who would be their father?" he'd murmured. "Is someone . . . waiting for you, back in London?"

"No chance of that," she'd whispered.

That he thought there might be made her want to cry. She told him how she sometimes dreamed of a man of her own. Just one. Someone who didn't mind her past and would love her like any other woman. Who desired her body but her soul moreover.

"You'll find him," Eden had said tenderly. "And he'll be such a lucky man."

She was not so feverish she told him that in her visions the man had come to look like him. Tall and olive-skinned with the kindest eyes she'd ever seen.

Instead, she reached for him and told him that she wanted him.

She wanted him to kiss her throat and rub his hands

down her body. To hold her in the dark. To enter her and claim her.

They spent the night tangled in each other's limbs. She prayed he would not catch her illness, but she could not bear to let him go. She wanted his mouth and hands on her, his cock inside her. She let herself give way to it. To disappear in him. To be known, in her mind and in her body.

She cried when it was over, and he brushed away her tears and asked why she was sad.

She would not—could not—tell him.

She woke up in the middle of the night feeling sick for all that she'd revealed.

Stupid, stupid girl, treating a trick like he was her soulmate.

Letting herself believe, even if only for a night, that the man lying beside her thought her better than she was.

And then it was the morning, and she woke up to the crowing of the cocks.

Her skin was cool, her eyes were clear, and Eden was no longer in her bed.

Which was for the better.

She only had three days before she'd have to give him up for good.

He'd be ready to go back to London and marry some prim young thing, some milk-fresh girl who'd fall in love with him on sight, because who wouldn't? He'd be ready to be a caring husband and a most attentive lover. Just the kind of man he'd paid her to help him become.

And foulmouthed harridan or not, it broke her heart.

Chapter Thirty-Two

Eden walked along the lane as the sun rose, taking in fresh air while Thaïs slept.

He had not slept at all.

Not since she'd wept in his arms.

He'd begged her to open up and be her freest self with him. To let him truly pleasure her. And she had. But it had not been in an operatic display of erotic theater.

It had begun in whispered secrets and grown into an urgent need to be connected with each other. Crested in two desperate bodies joined together, bringing comfort and acceptance in the dark. He'd thought it wonderful that she'd truly let him see her, shown him exactly what was under her pose as a brazen lady of the night. He'd felt his heart expanding.

That is, until he realized it had made her sad.

Made her *cry*, in great, racking sobs.

Had he been wrong to ask her questions? To pry into who she was behind what he had begun to understand was a mask of flippant humor? To wish to understand her—and maybe even to succeed?

He turned back to the cottage. He should check on her.

Perhaps she would let him touch her tenderly again.

Assuage his worry that she regretted how much she'd revealed.

He went into her room without knocking, as he'd been doing for days while he had nursed her, and found her sitting at her dressing table plaiting her hair. Her color was not high, but she was no longer deathly wan, and her eyes were clear from the haze of fever.

"Well, look at you," he said, smiling.

"Feast your eyes, milord."

Milord. An odd thing for her to call him in the light of day, after she'd whispered his given name all night.

He bent down and kissed her on the crown of her head. "You look like you're feeling better."

She ducked off his kiss. "I am. I want a solid meal for once, and you best have one too. Now that I've got my vim, it's time to put you to your paces."

"My paces?"

"Three days left to practice," she said, winking at him in the mirror. "Then you're off to set the *ton* on fire with your cock."

He had to fight to keep from frowning. After what they'd shared last night, this talk seemed coarse and insincere.

"You rest, and I'll bring you breakfast on a tray," he said. "No need to tire yourself."

"Eating at a table isn't likely to kill me after what I've been through. And I want to see Hattie. Nice to set eyes on another soul after being trapped with you."

She said it playfully, but he wasn't feeling playful. Her mood was too sharp, unnatural.

She was pretending. He was sure of it.

It had to be about last night.

She *did* regret the intimacy they'd shared.

And as much as it crushed him, perhaps she was right to.

Perhaps it had been wrong of him to allow himself to tease out her secrets and make love to her when she was ill and vulnerable. Perhaps he was no better than the other men who'd used her.

And if he were, he'd have to find a way to make it up to her.

But right now, he wouldn't press her on the point. If she wanted a morning to herself, he would grant her one. God knew he had enough correspondence to catch up on to keep him occupied for days.

"Yes, it will be nice for you to move about the house, I'm sure," he said. "Let's go downstairs. I think I hear Hattie at the gate."

He made a pot of tea while Hattie clucked about Thaïs, then left them in the kitchen. He set about sorting through his towering stack of letters, arranging them in separate piles—estate matters, a note to Thaïs from Elinor, and a few new reports on potential brides.

The reports filled him with dread. He didn't want to read about the young women he'd begin to court in a few weeks' time.

So he read about sheep.

For hours.

Until his mind was numb.

The sound of the women's conversation faded, and Thaïs came ambling through the door.

"Time for lessons," she said merrily.

He did not believe her jauntiness. Not after last night. He looked up, wary.

"Aren't you tired? You're still recovering. You should have a nap."

"I feel right as rain."

He did not. He felt confused and wobbly.

He held up the letter from Elinor, addressed to *Miss Smith*. "This came for you."

"Read it to the dullard."

He winced at her. "You're not a dullard. You're one of the quickest people I've ever met."

"Not quick with me letters."

"I don't like it when you denigrate yourself."

"Well, only a few days left to tolerate it. Will you read it or not?"

He slashed open the letter with his knife and unfolded the paper. It was short.

"My darling," he read aloud, "I write with good news. Without going into detail, I found the boy. There was no way to visit him, but I know from a trusted person that he's safe, and that's a comfort. I'm so grateful to you for helping me see my two lost loves."

He glanced down at the next line and his cheeks went hot. He cleared his throat.

"Is that it?" Thaïs asked.

"Erm, no. She goes on, I hope you are enjoying your last days with X. It was such a pleasure to see the two of you together and the friendship you have built. Be kind to him. He cares for you."

He glanced at her. She was looking at her hands.

"I'm making my way back to London on the mail coach tomorrow," he finished reading. "Call on me when you return.

"All my—" he cleared his throat again "—All my, erm, love."

He stared at Thaïs, wondering if those words—*all my love*—jarred her the way they did him.

Wondering if she knew the sentiment was true.

He did love her. He could deny it to himself as he'd done last night, but he knew in his bones what she was to him.

She lifted her gaze back up.

"Thanks," she said brightly. "Now, I was thinking we should get you fucking standing up."

Something was seriously amiss here.

"Are you well?"

"Right as rain."

"I'd rather not tire you with acrobatics just now. You were quite . . . faint . . . last night."

He searched her eyes, pleading with her to acknowledge all they'd shared.

But she just shrugged. "Nothing like a little sleep. Come. Time for a screw."

He wanted to be more direct. To say, *I know I'm more to you than a randy student, and you know you're more to me than a one-night patron.*

But there was no trace of the woman who'd wept in his arms the night before. She was every inch the Thaïs Magdalene who'd arrived here nearly a month before, when she'd been expecting Camberwell.

He brushed his hair into his eyes, trying not to show how hurt he felt by this.

"Let me just finish up here, and then perhaps—"

"Oooh," she interrupted him, pointing at his stack

of reports on other women. "Are those more of your ladies?"

He nodded.

She clapped her hands excitedly. "Let's read them."

"My eyes are tired," he said. "Maybe later."

All he needed was for Thaïs to finally find a gem. Someone to her liking, to whom she could jauntily marry him off in a morning's work.

"Well then, there's something else we can do behind that desk."

He once again recalled the first day she'd come here. When she'd offered to pleasure him under it. His utter shock and horror. He'd grown accustomed to her taking him in his mouth—he enjoyed it immensely— but the act seemed off after what they'd shared the night before.

"I'd rather take you to bed," he said softly. "Like last night."

She made absolutely no sign she knew what he was talking about.

"No use repeating old tricks when there's new ones to learn," she said, without acknowledging the emotion in his voice.

And that was as far as he would go. He'd taken too much from her, and she regretted granting it. *We are not lovers*, she was telling him. *I am your whore.*

He was delusional to think she'd ever think of him as more. And unfair to sow such feelings, when they'd so soon have to say farewell forever.

So he did exactly as she asked for the rest of the day.

And she asked a lot of him.

She went through his erotic books and made him

test out positions they had not yet tried. Her riding backward on his lap, standing propped up against a wall, lying on a table with her feet resting on his shoulders. He knew she was faking her pleasure, and while he could not stop himself from spending—he desired her too much—it was joyless. He felt like a sexual performing monkey ordered about by an organ-grinder, pretending to have a merry time.

By late afternoon he was exhausted, and she looked so peaked it would have been a crime to join with her again, no matter what she asked of him.

"That's enough for the day," he said wearily. "I'll make you supper. Please, take a nap. I'm worried you'll grow ill again."

He could tell he was right because she didn't argue. She went upstairs slowly, like she was sore. And how could she not be after what his much larger body had just put her through?

He prepared a chicken soup. Heartier than the broth he'd been giving her, but still nourishing and gentle on the stomach. When it was done, he called her name. He didn't hear her footsteps, so he went upstairs to check on her.

She was in bed, eyes closed.

He sat down beside her and touched her shoulder.

Her eyes fluttered open. "Sorry," she said. "I fell asleep."

"Good. That was the idea. Do you feel up to eating?"

"Maybe just a bit."

"I'll bring you something. Stay in bed."

"No, no," she objected, dragging herself up. "Better for me to be on my feet so I sleep through the night."

She followed him downstairs, and he brought two bowls and a loaf of bread to the table in the parlor. She sank down into her chair and closed her eyes, breathing in the steam.

"Smells delicious," she said.

She barely ate, however, slurping at the broth and picking bits of bread from inside the crust.

"You don't like it?" he asked.

"It's good. But I'm not hungry."

"Perhaps you should go back to bed."

"You should come with me," she said. "Get in a bit more practice."

Even looking pale and clammy, she would not give up this charade. It was beginning to try his patience.

"I've had quite enough practice for one day," he said. "And so have you. I'll clean this up. You get some sleep."

She shook her head. "I'm not ready for bed, I swear."

"Then play patience."

"Why don't you read to me?"

Finally, a reasonable suggestion. "My pleasure," he said. "What would you like to hear? Perhaps some poetry? I have a new volume by—"

"Read to me about your girls."

He sighed. It was like she wanted to twist the knife. Insist in every way she could that he meant nothing to her. "Is that *really* what you want?" he asked.

"I want to be useful to you after days of rotting in bed, wasting your money."

"You know I don't care about the money."

"Well, I do. Besides, I like hearing about the innocent little things. Always did like stories about princesses."

"Fine," he said. "But get back in bed. I'll come join you."

He retrieved the final batch of letters from his study. When he went upstairs Thaïs was propped up in bed.

"Oh good," she said. "I was about to come and find you."

He held up the papers. "Just gathering the entertainment you requested."

He moved to sit down in the chair across from the bed, but she patted the sheets beside her. "Come sit with me."

She probably intended to take liberties he had every intention of resisting, but he was too tired to argue. He perched on the bed and broke the seal on the first letter.

"Miss Amelia Landslough," he began. "Seventeen years old—"

"Far too young," Thaïs said. "Next."

He agreed. There was no point in reading on.

He unsealed another missive. "Lady Honor Hastings."

"Lady Honor. How dignified."

"Lady Honor, twenty-one years old," he read on, "is the second-eldest daughter of Lord Lyle Hastings."

"Seasoned enough," Thaïs allowed.

"She is blonde, and at four feet eleven, considered quite dainty."

Thaïs sighed, took the letter from his hands, and tossed it onto the floor. "Well, she won't do, will she?"

He could not see why not. She sounded unobjectionable.

"What could possibly be the problem?"

"She's much too short for you."

He was growing so, so tired of this.

"What does her height matter?"

"How will you talk to her? She won't be able to hear you."

"I can speak up."

"Speak down, you mean. Toward her ears."

"You are being ridiculous. What is the purpose of me reading these to you if you object to every girl on the smallest grounds?"

"The only thing small is Lady Honor. You like walking, but she'll have a tiny stride. You like riding, but she'll only be able to mount a little pony."

"Pure speculation. You're rejecting these women just to irritate me."

"Do you want my feminine wisdom or not?"

"I'm beginning to think not."

"Oh, don't be cross. Read me another."

He agreed only because this was the final letter of the batch.

"Miss Edwina Lawrence," he said. "Twenty-four years old, eldest daughter of Mr. William Lawrence of Blyth, in Northumberland."

Thaïs nodded for him to go on.

"Considered a striking beauty, Miss Lawrence has raven hair, blue eyes, a slim physique, and is of medium height."

"No," Thaïs said immediately. "She's not the right look."

He gritted his teeth. "I've *told* you, looks are of minimal importance."

"You're dead wrong. You feast with your eyes more than most."

"What does that mean?"

"Looking upon a woman—the right kind of woman—makes you randy."

"You make me sound like a lech. Is that what you think of me?"

"You're a gentleman through and through. But one who likes hips, breasts, and an arse."

This was utterly exasperating. He tossed the letter aside.

"This is the last of forty girls I've told you about, and you've ruled out every one of them. For all you know, this woman could be perfect."

She snorted. "I keep telling you, there's no such *thing* as perfect. You're a fool to think there is. There's only perfect for *you*."

"Well then, who exactly do you think I'm supposed to marry?" he snapped. "How am I possibly supposed to find her, in your infinite wisdom?"

"She probably doesn't exist," she said in a singsong voice. "I guess you better just marry me."

"Can you be *serious*, for once, Thaïs?" he said, pounding the mattress with all the frustration and disappointment this day had built up in him. "I could sooner marry one of my sheep."

She gasped so sharply his neck cracked as he looked over at her.

Her face was contorted, like he'd lashed her.

He froze. The contents of his stomach churned.

Oh God, he'd said that. Aloud. To *her*.

And after what she'd confided to him last night, about her desire to be a wife and mother.

It was cruel.

He took her by the shoulders urgently. "Thaïs," he said, "that came out wrong. So bloody wrong. I meant only that the *ton* would never accept such a thing. You would make a fine—"

"A fine sheep, eh?" she interrupted him, with a forced chuckle. "Better than a pig, I suppose."

He had never felt more nauseated.

"I'm so—*so* sorry," he stammered. "I didn't mean it that way. Not that *I* perceive you, or a match between us, in such a fashion, only that—"

"Alastair," she said, "it was a joke."

But even if it had been meant as such, the way he'd replied to it was unspeakable.

And worse, now that he'd made such a terrible error, he had the most arresting thought. What would it be like if he *did* marry her? If he could be that man she longed for, who chose her and only her, who gave her babies and a home and—

Stop, he commanded himself.

He couldn't.

If his mad parents had taught him anything, it was that a respectable alliance was the bedrock of stability. He could not allow his most intimate relationship to cause chaos in his life. He did not want a homelife like the one he had grown up in.

He wanted an existence he could control to the point of absolute perfection.

And marrying a person like Thaïs—a woman

whose reputation alone would thrust his life into a turbulent storm, let alone her mannerisms and passionate personality—was out of the question.

But he'd never felt as terrible as he did right now, realizing he'd killed the tenderness between them.

The loss of it provoked a sadness unlike anything he'd ever felt.

Chapter Thirty-Three

Thaïs tried not to let Alastair—Lord Eden—see that she felt like he'd slapped her.

After all, she was foolish to be stung by his words. The quip he'd made had been exactly like one she'd have made herself.

But she could tell that despite her laughter, he saw through her.

His eyes were liquid, tortured. He kept trying to touch her, to soothe her.

It was humiliating.

Why had she *said* that?

Why would she think a man like him, who prized respectability and perfection, would even *joke* about marrying a woman who slept with men for money? Hundreds of men, decades' and tens of thousands of pounds' worth of them.

She believed that there might be a man out there who would marry her. But he would not be a man like Lord Alastair Eden. And she'd been a foolish hussy to forget it.

She was usually blunt to herself about how she was seen in the world. The way people looked at her, and always would, for how she made her living.

Alastair was one of those people.

And she'd been mad to forget it, even for a moment, even in jest.

What was *wrong* with her?

All day, she'd taken pains to remind herself that last night wasn't real. She'd thrown herself into sex with so much false exuberance she had almost collapsed, just to remind herself why she was here. Why they both were.

To fuck.

That was it.

Not to whisper secrets in the dark.

Not to fall in bloody love.

She was so ashamed she wanted to hide in the privy. Maybe then he'd stop looking at her like she was a child he'd kicked. He was still fervently apologizing, which only made her more embarrassed. She had to make him stop before she cried.

"By God, enough," she moaned, a smile plastered on her face. "Don't squawk yourself into a lather, milord. You'll bring back my fever."

He stopped talking. Instead, he pulled her close to him, holding her tenderly, and looked her in the eye.

"Please accept my apology."

"Of course I don't accept, when none is needed."

To end the torment, she grabbed his hands and squeezed them to her breasts and wiggled her hips to get closer to his groin.

He reared away from her like a horse startled by a crack of lightning.

"Please don't. That's not what I want right now,"

he said. "And I don't think it's what you want either."

It wasn't. What she wanted was to leave this place and promptly begin forgetting it.

Forgetting him.

"What I want is to give you what you paid for," she said.

"Well, you've given me that handsomely all day," he replied darkly. "You're becoming an incredible value."

"That's what she likes to hear."

"I'm going to sleep in my own bed," he said. "I'm tired. And you should get some rest. I'll see you in the morning."

They'd slept together every night for weeks, even during her illness, but she didn't argue. She'd just as soon be alone with her scalded feelings and her blushing heart.

She wished her friends were here. She'd have loved to moan to Cornelia and Seraphina about how he'd said such hurtful words, and how her own reaction had made the whole thing worse.

How she'd ruined a lovely month.

But then again, maybe it was better they *weren't* here to complain to.

They'd no doubt have told her Eden was a prig, or mean-spirited, and written him off for dead.

But they'd be wrong about him.

She knew deep in her bones that he felt worse than she did. That if he'd not been so annoyed with her peevish ways he'd never have tossed off words so thoughtlessly. That he'd probably never forgive himself for the lapse, being as focused as he was on being the best at everything he tried, including charming whores.

But that didn't mean his words had not been true. The most honest things were often said when you weren't thinking.

"Stupid girl," she whispered to herself, wiping away the tears that had begun to fall the moment he'd turned his back.

She cried herself to sleep.

She felt sick again when she woke up in the morning. Sick with fever, sick with dread at facing Eden.

When she didn't come down for tea, he knocked and entered with a tray for her. "How are you?" he asked, his face drawn with concern.

"I might have worn myself out yesterday," she admitted.

"I imagine so. You feel ill?"

"Tired, mostly."

The painfulness of their conversation the night before made every word hang heavy in the air.

"Stay in bed," he said. "Rest. I'll check on you when Hattie leaves."

She was too defeated to object. She fell back asleep, as much to escape the day as out of fatigue.

When she awoke it was almost evening.

She must still be sicker than she'd thought.

She went downstairs to find Eden. He was in the kitchen, covered in flour up to his elbows. There was a streak of white slashed across his cheekbone.

She wanted to reach out and brush it away, as she'd done so many times before. But she couldn't touch him. Not even chastely.

She didn't know how she'd stand to sleep with him again.

"What are you making?" she asked.

"A lamb pie for our supper." He gave her a tentative smile. "I thought you might recover your appetite if I made you your favorite."

It was her favorite. He was stewing the lamb with a savory combination of carrots and tomatoes and onions and herbs that filled the kitchen with the aroma of comfort itself.

"I'm sorry I slept the day away," she said.

"Sleep all you want, Thaïs. My lessons have concluded."

As much as she was relieved to be spared the pain of touching him, she didn't want to fail at what she'd come for.

"Your math is wrong," she said. "We still have tonight and tomorrow. You hired me for a month."

"I hired me to teach me how to please a woman. And you have. I feel confident as a lover. You've more than fulfilled your obligation."

He said this to the pie crust he was rolling out rather than to her.

He didn't want to be with her again, it was clear.

And the knowledge it was over—that the final time had passed, and she hadn't even known to cherish the last moments—made tears sting her eyes.

She was glad he wasn't looking at her.

"Your loss," she said with cheer she didn't feel. She *felt* like learning the bagpipes so she could play a mournful bloody dirge, loud and jangled and off-key. Give the cocks a taste of their own medicine.

She left the room and lost at patience for an hour until he came into the parlor with two steaming plates.

They ate in silence. Though the meal was probably scrumptious, it tasted sour in her mouth. She could barely swallow.

Out of duty, she asked Eden one last time if he was certain he'd not join her in her bed.

He shook his head. "Thank you," he said politcly. "But I'll leave you to your rest."

Her bloody rest. Dog's blood, but she was sick of him talking about her rest. She'd had enough rest this past week to raise the dead. She wasn't some flimsy violet he had to keep from wilting.

But fine. He'd relieved her of her duty, and she'd drop the matter.

If there was one thing a whore must know, it was that your patron had no obligation to you. You were there at his convenience. And she was no longer convenient for Lord Eden.

She went to bed, and when she woke up with the roosters she immediately knocked on Eden's door.

"Yes?" he called.

She walked in and found him in his nightshirt, still in bed. She fought the urge to dive in beneath the sheets with him. She missed his morning warmth.

"Seeing if you're still abed," she said. "When you're up, I'll pack my trunks."

"Wait until Hattie leaves," he said. "I'll help you."

"Fine."

She whiled away the morning chatting to Hattie about her supposed return to her genteel charges, and gathering all her brochures and notes from the places she'd left them strewn about the house. The concerns of the Institute felt like a lifetime away after a month in the countryside. She took comfort in the fact that soon she'd be back in London, back to her friends, back to having a purpose in life aside from Alastair Eden.

When Hattie left she went upstairs to pack. She was tearing her clothes out of the wardrobe and the bureaus and piling them on the bed when Eden entered and winced.

"You'll make a mess of your nice things," he said.

"My things aren't so nice."

"Of course they are. Don't be impatient. There's not that much to pack. Here." He took a chemise and carefully folded it, then repeated it with another and another until he had a tidy stack.

"See?" he said. "They'll fit better in your trunks."

"I'll add *valeting* to your list of services."

"I hope you'll provide a reference."

"Perfect man," she said.

"Not perfect. But a better one, thanks to you."

She grunted.

"I'm very grateful to you, Thaïs," he said. "For everything you've taught me. I consider this a great success."

"Glad you got your money's worth."

"Stop saying that. I'm being sincere."

"So am I. You paid a fortune."

He sighed and continued to fold in silence, handing her garments to place inside the trunks.

"The carriage will arrive first thing in the morning to retrieve you," he said when they were done.

Good. It couldn't come soon enough. She wished it were here right now.

She shut herself in her room for the afternoon, to avoid the awkwardness of bumbling around the house with a man who didn't want her there. A kind man who no longer had a use for her.

She kept fighting the urge to cry. She knew she was about to get her monthly and blamed it for her infernal weepiness.

They ate leftover pie for supper, and this time Thaïs did not offer to take Eden to bed a final time.

Even a whore didn't like to be rejected.

Even a whore no better than a sheep had her pride.

She slept fitfully and woke to a smear of blood between her legs.

A fitting way to end the month.

When Eden took her in his arms in the doorway after the carriage was loaded, she allowed him a polite kiss on the cheek but did not return it.

And she cried, hunched and aching in her womb, the entire journey back to London.

Chapter Thirty-Four

"You're out of sorts," Eden's sister, Anna, observed at dinner his first week back in London. "Even more so than usual. You've barely said a word all evening."

Out of sorts. If Anna thought he was merely *out of sorts* he was doing an excellent job of pretending to be in high spirits.

He could not recall a time since childhood that he'd ever been so at a loss for joy.

It wore on him, feigning normalcy each day as he went about his business, when all he wanted was to be left alone.

"I'm unenthusiastic about being here in town," he said, which was true, but not the reason for the relentlessly gray way he felt. "I was enjoying my time in the country."

"Dogs, horses, and fresh air," Anna said drily to her husband, Gilby Howe. "The only things my brother truly longs for."

No. What he longed for was waking up beside a certain kindhearted, foulmouthed woman he could not stop thinking about.

Gilby gave him a sympathetic look, though Eden knew Gilby was a Londoner through and through, and found the countryside as dull as Thaïs did.

Thaïs. He longed to say her name out loud. He missed the feeling of it on his tongue. But who could he speak of her to, even in passing? No one knew they were acquainted in any more than the most cursory way.

"I'm fine," he assured his sister. "Merely tired from the opening of Parliament."

"Well," Anna said, "whatever you are, it's time to summon some enthusiasm. You can't be morose while courting at a ball. You have to show the ladies your charming side." She paused and grinned at him. "If you *possess* a charming side, that is."

He shot her a withering look.

"No," she said and laughed. "Certainly not that one. Try a smile."

He humorlessly bared his teeth at her, and she dissolved into laughter.

"How's work going, Gilby?" he asked his brother-in-law, to change the subject. Gilby was preparing evidence against a slave trader accused of attempting to kidnap a group of free Black men on a ship bound for the West Indies.

Gilby opened his mouth to reply, but Anna held up a finger to stop him.

"Didn't Mathson prepare notes for you on potential brides?" she asked. "Surely you must be excited to meet a few of the young ladies tonight."

"Of course," he said, though he could not summon much conviction, even for show. He could barely remember the specifics of any of the girls he'd read about. What he remembered was Thaïs's responses to them.

Particularly that final one.

"Try a little harder to convince me," his sister said.

"In truth, no one caught my particular interest."

"Well, anyone will seem uninteresting when her characteristics are inventoried in a list by a man more accustomed to sending reports on sheep," Anna said. "You should have let me write the reports. I'm much more florid."

"It doesn't matter. If I'm not struck in person, a list of accomplishments is meaningless."

She looked at him with mild surprise. "But you *love* lists of accomplishments. What has come over you?"

Thaïs was what had come over him. He could no longer think about courtship without hearing her voice admonishing him. *There's no such thing as perfect. Only perfect for you.*

He wondered what would happen if *she* escorted him through the capital's ballrooms, observing his interactions with potential brides. Would she dismiss all the girls out of hand, the same way she'd done when she'd read about them in his letters?

Of course, none of the young ladies in question would associate with him—perfect for him or not—if he showed up with a courtesan on his arm.

He needed to stop thinking about her.

But he couldn't.

He *hated* how things had ended. How they'd formed an intimacy unlike any he had ever known, only to end in a bitter détente. At least when she'd arrived they'd been cordial acquaintances. Now he suspected that if he met her in the street, she'd walk the other way.

And after that brutal remark he'd made, she deserved to feel that way.

She'd recognized his words for exactly what they were: evidence of an instinctive thought that she was less than him.

The torment of it was he didn't even actually *believe* that it was true. The more he thought about the impulse that had made him laugh off the idea of marriage to her, the more it seemed archaic and revolting. He *knew* Thaïs, and he knew that she was every bit as deserving of his respect and kindness as any other woman. *More* deserving because she'd given him so much and taken nothing back from him, save coin he could easily afford to spend. Aside from Anna and his mother, no other woman—no other *person*—had ever been so close to him.

He was grateful to her.

He missed her.

Her enormous personality. Her intelligence, which came at him fierce and sideways. Her raucous laugh and wretched language and tumbling red hair. Her body, warm beside him in bed.

What he'd give for even one more day with her. A chance to undo what he'd done.

A chance to tell her he was sorry that he'd hurt her.

That it was *he* who was the undeserving one between them.

But the truth was, however deeply he regretted his snobbery, a hard fact underlay it: he could not be with her. It was not merited or fair, but it was incontrovertible. He was an earl, and she was a whore.

Their time was over.

And he was being ridiculous, letting himself brood on the past, when he should be welcoming the future.

The future that started tonight, at the opening ball of the season.

Anna chattered the entire carriage ride to Lady Rasby's gracious St. James's town house, peppering him with tips on how to behave and whom to talk to. As soon as they were announced, she delivered him to Lady Rasby herself, who had evidently promised Anna to introduce him to every mama and daughter in the room.

He poured himself into the task of seeming like an eligible gentleman. He smiled, bowed, asked polite questions. But the girls all seemed so young, so nervous, so inexperienced. Though he was far from the eldest bachelor in the room, they made him feel ancient. In such formal confines, with such perfectly mannered women, he found himself reverting to exactly the same behaviors Thaïs had called *stiff* and *remote*. (Or, in her parlance, *priggish* and *cold as a witch's kitty*.)

And though he felt crass for thinking of it, none of the girls he met drew the interest of his body. He scanned the crowd for more curvaceous figures or tumbles of red hair. But Thaïs's figure was not in fashion among the upper crust. Many of the girls were whippet-thin, their hair arranged in tight ringlets pinned atop their heads with pearls and flowers. Some were gorgeous, some were plain, but none of them tempted his eye to linger.

He retreated to the billiards room and drank a brandy with a few acquaintances from his club to fortify himself.

"On the hunt?" Lord Zachary, an occasional ally in Parliament, asked him. "Don't usually see you at these evening dos."

"I've decided to marry," Eden said.

Zachary laughed at him, though not unkindly. "You sound awfully morose about it. Women are not illnesses, you know."

Eden rolled his eyes at himself. "You're right. It's just that I hate these things. Circulating among the crowds, meeting so many people all at once. I can't believe anyone comes to balls for enjoyment."

"Oh, they're not all bad. Finish your drink, and I'll take you for a spin. We'll find you a pretty girl to dance with."

Eden had no desire to dance with any girl, pretty or not, unless she were Thaïs. But this was not an attitude that was going to lead to him being settled with a family, so he threw back the last of his drink and followed Zachary from the room and back out into the swirl.

Zachary frowned at a very young lady sitting alone in the corner. "Oh dear," he said. "Poor Miss Clark is unattended. She's a friend of my sister's. Let's go rescue her. I'll introduce you."

Eden was struck by Zachary's kindness. As a sought-after gentleman, there were plenty of people waving him over and competing for his interest. Nevertheless, he went directly to the young lady all but shivering from fear in the corner of the room.

"Miss Clark," Zachary said warmly, "I was not aware you were out this season."

"Yes," she said in a voice scarcely louder than a

whisper. "My first ball." She lowered her eyes. "I don't think I'm very good at it."

"Ah, well then, you should meet my friend here. Lord Eden, this is Miss Emily Clark. Miss Clark, Eden here detests socializing and is perfectly miserable."

Oh. Miss *Emily* Clark. This was the young lady he'd heard Lord Bell had taken an interest in. The woman to whose uncle he had written a letter of warning and from whom he'd heard nothing back.

Looking at her in the flesh, he was even more appalled by Bell's intentions. Though Miss Clark was of age to marry, she had the appearance and demeanor of a girl still in the nursery. She could easily be fourteen years old.

"A pleasure to meet you, Miss Clark," Eden said.

He felt so bad for her cowering here all alone that he impulsively decided to ask her for a dance. She accepted, looking exceedingly relieved, and he led her out onto the floor.

He noticed many eyes glancing at them in surprise. He was not sure if it was because people were unused to him joining the dancing or if they were expecting to see Miss Clark on Lord Bell's arm.

Miss Clark was an able dancer, nimble on her tiny feet. Eden led her across the floor with the competence he'd possessed since childhood.

He did not, as Thaïs had instructed, make a promise to her with his body. He could not fathom doing such a thing with *any* of the proper young ladies in this room. Surely, they'd be as horrified as he was uncomfortable and insincere.

They were like pristine little angels.

He'd come to find he had a taste for devils.

When the movement was over, he and Miss Clark adjourned for the refreshments table.

"Thank you for the dance," he said. "You do it well."

"As do you, milord. Though, you are being kind. In truth, I am better in the library than the ballroom. I prefer reading to dancing."

He was surprised by her candor, not to mention her rueful tone. "Is that right? I will confess I share your taste. What do you like to read?"

"Modern philosophy," she said. "I recently enjoyed the work of Mr. Adam Smith. And—" she glanced around them and lowered her voice "—Mary Wollstonecraft."

He could not stop himself from raising a brow at her. "Miss Clark. You are a scandal."

"I only tell you because I know your sister is a friend to the Duchess of Rosemere."

Her implication being that if he allowed his sister to associate with Cornelia Ludgate and her ilk, he must have progressive views.

Which he did.

Unlike the man who Miss Clark was reputedly fated to marry. Bell took an almost sadistic pleasure in persecuting Cornelia and Seraphina for their radical views and close friendship with his estranged wife. He'd led a faction against them and their Institute in the papers and was suspected to have done much worse.

What a ghastly match.

Before he could offer a discreet word of warning, they were joined by a Mrs. Perth, Miss Clark's chaperone, who appeared old enough to be Eden's grandmother. Mrs. Perth announced their carriage was waiting.

He felt fond of the girl as he watched her walk away. And could not imagine her in the clutches of a brute like Lord Bell.

It made Eden wonder if *he* should marry her, just to protect her from such a fate.

It was exactly the kind of match Thaïs had warned him away from. After all, there was no way he would want to consummate a marriage with such a girl for years. It would essentially defeat the purpose of marrying at all, given that he was only doing so to have a family.

But if tonight had proven anything, it was that there were no women in this milieu who moved him like Thaïs. She had said he needed to find a woman perfect for *him*.

He'd already found her and lost her.

Protecting a woman might be the best that he could do as a husband.

It would stand in place of loving her.

He resolved to send Miss Clark flowers and call on her the following afternoon.

Chapter Thirty-Five

Dear, are you listening?" Thaïs's friend Marianne Anderson asked, holding up two squares of fabric. "Rose or violet for the curtains in the dormitory?"

Thaïs had not been listening. She had been staring at her fingernails, which were bitten to the quick, and wishing she would stop gnawing at them, which she could not do owing to her never-ending foul mood, which she could only blame herself for since she'd gone and liked a *man* too much.

"I don't care," she said, picking at a cuticle. "You choose."

"Are you feeling well?" Marianne asked. "You seem quite—"

"Bitchy," Cornelia provided.

"I'll take that as a compliment," Thaïs muttered.

"I was going to say *irritable*," Marianne said gently. "You've not been yourself since you returned from the country."

Thaïs was surprised they'd noticed. There had scarcely been time to talk to one another since she'd gotten back a month ago. They were all too busy dashing around the Institute, trying to ready the place for its opening in a few months' time. The building was aswarm from dawn to dark with builders and decorators, deliveries of furnishings and supplies, interviews of students and training sessions for the teachers, and meetings between the founders and the patrons who had agreed to take on female apprentices.

The craze was welcome, as it kept her friends from interrogating her about the weeks she'd spent away. They still thought she'd been gallivanting around a grand estate with Colin Camberwell. Only Elinor knew she'd been with Eden.

There would be no harm in telling them—they'd never violate Eden's privacy by gossiping—but she didn't want them to look too closely at her. Especially not when Eden's sister, Anna, was so frequently around.

As she was this bloody afternoon.

Thaïs liked the girl, and her help around the Institute was sorely needed. But Thaïs couldn't look at her without thinking of her brother.

"I like the violet," Anna said.

"Me too," Seraphina agreed.

"Violet it is," Marianne said, writing it down in her notebook.

"That's the final question from the decorator," Marianne said. "Why don't we all sit down and have lunch."

"Yes, let's," Cornelia said. "Maybe food will improve this one's temperament." She gestured at Thaïs.

It did, at first. The cook they'd hired was very talented.

But then Cornelia turned the conversation to the

topic Thaïs had avoided thinking about all month: Lord Eden's success in the marriage mart.

"How is your brother faring with the ladies?" Cornelia asked Anna. "I must admit the idea of such a serious man going about to balls and musicales is rather amusing."

It certainly did not amuse Thaïs.

And Eden was not as serious as they thought. He only appeared that way when you didn't know him well. As some very lucky woman was bound to discover very soon. The wench.

"Well," Anna said, "Alastair's not hopeless, exactly. He's quite good at conversing with women. He takes a sincere interest, and he's even rather funny."

Yes, because *she'd* taught him how to be natural and ask questions and not talk about his sheep all day, Thaïs thought darkly.

"And he's a good dancer," Anna went on. "He claims to loathe it, but he at least puts on a decent show."

Thaïs wondered what that meant. Whispering to his partner? Seducing her with his eyes and body as he did the outwardly innocent steps? With the handsome face and perfect manners he'd come to her with, combined with the things she'd taught him, she'd made him deadly. The whole *ton* was likely clamoring to marry him.

She hated it.

"Sounds like he's a success," Seraphina said.

"Not quite," Anna said. "I suspect he could have any woman he offered for, but he's morose when he's at home. He barely eats and has gotten so thin I had to summon the tailor. He hates the town air and says it does not agree with him, but he's here every season for Parliament and I've never seen him quite so pale or grim."

Good, Thaïs thought. Maybe he'd be so pale and grim no one would be willing to marry him, and she'd not have to be brokenhearted for the rest of her damned life.

She was instantly annoyed at herself for wishing him ill.

And then forgave herself because Eden deserved her ire.

"Is there anyone he's taken a particular interest in?" Marianne asked.

Thaïs held her breath. The very idea of him feeling tenderly toward someone else was like a trowel to the chest.

"It's difficult to say," Anna said. "He seems to be courting half the girls in town. He's out every night and assures me he spends every moment he's not in the Lords or working calling on ladies."

This was not the answer Thaïs had been hoping for.

"Which chits is he visiting?" Thaïs asked, despite herself. The specifics would not help her mood, God knew, but she could not bury her curiosity.

Seraphina chortled. "Are you familiar with the virgins of the *ton* by name, Thaïs?"

Well, in fact of it, she was. And she was very curious which of the girls from the letters had caught his interest, even if thinking of him with them made her feel like the devil was lying on her grave.

"I like to know the gossip," Thaïs said.

Anna tapped her chin. "Well, let's see. He's called

on Letty Pettigrew a few times. He appreciates her skill with music. Apparently her voice is like an angel's, and she's a genius on the harp."

Thaïs remembered the letter about Miss Pettigrew. She'd deemed her too musical, likely to ruin Eden's beloved peace and quiet. He'd seemed to agree with her at the time. It annoyed her that her opinions were forgotten.

"A musical wife might be nice for him," Cornelia said. "He's a patron of the arts, after all."

Anna nodded. "And she could entertain us when I visit. His house in the country is so dreadfully quiet."

Because he hasn't any children yet, Thaïs thought. She tried not to gnash her teeth at the idea of some other woman giving them to him.

"So will he offer for the Pettigrew girl?" Cornelia asked.

"I haven't the slightest idea," Anna said. "He sent flowers to Lord Bollinger's daughter, Ellie, just this morning after dancing with her twice last night. He went riding with the Chambers sisters—I think he likes the elder one. She's quite good on a horse. And then there's Valencia Estes, whose father is the ambassador from Spain. She's interested in politics and—"

Anna went on for a quarter hour, describing the charms of woman after woman Thaïs had told Eden not to bother with.

It turned her off her food.

"I'm going home," Thaïs said when lunch was over and Anna had finally stopped talking.

"But it's only two o'clock," Seraphina said. "Don't you want to help interview the next four girls?"

"I have a pounding headache," she said. Not to mention a sour heart.

She took a hackney coach back to her house. She wasn't up to walking.

At home, she lay down in her bed and closed her eyes.

It was rot to feel this way. If she was this upset hearing about Eden *riding* with someone in the park, how would she be able to bear it when he *married*?

She needed to focus on her own life, not his.

Which meant taking on new patrons.

She had not entertained a man since she'd come home. She told herself that she was too busy with the Institute, but that wasn't true. She could easily take an evening to herself once a week to pad her savings. She wasn't desperate for the coin. Over the years, she'd squirreled away enough to keep her fed and housed when she eventually stopped whoring—but the extras could go to her charity girls.

Besides, harlotry had been her calling since she was fifteen years old. Without it, who would she even be? She'd spent her whole life becoming Thaïs Magdalene. Her work had given her a purpose, and it was good for her.

This dithering was because no one in her queue of patrons was Alastair Eden. It was sentimental drivel, and it was going to ruin her whole life if she didn't cast it from her mind.

"Fine," she said aloud. "Now is as good a time as any."

She found the pile of solicitations from men who'd requested an evening of her company. She plucked one from the top. Lord Alfred Quirke. She knew him by reputation. He was the third son of a marquess. Not particularly rich or distinguished in any pursuit besides leisure, but he was said to be handsome. He'd do.

She sent him a note inviting him for the evening. Normally she gave more notice, but now that she'd made the decision to take a patron, she didn't want to wait. Besides, she was the kind of woman men dropped everything for.

It would do her well to remember it.

Quirke replied that he'd visit her at ten o'clock, which was perfect, as it left her time to visit her favorite bathhouse. It was her ritual to bathe before and after each man that she took.

Once she'd soaked, she went back home and spent two hours making herself beautiful. She dabbed her body with scent and rouged her lips and cheeks. Rubbed oil into her skin to make it soft and supple. Put on a gown that would make a madam blush.

Once her body was done up to perfection, she laid out a spread of wine and fruit and cheese and spirits for her guest.

He arrived promptly at ten.

She opened the door and stood in such a way to show off her body as she greeted him. The candlelight, she knew, made her gauzy gown transparent, revealing the outline of her breasts and arse almost as well as if she were naked.

"You're a vision," Quirke said. "Turn around."

She did, and he growled and cupped her bum in his hands. "Just as good as they say."

"Better, even," she purred.

"Better, even," he concurred.

"And you're a fine specimen of man yourself," she told him, leaning back against his chest as his hands explored her waist.

"So they tell me," he said.

"Lucky me."

Patrons loved flattery. She was good at making even the ugly, stinking ones feel wanted. But tonight the pretense of enjoyment was a strain. She keenly felt the work of every smile.

Quirke's cock pressed into the small of her back. She was glad he was already hard. Less work for her to get him there. Usually she didn't mind putting in the effort—enjoyed the satisfaction of making a man want her—but tonight she wasn't interested.

She slid her hand over his prick.

"What a rod you've got," she said. "Can't wait to feel you inside me."

She wished she hadn't said that. The last time she'd uttered it had been to Alastair. And damn her, it'd been true.

Quirke's hands climbed up to her breasts.

"Can't wait myself," he said.

She turned around and began undressing him.

He was of medium height and broad build, with sandy hair and blue eyes. He was clean-smelling, attractive, nice enough, clearly aroused by her.

He was as close to a perfect patron as she could imagine. She owed him a good night.

She rid him of his coat, cravat, and waistcoat, taking her time and running her hands over his body until he was bare-chested. Then she dropped to her knees to shimmy off his boots and breeches.

He pressed his cock into her face as she did so.

A bit rude, but at least he knew what he wanted.

Normally she'd be happy enough to give it to him. She'd not bother undressing him, just take his prick out of his smalls and suck him off to get the evening going. Part of her charm was her exuberance, after all. Men did not pay her small fortunes to be reluctant.

Yet she ignored the cock in her face and took her time getting him undressed.

When she finally had him nude, she lowered her head and took his penis in her mouth.

He groaned.

This was the part where she should put her hands to his arse and pull him closer to take him deeper. The part where she should lick and suck his knob to get him going. The part where she should make her own sounds of pleasure.

But she didn't bloody want to.

She didn't want a damned dick in her mouth.

At least, not this one.

She popped it out, pulled back, and stood up.

Quirke looked at her in confusion.

"I'm afraid it won't be happening tonight," she said.

"Pardon me?"

"I think I'm getting sick. You should go."

He gaped at her. "But you summoned me here just this afternoon."

"I'll have you back some other time."

He gave her a disgusted look. "I'm not paying."

"Wouldn't ask you to."

He shook his head, dressed quickly, and left without a word.

Which was quite polite, really. Many men would have wanted to give her a slap for kicking them out without their getting any satisfaction.

But it was worth the risk to be alone.

She simply could not put on her usual show with a strange man when she wanted a specific one so badly.

She lay down in her bed, alone, and ached for Alastair.

Chapter Thirty-Six

Eden arrived at the Institute for the Equality of Women grateful for a day away from the unpleasantness of courtship. It was six weeks since the opening of the season, and he had now met every girl on the marriage mart, plus her mother and sisters. He had danced every dance he knew a hundred times with fifty different people. He had attended suppers, picnics, musicales. Gone calling, riding, walking. Sent flowers, sweets, cards. He'd not had a night to himself in weeks.

He was exhausted and no closer to finding a wife than he had been when he started.

He could not blame the situation on the women that he met. Most of them were lovely, and the few that were not were at least memorable. But no one called out to him in the way Thaïs had insisted the right woman would.

He was haunted by the advice she'd given him. That he should be drawn to a woman's smell. That he should be captivated by her body as much as by her mind. That there should be a spark in his heart when he thought of her, looked at her, spoke to her, held her.

He could not dismiss this advice, because he knew what these things felt like.

It was the way he'd felt when he was with Thaïs.

He missed her to the point of distraction. He still reached out for her in bed as soon as his eyes opened, only to be greeted by a cold space where her body should have been. His thoughts drifted to her even when he was in Parliament, at his club, dancing with other women.

He wanted to visit her. More than once, he had begun drafting a note asking permission to call on her to discuss his troubles finding a bride.

But that was simply an excuse. He didn't want to hear her opinions on the girls who didn't move him to affection. He simply wanted to hear about her days, to listen to her jokes, to be near her, even if he couldn't touch her, now that their time in that way was over.

He did not send a note. Indulging himself would only increase his longing. He needed to move forward.

Which kept leading him to Emily Clark.

It was now common knowledge about the men's clubs in town that Lord Bell planned to offer for her as soon as he was divorced. Bell had warned others to stay away from her, and given his power and lack of scruples, few were eager to cross him in the matter.

Eden was not scared of Bell. He already had the enmity of the man due to his friendship with the Equalist Society and Jack Willow, whom Bell had harassed, sued, and threatened since Elinor had left him. Few men of Eden's station could afford to exercise such nonchalance. If he did not save Emily Clark, he did not know who would.

He made a point to dance with her each time he saw

her out, as she was so frequently alone. He'd visited her several times at her guardian's house—a rambling town house in Chelsea crammed with Lord Hoover's collection of sabers and ornamental knives. Each time he'd been there he'd asked for an audience with Hoover and been told he was ill. Miss Clark did not speak ill of him, but when she mentioned him to Eden during their conversations, he inferred a faint implication that the man might be mentally unwell. *Foggy* was how she put it.

So she was unprotected. Ripe for Bell to snatch her up for the sake of her fortune, which everyone knew he needed as he had squandered so much of his money in his legal battle against Elinor and Jack.

The idea of Emily's future being consigned away to Bell at the age of eighteen made Eden sick. She was a smart girl. A kind one. He enjoyed talking to her. She had a wry wit, a natural way with dogs, and a fondness for the countryside. Her quiet nature reminded him of himself.

He was not attracted to her physically and could not imagine taking her to bed given her innocence. But if there was no other woman he wanted to marry, and he could save Emily by offering his hand, perhaps it was the best for both of them.

He could give her sanctuary while she matured, and eventually they could move from friends to spouses. Two, three years from now was not so long to wait to start a family.

He knew Thaïs would be appalled at this plan. She'd say he was wasting everything she'd taught him. That he was marrying exactly the wrong kind of woman.

She would probably be right.

But the problem was there was *not* a perfect woman out there waiting to be found.

He'd already found her.

And he could not marry her any more than he could let Lord Bell marry Emily Clark.

Some things were simply sad and difficult in life, and this was one of them.

"Ah, Lord Eden," Seraphina Arden said as he walked into the lobby of the building. "You're right on time. The meeting is just this way."

He immediately recognized the grand chandelier overhead as the one Thaïs had chosen from the iron-monger. He'd written the letter placing the order for it himself. It looked handsome in the room. He wondered what Thaïs would think of the furnishings in his homes. How she might improve the atmosphere with her eye for careful touches.

Seraphina led him through an airy hallway with views of the greenery in the courtyard of the building. It was beautifully furnished, every doorknob and table and pattern reflecting Thaïs's taste. Among these things, he could feel her presence so keenly it was like she was beside him.

He wondered if she would attend the meeting.

He was annoyed with himself for how disappointed he felt when he walked into the assembly room and saw she wasn't there.

About thirty people, mostly men, were gathered to learn of their new duties. Like him, they had agreed to take female apprentices to train in their trades. Eden was going to be assigned two women to educate in land management.

He waved at Seraphina's lover, Adam Anderson, who would apprentice women in architecture, and sat down beside his brother-in-law, Gilby Howe, who had agreed to take a female law clerk.

"Good morning, gentleman," Seraphina said. "I think we're all here. I'd like to thank each of you for your support. Our students are thrilled at the chance to work with you. And they are a marvelous class of women who will be brilliant in their roles."

Eden jotted down a few notes as she explained how the program would work. He would receive applications next week and would interview the qualified candidates personally. They would then live at the Institute while they did their initial studies and take up posts at his estate for hands-on training with him and his stewards once Parliament let out for the summer.

He was impressed by how detailed and orderly the program was and by the qualifications of the women the Institute was welcoming in their first class. He said as much to Gilby as they adjourned back to the lobby. They were about to leave when a voice called their names.

He looked behind him to find Cornelia Ludgate walking toward them, waving. "Gentlemen!" she said. "It's been ages since I've seen you. Have you been to the Institute before?"

"No, it's our first time," Eden said. "What you've built here is incredible."

"Yes, we're very proud," she said. "Would you like a tour before you leave?"

"I'm afraid I have to get to court," Gilby said. "Next time."

"I'd love a walk about," Eden said. He wanted to see more of the furnishings Thaïs had chosen. They were perhaps his lone connection to her that was appropriate.

Cornelia offered him her arm. "Shall we?"

He took it and let her guide him through the building. She showed him an auditorium where lectures would be held. Classrooms where students would learn literacy and other skills they needed before they could advance into apprenticeships and jobs. A handsome dining hall equipped to serve one hundred people. The beautiful garden in the courtyard, where herbs were grown for the kitchens, which would be staffed by a mix of cooks and students taking shifts.

The second floor had a homelier atmosphere. There was a large parlor for socializing and lounging. An enviably equipped music room. A spacious nursery for children.

"You've done a remarkable job," Eden said. "It's so comfortable and welcoming."

"Oh, we have Thaïs to thank for that. It's her vision. She was determined the place should feel like a home."

"She's a marvel," he said. It felt so good to speak of her.

"That she is," Cornelia agreed as she led him up a staircase. "The third floor is the dormitory. It's quite lovely. Each woman has a bit of privacy, yet the whole floor comfortably sleeps eighty. With room for more in the attic if we grow."

She opened a door off the landing, and it thumped against something large and solid. He heard a familiar squawk.

The door flew open, and Thaïs burst through it.

She was wearing the yellow dress he'd bought for her.

That dress made everything come back.

Her licking butter off her fingers over breakfast in the parlor in that yellow dress as the light shone on her hair. Telling him a bawdy story in the evening over cards. Walking sullenly beside him in the rose garden, sneezing. Dictating letters about chairs. Lecturing him on women.

But above all, he was stricken with the memory of all the times he'd taken that dress off her.

"God's toenails, wench!" Thaïs cried at Cornelia.

"Sorry!" Cornelia said. "I didn't know there was anyone coming. We really need a transom at the door. I was just showing Lord Eden—"

He stepped forward, and Thaïs's eyes went wide.

"Oh!" she exclaimed. "Eden! Didn't see you standing there with my brains all rattled."

"Good afternoon, Miss Magdalene," he said, because his own brain was rattled at the sight of her, and he could think of nothing better.

"I was just giving Eden here a tour," Cornelia said. "Could you show him around the dormitories before he goes? I need to prepare for an interview."

"Can, indeed."

"Thank you. Farewell, Eden," Cornelia said. "It was good to see you."

"Always a pleasure," he said, bowing.

Cornelia hurried away and closed the door behind her, leaving him and Thaïs alone together in the vast room.

His impulse was to embrace her, but he knew he could not.

His fingers vibrated with the desire nonetheless.

"Well, look who it is," Thaïs said quietly. "The quiet bachelor teacher from Gloucestershire. Mr. Smith, I think it was?"

He smiled. "Never heard of him."

"Ah, no loss. He's a bit boring. Always in the kitchen, cooking, or in his study, reading about sheep."

He swallowed hard at the recollection of their awful conversation.

"He sounds terrible," he said and hoped his voice conveyed the grave regret he felt.

Her face softened. "Oh, don't be too harsh on him. He did have his appeals."

He wanted to ask what they were. What she valued in him. For at the moment, he saw little in himself to like—at least from her perspective.

"How have you been, Thaïs?" he asked.

She shrugged. "Uncomplaining."

He gave her a wry smile. "I *highly* doubt that."

She laughed. "Well, perhaps complaining a fair amount. But I'm right as rain. And you?"

"I'm well."

"Found yourself a wife?"

"Not quite yet, I'm afraid."

"What! After all I taught you I'd have thought you'd be wed twice over by now."

He jerked his head to scan the room, worried someone might overhear and gather that they knew each other better than would make sense to an observer. He did not want to raise suspicion.

"Could you lower your voice?" he asked.

She looked at him with irritation. "There's no one around to hear me," she said.

Ugh, he'd made her angry. The last thing he wanted.

"I only meant that perhaps there's somewhere more private where we could talk. Would you mind?"

She pointed at a door. "In there."

He followed her inside.

It was a linen pantry.

A *small* linen pantry with little room to stand without brushing up against her.

He knew she'd brought him here to rankle him, but it had the opposite effect. Her familiar scent aroused a wave of tender feeling. A longing so deep his throat ached.

"I didn't mean a closet," he said.

"The other option is the privy."

"Closet it is."

"So tell me everything," she said, leaning back against a shelf. "Anna says you're courting half the girls in town. Enjoying yourself?"

He shook his head. "Not at all. I'm failing utterly."

"Failing?" She snorted. "Impossible. You were my star pupil. Surely you can trick *some* lady into marrying you."

"Oh, I think several of them might accept my hand. The trouble is I can't seem to form a connection with anyone. I keep thinking of what you said. That when

I met my wife I would feel something and know she was the perfect person."

"Perfect for *you*, that is," she corrected.

"Perfect for me," he agreed. "And I haven't felt it."

He did not add *except with you*.

He wondered if she knew that he was thinking it because her gaze went soft. She reached out and touched his shoulder.

"That's too bad," she said. "But maybe it's not the women. Maybe you need a reminder of your lessons."

He had to remind himself to breathe.

"Oh, there's very little I've forgotten," he assured her. "You're a memorable teacher."

They looked into each other's eyes. He couldn't read her expression. Were her irises dark because she wanted to touch him as badly as he wanted to touch her? Or was she guarded, worried he might say something hurtful?

The thought made a lump rise in his throat. He needed to change the subject.

"The Institute is stunning," he said. "I see your touches everywhere. You must be so proud."

She smiled. "That I am."

She did not say anything further.

He could tell she was not sure what to talk to him about, the circumstances being what they were. The natural thing would be to excuse himself.

But he could not bring himself to do so.

"And how's your health?" he asked, to extend the conversation.

She furrowed her brow. "My health? I'm not pregnant, if that's what you mean."

The thought had not occurred to him. But now that she raised it, he almost wished she were. Because then . . . well, he'd have a reason not to let her go.

"Oh," he sputtered. "No, I . . . I was not implying . . . that is, if you were, I'd imagine you would have told me, and of course I would see that you were—"

She started laughing. "Look at you, all flustered."

"You were recovering from an illness when you left. That's what I meant."

"I was low for a while," she said.

There was something in her eyes that made him wonder if she was telling him more than she was saying. If she meant her mood and not her physical health.

"But you're better now?"

"Perfect as a pig in shit. And you?"

Miserable, he wanted to say.

"Very well," he said. "Thank you."

"Well, best we return you to your day, no?" Thaïs asked.

He was dismissed.

How painful.

"Of course," he said quickly. He turned to go.

But then he stopped.

He simply could not bear to open the door and leave her.

He turned back. "I don't wish to waste your time, Thaïs," he said quietly. "But I can't go without saying I have missed you dreadfully."

Something ripped across her face—something like anguish—and he knew that expression because he'd felt himself making it day after day when he thought of her.

She missed him too.

My God, the relief. *She missed him too.*

He opened his arms. "Come here."

She stepped forward, and he pulled her close without even thinking about the reasons why he shouldn't.

She tucked her head under his chin and squeezed him back.

God, her hugs. *Their* hugs. There was no more comforting feeling in the world.

"I've missed you," he murmured again. "God, how I've missed you."

"Show me how much," she said.

He picked her up, held her against the shelves, and kissed her. She buckled, her form welcoming his.

And this, *this* was what he had not felt in weeks. *This* was what he had so naively thought he could recreate with someone else.

It made him frantic to be closer to her.

He bent down and took her face in his hands and kissed her softly on the lips. Her body relaxed in a luxuriant way that instantly made him hard. He deepened the kiss, and when she met him with the same urgency overtaking him, he slid his hand beneath her skirts and found her pussy.

God, the feel of it. Hot and slick and wet.

He put his fingers to her pearl and used the motions she had taught him to pleasure some other woman and prayed that it would work on her because he needed to leave her with something of himself.

She cried out, and then he felt it. A trickle of warm liquid squirting from her quim into his palm.

She was spending.

The one thing she could not control.

It meant she was not pretending to wilt with pleasure in his arms. She was letting herself go, letting him make love to her, in this tiny little room after weeks apart.

He didn't know what it meant, except that he loved it, he *loved* it, and also that he needed to put his cock inside her right now or he would die.

They didn't have a condom, but he didn't care.

The moment that he entered her they both froze, eyes locked together, and simply *felt* it. Felt *them*.

It was so right and good and overwhelming that Eden began to spill.

And then the door swung open, and the confused face of Cornelia Ludgate greeted them.

"Oh," she said.

Chapter Thirty-Seven

For a moment, all three of them were still and silent, locked in shock.

"Mind closing the door?" Thaïs finally found the wits to say. "I've got a prick inside me."

Cornelia slammed the door immediately.

Alastair, still holding her, looked like he might faint.

She didn't blame him. She was shaken up by what had just happened between them. It was like not a minute had passed since they'd left the cottage.

It was like coming home.

But she couldn't let herself get weepy. It was just sex, just a frig in a damned closet, not something that should break her heart.

"I'm so sorry," Alastair said. "Christ."

"Don't worry. Not the first time Cornelia's caught me fucking in a linen room."

"Really?"

"Well, no. I don't usually fuck in linen rooms unless it's by special request."

"A request you get a lot?"

"You're my first."

He tightened his arms around her. "Glad to be your first in something."

"A rarity indeed."

He kissed her cheek. Oddly, he seemed to have calmed down. He seemed almost happy.

"You're not having a fit over this?" she asked.

"I'm not sure that that would help. The damage is done."

The damage.

That cut through her. Reminded her how he thought of her. More like a risk than a woman.

She parted from him and handed him a towel. For two people who hadn't even used a bed, they'd both managed to get extremely sticky. She'd have to come back in here later with a mop and clean.

But first she had to get Eden out of this building so that she could be upset in peace.

"Don't worry," she said. "Cornelia won't say anything. Nothing shocks her."

"She looked and sounded plenty shocked to me."

"I'll threaten her. She's scared of me. Now come, let's sneak you downstairs."

She moved to open the door, but he put his hand on her arm to stop her. "Wait," he said.

God, she loved his touch. Even the light pressure of his fingers on her arm made her body brighten.

"What?" she asked.

"Thaïs, I was thinking about something. I've been thinking about it for a while, actually, and seeing you today makes me wonder if perhaps there's something to it."

He looked at her intently, boring into her with his eyes in a way that made her nervous.

"Well, what is it?"

"Say I can't find a wife this season," he said.

She just about stopped breathing.

Was it possible he felt the same way she did? That life was simply less when they were not together? That the sun was not as bright and the air caught in your lungs?

Could it be he wanted forever, damn the consequences?

"What if I took a mistress instead and tried again later on?" he asked.

Oh.

How stupid of her.

Of course he was not proposing marriage.

He wouldn't.

Ever.

Nothing had changed.

"Well, that's a question for yourself to answer, I'd reckon," she said, trying to hide her disappointment.

He swallowed, hard. "I think I have. I'm asking *you.* What if you were my mistress?"

Her?

He had a slight smile on his face, like he expected her to be pleased by this invitation. And that almost brought her to her knees. How could he ask her this, when he was one of the few people she'd spoken to about her dreams?

He might as well have called her a sheep again.

She wanted to slap him.

"Eden," she said sharply.

"Alastair," he corrected.

"*Alastair*," she bit out, "the answer is *no*."

His face fell. Like he was *surprised*. Like he really thought that after everything, she'd just happily agree to be his hired woman.

"Why not?" he asked. He looked crestfallen.

It was infuriating.

"Because I don't want to be a mistress," she cried. "And I told you that, and told you why. Weren't you listening?"

"I was, Thaïs." He took her hand and squeezed it. "I *was*. I've listened to everything you've said, and I know that you didn't like being kept by a single man in the past. But it wouldn't be like that with me. I wouldn't own you or ask you to obey me. You could do whatever you like. But at night, you could come home to me."

The idea of coming home to him made her guts twist. It was everything she wanted.

But she wouldn't come home to a man who could only ever think of her company as something he could buy.

After the bungled night with her last patron, she'd made a firm decision. She was retiring.

"No," she said. "I've stopped taking paid lovers. You were my last one."

"You've what?" He looked at her like she'd said she had become a sea captain and sailed to the Arctic. Which cut her to the bone. That he could only see her on her back.

"But what will you do instead?" he asked.

"I'll help look after this place. Tend to the girls."

He nodded slowly. "I see. You'll be wonderful at that."

"I'm wonderful at most things."

"You are," he said. "But perhaps you could do both. You could be my companion and still—"

"I don't want to be a mistress, Alastair," she said. "I want to be a wife. And if I'm your companion, I won't be able to meet a man who loves me. And you won't meet your lady either. So let's call this what it is. A nice affair that ran its course."

He closed his eyes. A muscle twitched in the side of his face. She could see he was truly pained by this.

For a second, she wondered if he would do the thing she'd fantasized about. Tell her that *she* was the woman he wanted to marry.

But when he opened his eyes, they were full of disappointment. Not hope for some imagined future. Alastair Eden was a realist. He knew they could not be together.

He'd known it all along.

They both had.

"Yes," he said. "Of course. I'm being foolish."

His pain was obvious. It almost made her want to weep. For how foolish this all was. Two people who wanted each other, kept apart by mores and rules.

But she would not cry in front of him. She'd do it later. Mourn this thing that couldn't be, alone.

"I'll see you out," she said.

"No need. Take care, Thaïs."

He bowed to her deeply and left the little room.

She waited until the sound of his footsteps faded before exiting the closet.

Then she collapsed on one of the dormitory beds and let the tears roll down her cheeks.

It was no time at all before Cornelia and Seraphina were beside her.

"What in the name of God is going on?" Seraphina said. "Cornelia says you were fucking Lord Eden in the linen pantry? He just ran out of here without saying a word of goodbye. Now you're in tears? Did he do something to you?"

"He asked me to be his mistress," Thaïs said, wiping away the tears.

"Just today? Out of the blue? While swiving you?" Cornelia asked.

"Well, he waited 'til the swiving part was over."

"And this made you sad enough to cry?" Seraphina asked.

"Darling, what is *wrong*?" Cornelia said. "I didn't know you even *liked* Eden. Have you even seen him since last year? None of this makes sense."

"Camberwell didn't really win me in the auction," Thaïs admitted. "It was a ruse to cover up the fact that Eden did."

"What?" her friends gasped out at once.

"When I was in Gloucestershire, it was with Eden. I was with him for the month. He asked Camberwell to bid on his behalf, to keep the whole thing secret." She paused. "Don't tell anyone. It's important to him that no one knows."

She might be angry with him, but she would not break her word.

"Of course we won't tell," Seraphina said. "But how

strange. He doesn't strike me as the type to keep a mistress. Much less pay exorbitantly for one."

"He's not. He hired me to train him how to be a good husband before he goes off to find a bride."

"Oh," Cornelia said. "How . . ."

"Considerate?" Seraphina offered.

"Yes. Even rather sweet," Cornelia said, as if she were confused.

"He's very sweet," Thaïs wailed. "So sweet that I fell in bloody love with him."

"In *love* with him!" Cornelia erupted.

"I can't explain it either. It just happened. I taught him to rut, and something went wrong in my brain."

"Eden didn't know how to have sex?" Seraphina asked.

"Well, he thought he wasn't good at it, and he wanted to be perfect before he married. No harm in that."

"It's rather romantic," Seraphina said.

Thaïs sighed. "I *know.*"

"Did it work?" Cornelia asked.

"Yes," Thaïs said. "He's very, very good. I miss him."

"Well, why not agree to be his mistress? What's the harm?"

"I don't *want* to be a mistress. I want to have a man of my own. Just one. I want to make a family with him. Be a wife. Be *chosen*. I know neither of you ever wanted to marry, and it must sound crazed from the likes of me, given what I am, but it's what I want."

She braced for them to give her all their arguments against it. To say she'd lose what rights she had, that she'd not have independence, that love was not a question of binding herself into unfair laws.

But neither of them said a word in judgment.

"You don't sound crazed," Seraphina said. "Or unworthy. If that's what you want, then you should have it."

"Maybe if you told Eden how you feel, he *would* marry you," Cornelia said.

She laughed bitterly. "I *did* tell Eden that, and he said—and these were his exact words—'I could sooner marry one of my sheep.'"

The two of them looked aghast.

"A bloody *sheep*?" Seraphina said.

"I will snip off his balls," Cornelia said. "Immediately."

"It's fine," Thaïs said. "He didn't mean it in a hateful way. It's not that he scorns me. I think he cares for me. But he isn't the type to flout the rules. He's too proper. He values his reputation, wants to be perfect. He's the last man in England who'd make a whore his wife. And I won't be with a man who wants someone else to have his family."

"Nor should you," Cornelia said. "You deserve a man who cherishes you exactly as you are and who'd consider it the honor of his life to marry you."

The words were kind. But they didn't make it hurt less that Alastair would never be that man.

"I hope you're right," Thaïs said.

"I know she's right," Seraphina said.

"I'm rarely wrong," Cornelia said.

"Don't puff yourself, Duchess," Thaïs retorted.

"Don't call me Duchess," Cornelia said.

"Let's not spar just now," said Seraphina. "Thaïs might cry again."

"Only because I love you," Thaïs said.

"As much as it pains me to admit it, the feeling is mutual," Cornelia said, taking Thaïs's hand and kissing it.

"Well, let's get on with it," Thaïs said. "Day's going stale on us, and I need to clean up the linen pantry. Made a mess of it."

"Don't forget we're leaving at six to go to Jack's," said Cornelia.

Elinor's husband's petition for divorce was to be voted on by the House of Lords tomorrow. Elinor was in a state, knowing that the chances of it passing were nearly certain. She didn't have a lick of desire to stay with Bell, but the divorce would leave her arsed: without the legal rights of a single woman or the benefits of her marriage contract, and no hope of seeing her children until they came of age.

Thaïs was worried about her. Every time she saw her, Elinor looked worse. Pale and watery-eyed and tired and so thin that Thaïs had taken to bringing her sweets whenever she visited.

At six, she joined the other women in Cornelia's carriage, which took them to Jack's rooms in Mary-le-Bone.

They rode in silence, knowing the mood at supper would be solemn. But when Cornelia knocked on the door, Elinor threw it open with a smile so big it showed her molars.

"Ah! You're here! Ha!" she cried. She held an open bottle of wine in her hand and raised it above her head. "Who wants spirits?"

The three of them exchanged a confused glance.

"I'll take a glass," Thaïs ventured. "What's the occasion?"

Elinor's eyes went wide. "You haven't heard?" She put her hand over her heart. "Oh, Jack," she called over her shoulder. "Come! They haven't heard. I thought everyone knew. It's been in the afternoon papers. But then I suppose you've been out at the Institute and—"

"What is it?" Seraphina cried.

"Bell is dead!"

"What?" Cornelia yelped.

"My husband, God rest his evil soul, was killed this afternoon." She looked at them with bright eyes. "Murdered," she whispered, though more in the manner of a killer than a mourner.

Cornelia braced herself against the wall. "You didn't—"

"Not *me*. A girl he was courting by the name of Emily Clark."

"Emily Clark!" Thaïs said, remembering the name from Eden's papers. "But she's a wisp of a thing, barely out of the nursery."

"She must have a great deal of mettle to her, wisp or not," Jack said, coming to put his arm around Elinor. "Stabbed the rotter right in the throat."

"Come in, come in," Elinor said. "I'll tell you everything."

They made themselves comfortable in Jack's small parlor, accepting drinks. Then Elinor produced a letter from her friend Lady Margaret DuMont.

"The story is in the papers, but Margaret has more

details. She lives across from Lord Hoover, you know. I'll read it to you."

"Bell called on Miss Clark this morning, bringing flowers," Elinor read from the letter. "He asked to be alone with her, and her chaperone excused herself. (Old Vanessa Perth. Not to be trusted with a pussycat, let alone a girl. Who knows what Hoover was thinking. I think he's gone a bit demented.) In any case, once they were alone, Bell said he'd be a single man tomorrow and asked for Emily's hand in marriage. When she demurred, he became enraged. He took her by the shoulders and attempted to force himself on her, saying he would take her virtue and then she would be compelled to marry him. Vanessa heard screaming and came back in the room, but she's an old woman, and Bell ignored her cries to stop. Emily tore herself away and grabbed an ornamental dagger from the wall. And when he tried to wrestle it away from her, she stabbed him with it.

"She didn't mean to kill him, only ward him off," Elinor concluded, "but in the scuffle, the knife happened to strike an artery. There was no saving him."

"Poor Miss Clark," said Seraphina. "She must be in pieces."

"But at least saved from a life with that cretin," Thaïs said.

"Will the girl be arrested?" Cornelia asked.

"Because there was a witness to see she was acting for her own protection, she won't be prosecuted," Elinor said.

"Thank God," said Seraphina.

"Yes," Elinor said. "I would hate for the poor girl to have to suffer more."

"So Bell is . . ." Cornelia trailed off.

They all looked at each other, shaking their heads.

"I don't want to tempt the devil celebrating his demise," Elinor said. "He is, of course, the father of my children, and they will be devastated to learn of what has happened."

"But now they have you," Seraphina said. "And you can all be together."

"And Elinor, you'll be a widow instead of a divorcée," Cornelia said. "You'll have your independence."

Elinor nodded. "The first thing I'm going to do is find my children. And then, Jack and I are going to have a wedding."

"Not getting married by law," Jack added. "Neither of us want that. But we'll say our vows to each other all the same."

Thaïs shed tears for the second time that day. And this time they were happy ones.

Chapter Thirty-Eight

Lord Alastair Eden walked into the wedding of the season with a headache so painful that it hurt to blink.

"Stop scowling," Anna hissed into his ear, pinching the skin above his elbow. "What has come over you? You love weddings."

Indeed he did, usually. And he was honored to be included on the small guest list for the breakfast celebrating that between Lady Elinor Bell and Jack Willow.

The trouble was that he knew who else was certain to be in attendance here.

"Sorry," he whispered. He relaxed his face into what he hoped was a less grim expression. An actual smile was beyond him. It had been so long since he'd smiled that his skin would likely crack if he attempted it.

They were greeted by a footman who showed them into a dining room set for thirty and led them to their seats.

Eden was between his sister and Seraphina Arden.

"Good morning, Miss Arden," he said with a bow. "How do you do?"

She nodded back coolly, then immediately turned

her head and began a conversation with the gentleman beside her.

She'd always been cordial in the past. She must know about him and Thaïs.

And if she did, she likely hated him.

And he deserved it.

A month had passed since he'd made his hog-minded proposition at the Institute. He'd spent the entirety of it awash in shame. He was not sure he'd ever be able to regard himself as a gentleman again.

He'd suspended his search for a bride. With Bell dead, there was no reason to pursue Emily Clark, and his feelings for Thaïs made it clear enough to him that he could not devote himself to any other woman. He could not pledge his hand when his heart was pledged elsewhere. And even if he wanted to, he would not trust himself with a woman again.

If he could hurt the one he loved as badly as he'd hurt Thaïs—twice—then imagine what pain he might cause a person he cared for less.

He had proven himself a brute when it came to sentiment—as sensitive as a battering ram. And it was shocking to know this of himself, after a lifetime of thinking he was a relatively gentlehearted man.

Lowering.

He deserved to be a bachelor. He deserved his empty home.

The man across the table from him, who Eden recognized as the bookseller from Jack's shop, smiled and stood up, greeting someone who'd just walked in.

Eden turned around to see it was Thaïs.

She was dressed in a bright orange gown that popped against her hair. She looked like the feeling of sunshine in a meadow.

He stood so quickly he nearly overturned his wineglass.

"Good morning, Miss Magdalene," he said to her, bowing.

"Lord Eden," she said politely. "How nice to see you." She quickly turned her attention to others around them, greeting them with far more warmth.

It was as though they'd never met. He felt the chill of her disinterest like a lash.

"You're right here next to me," Loudon, the bookseller, said to Thaïs, holding up her place card.

This meant she was one seat across the table from Eden. Close enough to touch. If he leaned forward, he could whisper to her.

But what would he say?

I'm sorry. I love you. I'm lost.

She instantly fell into an animated conversation with Loudon, and he was envious. He strained to hear what they were talking about.

The weather, it turned out.

What he would give to have a conversation with Thaïs about the weather.

Jack stood up and clinked his glass at the head of the table, and the buzz of conversation in the room quieted.

"Friends, thank you so much for gathering with us this morning," he said. "My *wife* and I are so grateful you've come to celebrate with us." At the word *wife*, everyone raised their glasses and cheered.

The bride and groom had already said their vows that morning in Jack's rooms in Mary-le-Bone with just Elinor's children in attendance.

"I'd like to tell you a story," Jack said. "I don't know how many of you know this, but Elinor and I have been friends since we were young, ever since she wandered into my bookstore, not knowing what it was."

"I knew more than I let on," Elinor said. "I always loved illicit things."

The crowd laughed.

"Well, you could have fooled me, for how innocent you looked," Jack said. "We struck up a conversation, and I was enchanted by her intelligence and beauty. That dry wit that we all love. The sparkle in her eyes and her warmth with everyone she meets."

"Jack, you'll embarrass me," Elinor protested.

"A woman deserves to be embarrassed by her husband on her wedding day," he said. "My bride here bought a few books to read, and I slipped a copy of the *Equalist Society* circular inside her bag. I don't know if I thought it would scandalize her or impress her, but it must have done the latter, for the next day she came back. Her color was high, and I worried I had offended her or gotten her in trouble with my views. But it turned out she was excited by what she'd read. She came back to see if I had older issues she could borrow."

"And perhaps to see you again," Elinor said. "See? A wicked girl."

Jack took her hand and kissed her knuckles. "Not a wicked bone in your whole being, but you were brave. You began to pass whole afternoons in the shop, along with your poor maid—what was her name?"

"Louise."

"Yes, poor Louise, eighty if she was a day, who always looked bored enough to fall asleep—and thank God, often did, so we could talk for hours. I was a poor man who wrote against the aristocracy, and you were a duke's daughter, but it never seemed to matter. Ours was the most natural friendship I ever formed in my life.

"I won't lie that I sometimes wished it could be more. But our Elinor here was like a princess, and I was living on day-old bread and broth in a garret above the shop, using every spare pence to fund the circular. And of course, leaving aside my origins, I was myself, and she was her. She could not match me in charm and looks."

"I still can't, sadly," Elinor sighed.

Everyone laughed, for Jack had a stocky boxer's frame and a broken nose to match, while Elinor was a seasoned beauty with the manners of a queen.

"So I never told my girl I loved her," Jack said. "I was too intimidated. Even I, who wrote of the hypocrisy of the social classes, felt I didn't deserve to cross them. I felt she wouldn't have me. That she'd have laughed me out of my own shop."

Elinor shook her head vehemently. "I wouldn't have. Oh, Jack. Of *course* I wouldn't have."

"Well, it's best I kept my mouth shut then. If I'd convinced you to be with me and live in poverty, you would not have gotten your two dear children. And the world would be a lesser place without them."

He smiled across the table at the boy and girl, who smiled back.

"I don't regret it, for that reason," Elinor said. "But I hope when it is their turn, my children will choose differently. We must change the world so that those who are meant to be together can feel free to be with whomever they want—society be damned."

The whole room cheered.

Eden was not among them.

He felt like the earth had turned to seawater beneath his feet.

All of these people were *cheering* at the concept of being with anyone—*society be damned.*

How could he sit here, in a room of people he respected no matter their lot in life or class, and make the choices he'd been making?

Why had he insisted to himself for months that certain rules were unquestionable, while others begged for reform?

He snuck a glance at Thaïs. She was smiling from ear to ear at Jack and Elinor, her eyes wet with unspilled tears. *She* knew the rules were foolish.

There had been that perfect moment when she'd suggested that they marry. He could have taken her hand right then and asked her to be his wife.

She'd have said *yes.*

He could have *had* her.

And then again, at the Institute, after they'd made love. *Again*, he'd had the chance to pledge himself to her, and instead he'd asked only for her body.

He'd put convention above his feelings for her—and for what? Why was he willing to defy so many rules, to push for change in society's most enshrined laws and customs, and yet too cowardly to apply this spirit to the deepest desires of his own heart?

He'd made himself miserable. And worse, he'd hurt Thaïs so deeply.

All because he'd not seen the simplicity of this truth that Elinor had put so plainly. That you could do what you wanted because of passion, simply because it made you happy.

He'd been so wedded to the idea of being a perfect husband in a perfect marriage. And it had led him to nothing but loneliness and despair. It had made him contemplate marrying women he knew would not make him happy just because he'd convinced himself he was not permitted to marry the woman who did. Where was the perfection in that?

He had certainly not been a perfect man to Thaïs. He had hurt her deeply. Insulted her. Willfully suggested a future he knew she didn't want because of his own prejudice.

But perhaps she could forgive him.

Perhaps she would let him be her imperfect husband.

Chapter Thirty-Nine

Thaïs slipped out of Elinor's wedding breakfast as soon as she could get away with it. She was happy for her friends. They were so in love.

But the trouble with people in love was that they were hard to watch when you had a broken heart. It was infernal torture to be so close to Alastair, knowing he did not return her feelings. Knowing he thought so much of her body and so little of her soul.

She walked home to her suite of rooms. She still adored it, but she'd be leaving this place soon. She didn't need such a sumptuous apartment if she was not using it to entertain patrons. She'd be moving to a cozy maisonette near the Institute to start her new life.

She took off her orange gown and hung it in her wardrobe. She'd chosen it at the dressmaker's because she knew it made her hair look lustrous, and she knew Alastair could not resist her hair. Since it wouldn't do to wear something that clung to her figure at a wedding breakfast, she'd shown off the next best thing.

It had worked, she reckoned. She'd felt his eyes on her, begging her to look at him.

She'd not obliged. Looking at him, or—Lord forbid it—talking to him, only made her sad.

She was tired of being sad. It was bone-wearying to feel so sorry for yourself.

She put on a dressing gown and climbed into her bed to take a nap, but she could not drift off. Blasted Alastair and his doleful eyes were keeping her awake.

It did not help when someone started pounding on her door.

"Crotch of Satan, stop that racket," she yelled. "I'm a-bloody-sleep."

But the pounding continued.

It must be Sera and Cornelia come to comfort her. They'd been especially soft on her since she'd told them of her insipid swollen heart, determined to make her cheerful.

Too bad for them she'd set herself on never being cheerful again.

She fumbled off her eye mask and marched to the parlor. "Who's there?" she called. "Is it you bloody harpies come to torment me?"

"It's me," Eden's voice answered. "Alastair."

Her heart, of course, stopped beating.

Not that she'd give him the satisfaction of knowing it.

"What do *you* want, Eden?" she yelled through the door.

"To speak to you," he replied. "Please, Thaïs."

She looked down at herself, barely dressed, and decided to let him in. At least he could feast his eyes on what he'd decided wasn't good enough for him.

She yanked the door open. He stood there pale and drawn but still so handsome it punched her in the guts.

He did not glance at her bosom, curse him. Instead, he looked into her eyes and swallowed, hard.

"What?" she asked, crossing her arms over her chest, like they might protect her from the sight of him. It didn't work. She couldn't see him without remembering how it felt when he held her. She wished she was not hemmed in by dignity and could throw herself into his arms.

"May I come in?" he asked.

She moved aside. "Make yourself happy."

"Thaïs," he said quietly, "the only thing on this earth that could make me happy is you."

Nice words from a man who'd made it his habit to reject her on grounds she wasn't good enough for him.

"You blister-cocked *bastard*, Eden," she erupted. "Whose fault do you think it is that you don't have me?"

He dropped to his knees right on the old wood floorboards, took her hands, and put them to his heart.

"Mine. Entirely mine. And I am the most abjectly brick-brained hypocrite who has ever lived. You have every right to loathe me and would be right to do so for the way I've treated you, for which there is no apology grave or fervent enough to possibly suffice. But please know that I am soaked in shame for how I've treated you."

He took her hand and brought it to his lips.

"If you want me to go," he whispered, "I'll go. But not before I ask the woman I love to be my wife."

She gaped at him, her hand limp in his. Love? *Wife?* Was he addled? Where had this come from?

She snatched her hand away. "Get up," she said. "I'm not rabbit-brained enough to swoon for handsome words. I know how you think of me, and it's not like a husband would. Have you forgotten who you are?"

"I haven't forgotten," he said. "And I despise myself for my snobbery and blindness. If I could take back the past, I would have married you in Gloucestershire."

His face was tight with pain, and for all her rancor toward him, she didn't like to see it. It was impossible not to notice how thin he'd grown. Between that and his pallor, she almost pitied him. Whatever had brought this on, the man was clearly miserable.

Which is what she'd thought she wanted—for him to feel as bad as she did. So why did she want to take him in her arms?

"Thaïs," he said quietly, "I don't know how to ask your forgiveness. I *know* I don't deserve it. It was my dream to be a perfect husband, and I've already failed you. But if you'd have me, I'd do anything to make it right."

He was sincere. She knew it by the way tears glimmered in his eyes. He'd never been able to hide his emotions from her.

It made her want to cry as well.

"Tell me why this madness has suddenly come over you," she said. "Were you clobbered in the head?"

"It's not madness, and it isn't sudden. I fell in love with you in that cottage in the Cotswolds and have not stopped thinking about you since. That has not changed. But I was so set in the belief that I had to wed within my station that I failed to see I had already met the person perfect for me. And this morning, at the wedding breakfast, I realized I was wrong."

She'd made a point to pay him no attention at the

breakfast. It was too painful. So she was not certain what about it had so altered his heart.

But the sincerity in his words softened her. Made her curious.

"I don't understand," she said. "But if you get up off the floor I'll sit with you, and you can try to solve the puzzle for me."

He rose, his knees cracking, and sat beside her on a sofa. She put a cushion between them, because her instinct was to be wary of him until she knew what had caused this change of heart.

"Thaïs, my father married a baker's daughter and eschewed the aristocracy for poetry, and they lived outside the mores of polite society. Their life was chaos. She went mad, and he drifted into opium, and they were loving but so unhappy. Our home was a shambles, and I suffered for it. And in my boy's mind, I thought that if they had only followed the rules, married the right people, behaved according to the letter, all the pain they endured could have been avoided. So in my life, I have tried to be upstanding and respectable in all the ways they weren't. Perfection is the antidote to anarchy, I thought. If I behaved exactly as I ought, pain could be avoided.

"And then I met you and felt free and content in a way I never imagined possible. Our month in the country was the happiest of my life. And since we parted, the pain of not having you near me has been the worst thing I have ever endured. And despite that, foolishly I told myself I was simply failing to meet the right woman. But this morning, I finally realized that the trouble was I had already met her and been too dead set on so-called perfection to realize what I should put above all else is love."

"You love *me*?" she said, pointing to herself.

He laughed brokenly. "I do. Madly. I ran all the way here to tell you just how much."

She could not hold back a smile. "So tell me."

He spoke in dizzying sentences about her cursing, her temper, and her tenderness. Her body, her touch, her smell. The way she made him laugh and the way she brought him to his knees in bed and the way she always seemed to know what he was thinking. The way her hugs made him feel like he was home at last.

It was that final thing that made her close the distance between them.

Because he was right.

She pulled her man into her arms. "You idiot," she whispered, burrowing her face into his neck.

"I know," he said. "If I court you with dancing and stolen kisses and walks along the Serpentine, will you give me another chance?"

"Seduction won't work on me. I taught you all the tricks."

"What if I simply say I want to be with you. To marry you and make a family with you. To take care of you and make love to you and cook for you. To fall asleep laughing with you and wake up beside you every morning."

She'd say he had her, were it not for the fear he'd change his mind when the scandal overtook them.

"You know the whole *ton* would turn on you for marrying me. Even earls can't get away with wedding whores."

"They can say whatever they like about us. I don't care about the opinions of a society I don't value. I don't care what people think about us. Unless—do you? Would it hurt you to be the subject of a scandal?"

"Oh, I couldn't say. Being infamous would be so fresh and new."

He snorted. "You do seem to have a knack for it."

"But what about perfection and all that? Because even if I listen to your wild plan, I'm not changing a hair on my head for the likes of you."

She said it hoarsely. Her voice was choked with tears.

He stood up and knelt before her. "Don't change your hair. It's perfect."

She wrapped her arms around him. "I told you, there's no such thing as perfect."

"Very well. Perfect for *me*. I'm just sorry I didn't see it sooner. But I hope that—"

"Oh, shut up. I love you too. I should have wrung your bloody neck two months ago and saved us both the agony."

"Would you like to wring it now?"

"Can't have you bruised on my wedding day. A lady only gets the one."

"I was thinking I'd get a special license. I could go this afternoon, and we could marry in a few days' time."

"Do it tomorrow. You'll be busy this afternoon."

"With what?"

She pointed at the bedchamber.

Epilogue

On a sunny day in Islington, a bright, white-painted auditorium smelled like the soap and perfume of the eighty ladies seated there, chatting quietly and peering at the stage for the first peek at their patronesses: the infamous radicals known in the papers as the Society of Sirens.

The women hailed from fine houses and farmhouses, from the Highlands down to Cornwall. There were whores and nuns, young mothers and old women, educated ladies and raw girls better versed in Cockney than the King's English. What they all had in common was their desire for independence, hunger for education, and belief in their own ambition.

"I'm so excited," Anna Howe whispered to Lady Elinor, who went by Willow now.

"It's a dream come true," Elinor said. "And I could not be more proud."

They cheered when Seraphina Arden, Cornelia Ludgate, and Lady Thaïs Eden took the stage. And in the back of the room, Adam, Rafe, and Alastair—the men who loved them—cheered just as loud.

"Welcome," Seraphina said, "to the Institute for the Equality of Women. I hope this is a place that will change your lives."

"The journey ahead may be difficult," Cornelia said. "You may face scorn and judgment. You will have to fight for your rightful place in the world, and true equality for our sex may take the work of generations."

"But we'll battle for our daughters," Thaïs said, thinking of the baby only she and Alastair knew would come the following summer. "And it will be worth the sweat and tears."

Acknowledgments

When I wrote the first installment of the Society of Sirens series—*The Rakess*—I was fueled by rage at the state of the world. The pandemic hit just as it came out, and it took me nearly two years to write Cornelia's book—*The Portrait of a Duchess*—as, like so many people, I was nearly paralyzed with sadness and isolation. And then the light came back, and with it came this final, most hopeful, volume of the series. Thaïs, who has always jumped onto the page so easily with her sharp tongue and tender heart, restored my belief that I could write.

Through it all, I have been sustained by the faith, patience, and passion of the readers of these books. Were it not for your belief in these characters and me, I may not have come back to the world of writing at all. I am so grateful for everyone who loves these women and their fight. And it has been an honor to put their story on the page.

I owe a huge debt of gratitude to Sarah Younger, Nicole Fischer, and Asanté Simons for helping to shape this series and giving it a home with Avon. You took a chance on *The Rukess*, and it expanded my ambition.

And as always, I am so indebted to the family and friends in my life whose love, support and encouragement sustains me. And thank you above all to my husband, Chris. Your faith in me never ceases to astound.